W9-AFZ-858

"I'm not a possessive man."

"Um . . . define possessive."

Brett shook his head as if trying to clear it. "This is crazy. Why are we arguing? You want me and you're not the kind of woman to play with two men at once."

"I don't want to play with anyone."

"Not true. You want to play with me."

Claire opened her mouth to deny it, but he didn't give her a chance. He kissed her instead, his lips molding hers, his tongue exploring her lips and the interior of her mouth with a thoroughness that made her tremble.

When he lifted his mouth, they were both breathing hard.

AND ABLE

LUCY MONROE

BRAVA

KENSINGTON PUBLISHING CORP.

http://www.kensingtonbooks.com

BRAVA BOOKS are published by

Kensington Publishing Corp.
850 Third Avenue
New York, NY 10022

Copyright © 2006 by Lucy Monroe

All rights reserved. No part of this book may be reproduced in any form or by any means without the prior written consent of the Publisher, excepting brief quotes used in reviews.

If you purchased this book without a cover you should be aware that this book is stolen property. It was reported as "unsold and destroyed" to the Publisher and neither the Author nor the Publisher has received any payment for this "stripped book."

All Kensington titles, imprints and distributed lines are available at special quantity discounts for bulk purchases for sales promotion, premiums, fund-raising, educational or institutional use.

Special book excerpts or customized printings can also be created to fit specific needs. For details, write or phone the office of the Kensington Special Sales Manager: Kensington Publishing Corp., 850 Third Avenue, New York, NY 10022. Attn. Special Sales Department. Phone: 1-800-221-2647.

Brava and the B logo Reg. U.S. Pat. & TM Off.

ISBN-13: 978-0-7582-1177-4
ISBN-10: 0-7582-1177-5

First Trade Paperback Printing: May 2006
First Mass Market Paperback Printing: September 2008
10 9 8 7 6 5 4 3 2 1

Printed in the United States of America

For my sisters' husbands, Paul, Tony, and Jason—
three incredible men who stand shoulder to shoulder with my
own gorgeous hubby in being real life heroes every day of their
lives.

Thank you all for what you add to our family and thank
you Paul especially for being such a great big brother from the
very beginning and such a super husband to my sister, show-
ing me what I wanted in my own hubby when the time came
and for caring enough to bring Tom into my life so I could
have it.

You are all my brothers, you are all my friends, and I thank
God daily for every single one of you.

Chapter 1

Did death before dishonor cover the maid of honor sneaking out of the wedding reception?

If it did, Claire Sharp's honor was in danger of extermination and she was ready to pull the trigger. She simply could not stand another minute of the torture, not another second.

Josette would understand . . . she hoped.

Claire slunk stealthily into the hall outside the reception room of the classy downtown Portland hotel. There were people out here, too, but only hotel staff . . . no one from the wedding party. No one to see and notice *her*.

She exhaled a sigh of relief as she cleared the room.

"Did you need something, Miss Sharp?"

She almost choked on her own breath. She could not believe it. Not out here . . .

"Miss Sharp?"

Tensing, she turned to find a black-clad waiter smiling at her inquiringly.

Whose idea had it been to introduce the wedding party to the hotel staff? Probably Wolf's. He was good at organizing things and had actually done a lot to help Claire's best friend and former roommate, Josette, plan her wedding. Ex-mercenaries were a strange breed.

Claire forced a smile for the waiter. "Um . . . no, just the . . . the . . ." Inspiration struck. "The restroom. I need the ladies' room."

He pointed to a deserted-looking—*Thank you, God*—red-carpeted hallway behind her. "Just that way, Miss Sharp."

"Thank you." And she scurried off as fast as she could, considering she was wearing the stiletto heels of death.

Would it be considered rude for the maid of honor to change into jeans and tennies at the wedding reception? She'd never been to one before, much less played a participating role. But she was almost certain that protocol dictated she keep her glad rags on. *Darn it.*

She just felt so exposed. The full skirt of the strapless, royal blue silk dress stopped four inches above her knees, and the back of the bodice, held together with thin velvet lacing tied in a very girlie bow right in the center of her back, dipped almost to her tailbone.

Josette had insisted it was perfectly respectable, but Claire was not used to going without a bra, and her breasts weren't exactly tiny. She felt like they jiggled every time she moved, and as the maid of honor, she ended up moving a lot. She'd worried it was going to be like this, but when Josette had asked her to wear both the dress and heels to be in the wedding, Claire had been unable to say no.

Josette was not only her *best* friend, but other than the elderly residents at the nursing home where she worked, Josette was pretty much her *only* friend. At least, that counted.

Josette had just married a man she loved and who adored her to distraction. Nitro thought she was everything a woman should be, which explained how Claire's friend could hook up with such a predator type. Both Josette and Nitro were former mercenaries, but he was a lot more dangerous, to Claire's way of thinking. The man oozed silent menace, but then so did his two closest friends, Wolf and Hotwire.

Wolf, at least, was domesticated. He had married Lise the winter before and they were expecting their first baby. Claire often marveled at how well the often vague and very imaginative author of kick-butt women's fiction got along with the ultra practical Wolf.

Hotwire was still single and making it very clear to anyone who cared to listen that he intended to stay that way.

No matter how attracted she was to him, Claire had no intention of trying to change his mind. However, something she'd said or done must have convinced him otherwise, because he had taken pains to let her know his stand on commitment.

He probably felt the need because of the way she stared at him like a love struck teenager whenever he was around. She couldn't seem to help herself, but it was so embarrassing . . . not to mention *unexpected*. She didn't do love struck, starstruck, or any other kind of struck.

Okay, sure, Hotwire had a body that rivaled Michelangelo's David and a southern charm that had the other female guests looking ready to swoon. He was also an inveterate flirt, and his honeyed Georgia drawl made her feel like she would melt in a puddle right at his feet.

Which was darn embarrassing, even if no one else knew about it.

But the worst deal was that underneath all that devastating charm, he was every bit as dangerous and aggressive as Nitro. The kind of man a woman knew could keep her safe and who actively made the world a better place. For Claire, that was a lethal combination. She could probably file that reaction under protector-type-struck, which was only marginally better than love struck.

He was so lethal, he made her feel downright lusty, and that took more doing than the whole protector-type-struck thing. A world-weary twenty-eight years old, she'd been around the block and back again and she did not do lust. It was a total waste of energy as far as she was concerned.

But darned if when Hotwire got within ten feet of her, she didn't go and get all shivery. The parts of her body she hadn't exposed to anyone except her doctor for longer than she wanted to keep track of *tingled*, for goodness' sake.

Standing around in a dress that made her feel half naked did not help.

She hovered uncertainly outside the bathroom. Did she have the nerve to go out to her car and get her regular clothes to change into? More importantly, would it upset Josette very much to have her maid of honor turn back into a computer geek with no style sense?

"Sugar, you look ready to bolt." The familiar Georgia accent went through her like a bolt of lightning.

Claire whirled around, her heart beating an irregular rat-a-tat-tat in her chest.

"I was thinking about changing my clothes," she admitted. "I'm not used to dressing up and don't really enjoy it."

Hotwire's blue gaze went over her like seeking hands, *really talented seeking hands*. "That'd be a real shame, Claire. You look beautiful."

She couldn't help it; she laughed. "Yeah, right."

Even on her best day, having had a stylist do her hair, a makeup artist do her makeup, and wearing the designer dress Josette had bought her, Claire knew she wasn't *beautiful.* Passable, sure—any woman could be passable—but beautiful was not something she'd ever aspired to. Nor was it something she was ever likely to achieve.

Unlike her mother, who had been broken on the inside but very beautiful on the outside, Claire had average looks and an average figure that was maybe a tad too curvy in places. Her hair was the color of cooked carrots, and what she knew about styling it wouldn't fill up the back of a cereal box. She was nothing like the women that flocked around Hotwire wherever he went.

And she really didn't mind. Beauty wasn't exactly a blessing for most women cursed with it. Look at her mom . . . look at half the actresses in Hollywood, for heaven's sake. Most of them had lives that would make your average family psychologist cringe.

Giving her a quizzical look, Hotwire reached out and adjusted the chain on her locket.

An heirloom that had been passed down for five generations in her family, it was the only thing Claire had left of the good times before her dad's death. She'd almost lost the necklace when the house she shared with Josette was burglarized, but Hotwire had gotten it back for her.

"Why'd you laugh?" he asked, his voice making her insides do that shivering thing again.

"No reason."

He traced the chain of her necklace until his fingertip rested over the locket, but he might as well have been touching her directly. The feeling was just as electric. "Come on, sugar, tell me why you laughed."

"Because it was funny," she croaked out, her normal insouciance apparently on vacation in the Bahamas at the moment.

"I didn't intend it to be."

She tried to affect a casual shrug, but ended up brushing her breasts against his forearm. Her, "Sorry," came out sounding suspiciously like a moan.

He didn't look in the least affected by their nearness. His to-die-for good looks were not marred by tension, sexual or otherwise. In fact, he seemed perfectly relaxed, though he wasn't smiling. He was a magnificent, golden lion at rest, the potential for powerful action there, but momentarily dormant.

"I'm not used to women dismissing my compliments," he said with a frown.

She couldn't tell if he was really angry with her or teasing. "Um . . . I'm *really* sorry."

He shook his head. "An apology won't cut it. You've besmirched my sense of honor. We take that seriously where I come from."

She laughed, still not sure from his unreadable expression and downright dangerous aura whether he was serious or not. "What do you expect me to say?"

"Nothing." Then he just stood there, silent and taking up more space than even his over-six-foot frame should occupy.

His hands rested against her neck, one thumb now brushing back and forth across her rapidly beating pulse. She began to wonder if her assessment of him as lion *at rest* was accurate. She realized he was coiled to spring at any moment, and like truly mesmerized prey, she didn't think she could lift a finger to stop him.

The heat of the locket warmed by his hand burned against her bare skin. "Thank you," she blurted out.

One brow rose. "For the compliment?"

She shook her head and then realized that might have been a mistake when his blue eyes narrowed.

"Then why?"

"For finding my locket and returning it to me. I know it's just a necklace, but it means a lot to me." It was her talisman, serving to remind her she did not have to follow in her mother's footsteps, that she had women in her lineage she could be proud of.

"Josie said it was your grandmother's."

"Yes, and her grandmother's before that."

"You must have loved her a lot."

"I did. She died when I was eight and I'll never forget her. She was a formidable woman." Unlike the daughter she'd given birth to.

"Who is Norene?"

"She was my mom."

"She's dead?"

"Yes."

"I'm sorry."

"Thank you." She didn't like talking about that part of her life. There was too much pain wrapped up in the memories, and pain meant a vulnerability she'd long ago rejected. "Josette said you finished installing the security system in the house."

"Right."

She tried to step back, away from him, but he moved with her, his hands continuing to caress her throat with subtle movements. It was all she could do to keep focused on their conversation. "I don't understand why she wants one now that she's not going to be living there."

"You live there, and a woman alone needs a good security system."

If he knew some of the places she'd lived in her life, he would realize the safety of a locked door in a decent neighborhood was a luxury she didn't take for granted. "Josette lived alone before I moved in."

"She was a merc."

"I'm not exactly helpless."

"Honey, if those terrorists we took down have friends, you'd be worse than helpless around them."

"What's worse than helpless?"

"Dead."

"Oh." She tried taking a deep breath to calm down, but all she inhaled was his scent and she had to bite back a moan of pleasure at the unexpected intimacy of it. What was it about this guy? He was just so darn male—even the way he smelled excited her previously happily dormant feminine sexual instincts. "There's no reason to believe anyone connected with them would have a grudge against me."

"Josie was part of the team that brought the bad guys to justice. People like that do not forgive and forget."

"But I'm not Josette."

"It's not like she took out an ad saying she was getting married and taking off on a month-long honeymoon. You are the one living in her house."

She thought the worry was far-fetched but didn't say so. She knew Josette had to agree because she would not have allowed Claire to continue living in the house if she believed doing so would put her at risk. The security system had been Nitro and Hotwire's idea, although Josette had gone along with it easily enough.

Claire didn't mention that to Hotwire, either. "I'm sure any security system you devised is more than adequate."

"No security system is fail-safe, even ones as complicated as what Wolf and Nitro have installed around their homes." He went on to describe the measures he and Wolf had implemented. "Oh, and I bought you a can of mace for every room of the house."

"For every room of the house?"

"I like to be thorough . . . *in every way.*"

The message that went through her had nothing to do with his intentional meaning, she was sure. But she could imagine him being thorough as all get-out, and her fantasies *were not* about alarm systems. So long as they stayed fantasies, it was okay.

"I see."

"A self-defense weapon won't do you any good if it's in the bedroom while you're accosted in the kitchen."

The only person she felt in danger of being accosted by right now was him, and if that happened, the last thing she'd want to do was fight. Which was a really dumb attitude she couldn't seem to shake.

Sex was not worth getting all shook up over, so why did hanging around this man make her feel like an Elvis Presley song?

"But mace?"

"Yes. Since you won't use a gun."

"You make that sound like a crime."

"It's just . . ." He paused as if searching for a word. "Different."

"I guess a mercenary would see things that way."

"Former mercenary."

"Right . . . now, you are a security specialist."

"Among other things."

She wanted to ask what other things, but suddenly, talking just wasn't an option.

The lion inside him was looking at her through his darkening blue eyes and the expression was one of a lethal predator deciding how best to devour his prey. "I know you tried to forget it, but you besmirched my honor and you need to do something to make up for it."

"I do?"

"Uh-huh."

How'd his face get so close? "Wh . . ." She had to clear her throat. "What do you mean?"

"I think a kiss would do it."

"What?" Kissing was the best part of sex, she supposed, but that wasn't saying a lot. So why did the prospect of locking lips with Hotwire sound so darn exciting?

"A kiss, Claire. You know what a kiss is—when a man and woman—"

She covered his mouth to stop the tantalizing words. "I know what it is, smarty pants, but why would you want one from me?" *That was her fantasy.*

And as she'd just reminded herself, fantasy was well and good . . . acting on it was not.

He licked her palm and she jerked her hand from his mouth.

He smiled that devil's smile that always sent her insides jumping. "Because you've offended me and now you must make up for it."

"You're crazy. Nitro and Wolf offend you all the time. I don't see you kissing them."

He smiled, his eyes so full of sensual suggestion, her knees went weak. "My friends are not beautiful women."

"Well, neither am I," she said sarcastically.

"There you go, besmirching my honor again. My mama would be appalled at your opinion of my veracity."

She wasn't going there. "You don't expect Josette to kiss you when she offends you."

"I would prefer not to end up in a fight to the death with Nitro. He's a scary son when he's riled."

"You're not afraid of anyone or anything," she scoffed. "Josette told me stories."

Something moved in his eyes and for a second she saw the mercenary who had gone into war-torn countries to bring out hostages. His was the face of a man who had killed, and would do so again, if it was necessary to preserve the safety of those he had committed to protecting.

But just as quickly as it surfaced, the look disappeared, and Hotwire's blue eyes burned with sexy challenge. "I want a kiss, Claire . . . are you going to give it to me?"

"Sure." She went up on her toes, intent on bussing his cheek.

He turned his head just enough, though, and her lips ended up pressed lightly to his. She didn't open her mouth, but she didn't pull away immediately like she'd planned to, either. She hung there, suspended by the connection between their mouths, her body humming with excitement. One second the kiss was soft and light, and the next he yanked her against his hard, male body and his mouth slammed down over hers with definite intent.

He took her mouth with the skill and power of an invading army . . . or one very formidable mercenary.

The man certainly knew how to kiss. He ate at her lips until she was dizzy from the pleasure of it. His fingers massaged her jaw, as if encouraging her complete surrender, the only kind she was sure he recognized. She'd never experienced anything so amazing in her life as Hotwire's kiss. She moaned out her approval while gripping the front of his white silk dress shirt in her fists.

He growled something she could not understand against her lips and then his hands skimmed down, over her naked shoulders and around to the exposed skin of her back. His fingertips touched bare skin between the velvet lacing and played tantalizingly with the bow.

Man alive, what would she do if he untied it? She'd

read about being branded by a man's touch, but had never known what it meant . . . until now. Her skin grew hot under his fingers, so hot she would swear burn marks would be left behind. Only it did not hurt like a burn.

It felt too darn good for her sanity.

Without really thinking about it, she opened her mouth. His tongue tangled instantly with hers and took immediate and absolute possession of the interior of her mouth. Pleasure jolted through her body, spearing her right between her legs and she arched her pelvis toward him.

His hands traveled down over her bottom to the backs of her legs below her skirt hem, then came up under her skirt and back up her legs. She almost jumped out of her skin when he touched the sensitive flesh of her inner thighs. He curled his big fingers around them, holding her while his thumbs kneaded her bottom and he lifted her into closer contact with his body.

She undulated against him in a move that felt entirely natural, but froze in shock as her mound brushed against the hard roll of his erection.

He wasn't so inhibited. He used his grip on her to move her up and down the length of his engorged and rigid penis, making a low, masculine sound of pleasure as he did so. Tremors more powerful than a Richter 10 earthquake went off inside her.

"Stop trying to seduce my maid of honor, Hotwire. It's time to throw the bouquet." Josette's voice crashed through the passionate haze surrounding Claire, bringing her back to reality with a thud.

What in the world had she been doing?

Hotwire jolted like a man shocked by a live electric wire and broke the kiss, practically tossing Claire away from him. She tottered on her unfamiliar heels and almost fell. He reached out to steady her, his expression pained, but snatched his hands back the moment she stopped wobbling.

The silence between them was more charged than the air after an electric storm.

"You have five minutes and then I'm tossing the bouquet," Josette said, her gaze faintly amused and assessing, before she turned to head back to the reception.

It would take Claire five minutes just to get her breath back. How was she supposed to walk back into the reception on top of that?

After several more seconds of charged silence, he said, "I'm sorry. That was way out of line."

"I liked it," she admitted. Way too much, but hot kisses were one thing, doing the deed another, and she really didn't want him thinking she was open for that kind of play.

"No doubt," he said, sounding terribly arrogant. "I've never had any complaints on my technique, but I was out of line all the same."

"If you say so."

"Look, I'm not in the market for a committed relationship, and you're not the type of woman to settle for a one-night stand or even a short affair."

"Of course not." Her distaste for the very thought had to have been written on her face because he winced.

The thing was, she didn't think Hotwire was a one-night stand kind of guy himself. Only, for some reason he wanted her to think he never got serious with women. She realized that was the message he'd been giving her since the day they met, but it simply did not ring true. He had too much integrity to be a true hound dog. Regardless, patently, he had no desire to get serious *with her*, and that's all that really mattered.

Besides which, she wanted a relationship with a man like she wanted to retake her finals from last semester and flunk them all. There was no place in her life for a man . . . not even a super-sexy stud who made her insides go nuts with something as simple as a kiss.

"Right, we're at opposite ends of this particular data array," he said. "So, no more soul kisses."

"That felt more like a groping, marauder kiss to me."

"I do not grope." Hotwire looked truly offended.

"So the fingers I felt on my behind were a spectral phenomenon?" she mocked.

"I'm not a ghost."

"I can vouch for that," she said with a small smile, still tingling in places *she* never talked about.

Chapter 2

"Claire," Josette yelled from the other room.
"That's my cue to go."

"Good luck," Hotwire said.

"Aren't you coming to watch?"

"No."

"Marriage isn't a disease, you know. You can't catch it being in the same room as Josette and Nitro."

He smiled a little. "It's a good thing, since I was at the wedding."

"You really are clinging to your freedom, aren't you?"

"I'm not ready to settle down, no."

She shrugged. Marriage wasn't her idea of life happily ever after, either, but his single status was almost a religion for Hotwire. "Thanks again . . . for getting me my locket back."

"Hey, no big deal."

Wolf had told her that Hotwire had spent precious extra minutes searching the offices of the terrorist group they brought down the month before, risking his very life to get her necklace back. Hotwire was hero material for sure . . . she, however, was no princess, and she didn't believe in fairy tales anyway.

"It is to me," was all she said, and then she turned and walked away, her hand rising of its own volition so her fingertips could press the swollen contours of her lips.

Hotwire watched Claire walk away and damn near went after her when she touched her mouth as if holding onto their kiss. He hadn't been this turned on in . . . hell, he wasn't sure he'd ever been this turned on.

Claire did nothing to entice him, and he spent every second in her company wanting to strip her naked.

If the near debilitating desire wasn't enough, he actually enjoyed her company. He'd once told Nitro that he and Claire had nothing in common. And in some ways that was true. The woman was a vegetarian *and* a pacifist. Not exactly best-buddy material for a former mercenary.

But she was also smart and understood computers with the same intrinsic ability as he did. She shared his passion for new technology as well. He'd never met another woman like her.

She didn't dress to her best advantage. He'd never seen her wearing makeup before today, but her lack of artifice didn't make her any less feminine to him. He felt more male hormones rampage through him in her company than he did surrounded by a gaggle of his mother's southern belle protégées.

But something about Claire held him back from acting on what those male hormones wanted him to do. Her ready confirmation that she was not the kind of woman to enjoy a no-commitment affair was only part of it. Even if she would accept those terms, he had a feeling that sex with her would be more than mind-numbing physical pleasure.

For all her lack of feminine wiles, Claire Sharp was a dangerous woman. She was so damn different from those southern belles his mama was so fond of. Any woman he knew from back home would accept whatever he chose to give her with a sweet smile and an attitude that said she was doing him a favor letting him give it to her.

Claire wasn't like that. At all. She said she refused to accept charity, but he didn't consider helping a friend charity.

Heck, it had taken some major fast-talking on Josie's part to get Claire to keep using the laptop he'd given her when she learned she wasn't getting hers back. The FBI had confiscated it as evidence the month before. Hotwire hadn't been surprised by the fed's action, which was why he'd made sure her grandmother's locket was off the premises when the FBI moved in on the bad guys.

She *was* his friend, even if maybe she didn't see herself that way.

There weren't many people he put in that category, and it irritated him she didn't consider herself one of them. He didn't get it, but there were a lot of things about Claire that mystified him and would continue to do so.

Because time spent in her company trying to figure her out was hazardous . . . both to his libido and his peace of mind.

"And this switch turns the outer lights on steady illumination." Hotwire pressed the small button and the backyard lit, exposing every shadowy recess.

He'd driven Claire home so he could go over the new security system with her.

"Great," Claire enthused, though he got the distinct impression she was humoring him. "I'm amazed you got it all done so quickly."

He shrugged. "No sweat. It's what we do."

She cocked her head to one side and looked at him. "Not exactly. Your new company specializes in hi-tech security on a much bigger scale."

"It's the same principle."

"There's nothing dangerous about installing outdoor lighting in a residential neighborhood."

"We're not mercs anymore, Claire. Our day jobs aren't that dangerous, either."

"Right. According to Josette, your latest client is an international politician who requested your expertise in keeping him alive because he'd received so many death threats in the past year."

"Coordinating protection for one politician is nothing compared to going into a war zone to bring out hostages."

"Agreed. But then, securing Josette's rental house is nothing in comparison to the politician, either."

"But no less important." Her safety mattered to all of them.

"Thanks." She smiled, her pretty pink lips void of the gloss she'd worn earlier.

The thought that he had kissed it off tormented him. He could still taste her on his lips, and the desire to kiss her again grew with every breath he took in her radius. Coming to her house alone had been a really bad idea. He hadn't reacted to a woman like this since Elena, and even then, he'd had more control of the physical desires riding him.

Her brown gaze was warm. "You did a great job. I really

like the way you set up remote access capability from my laptop."

"I figured you would."

"You know me so well." Which made her look wary, for some reason.

The temptation to touch her about overwhelmed him and he took a quick step back. "If you don't have any questions, I'll head back to the hotel."

"No questions, but if you don't mind waiting for just five minutes . . ." She smiled tentatively. "I would really appreciate a ride to the Max station. It's on the way, or I wouldn't ask."

His brow furrowed. "Why do you want a ride to the light-rail station?"

"Because it will save me a bus ride and two transfers. I'll only take a minute changing clothes. Really."

He didn't doubt it. Claire did not primp, but his libido rebelled at the thought of her changing out of the entirely feminine and extremely sexy dress she'd worn in the wedding. Though he didn't mind the idea of her taking the pins out of her silky red hair. The style was elegant, but not her. He liked her wild mop of auburn curls.

"I don't mind waiting for you, but if you need a ride somewhere, I'll take you." He wasn't dropping her off at some mass transit station at night.

"That's not necessary. It's only a short ride on the Max to Belmont Manor."

"Why are you going to the nursing home?"

"It's not a nursing home. Belmont Manor is an assisted living care facility." She grimaced. "Sorry. I didn't mean to get all politically correct on you, but the management has been really cracking down on how we refer to it."

"No problem, but you still haven't told me why you're going to the *assisted-care facility* tonight."

"I have to work."

"Josie didn't say anything about it." And that surprised him, almost as much as her not sending Claire home from the reception in time for her to take a nap before going in to work.

"I didn't tell her."

"Why not?"

"She would have insisted I take the night off."

"Considering the circumstances, that would have made the most sense."

"Maybe, but I can't afford to take off two nights in a row without pay. If I'd told Josette, she would have offered to pay me and then we would have argued. I didn't want to have a fight with her before her wedding."

"But you haven't slept." And if he knew women as well as he thought he did, she hadn't gotten much sleep the night before, either.

Her mouth curved in a quirky smile, though the shadows around her eyes betrayed her weariness. "Well, no . . . but sleep is overrated, anyway."

"Like hell it is. You have to take care of yourself."

"Oh, come on . . . don't tell me you've never gone without sleep on a mission."

"That's different." He'd trained his body to function on very little rest.

Claire was a civilian and a sweet, fragile one at that. Even if she didn't seem to realize it.

"You're right. It is different. Your missions are dangerous, and lack of sleep could impede your reaction times, putting your life at risk. For me, it's no more than a matter of maybe being tired and heavy-eyed. I don't even administer meds. So, nobody is at risk if I get a little groggy."

"How are you getting home in the morning?"

"Mass transit. How else?" she asked as if she thought a few of his synapses had malfunctioned.

"I'll pick you up."

"That's not necessary."

He ignored her disclaimer. He'd be there to pick her up and because she was a reasonable being, she would accept the ride. "What about dinner?"

Now, she looked confused. "What about it?"

"You haven't eaten."

"I ate at the reception."

"That was hours ago."

She rolled her eyes. "I'm fine. Now, if you are done grilling me on my eating and sleeping habits, I'll go change. These shoes are killing me."

His gaze skimmed down her legs to the sexy heels that were killing her feet. "My mama always said beauty comes with a price."

"No doubt *your* mother would know."

His eyes flicked back up to her face.

Her mouth was twisted wryly, her eyes teasing, and the look made him want to kiss her about ten times more than he had wanted to a second before. "Are you implying I got *my* good looks from my mama?"

"Did you?"

He grinned. "So you admit you think I'm good-looking?"

"Don't be vain, and it's impolite to answer a question with another question."

"Did your mama tell you that?"

"No, my mother wasn't one for wise bits of advice." And her expression said she wasn't going any further on that subject.

"So, you think I'm *hot.*"

"I did not say that."

"You inferred it and in answer to your question, yes, my mother is a very beautiful woman. But, sugar, you clean up real nice yourself."

"Meaning I look like a slob most of the time." She sighed. "I know I do, but I just can't make myself care about clothes and makeup and all that girlie stuff."

"I didn't say you looked like a slob." But she was probably the sloppiest dresser he'd ever met, certainly the least put-together woman he'd ever wanted to bed. "Besides, like something else my mama used to say, beauty is as beauty does."

"A lot of people never look beyond the surface."

"You do."

She shrugged. "Yes."

"I do, too."

"That's nice to know," but she sounded like she doubted his words.

If he argued about it, they'd probably end up kissing like they had at the reception and no way was he going there. "Go change."

She saluted smartly. "Yes, sir. On my way, sir." She turned and marched away, her delicious bottom swaying in a sexy rhythm.

He shook his head and went into the kitchen to make her something to eat in the car on the way to the nursing home. If she wasn't going to get any sleep tonight, she'd need all the energy she could get.

True to her word, he'd barely finished the quick meal preparations before she was back and saying she was ready to go.

She'd put on a pair of faded jeans that hugged her curves like a second skin and sent his blood pressure into the danger zone. The tank top she wore under a short-sleeved blouse clung to her generous breasts and he could tell she'd put a bra on. He should be relieved . . . her braless state had given him a perpetual boner at the reception. But all he could think about was peeling away her clothes and cupping the now modestly contained, but no doubt soft and resilient, flesh.

Something must have shown on his face because her mouth parted on a small gasp and she stepped back, putting distance between them.

"I'm not going to jump you, though you do make a tempting picture." She'd taken her hair down, as he expected, and it sprang around her head in a silky, curly mop he was dying to bury his fingers in.

She shook her head. "Did you have too much champagne at the reception? Maybe you shouldn't be driving."

"I had one glass and it was a long time ago. The only influence I'm under are my male hormones."

"Has it been too long since you had sex?" she asked in the same tone of voice she'd use to query how many gigabytes he had on his hard drive.

No matter how prosaic *she* was about it, having her ask such a question sent those tormenting hormones into a tailspin, which eroded his temper. "My sex life is none of your business."

She blushed, looking more than a little embarrassed. "No . . . of course it isn't. I have a real tendency to say what's on the top of my mind. Sorry. Forget I asked."

He wished he could forget the answer, but he hadn't had sex since the first time he fantasized about spreading Claire's legs and plunging into the heated wetness he knew he'd find between them.

"Um . . . are you ready to go?" she asked after a few seconds of his glowering silence.

He was acting like a bad-tempered SOB. It was not her fault he wanted her. For crying out loud, it wasn't even her fault he couldn't have her. From the way she had responded to his kiss, he knew it wouldn't take much to get her into his bed. It was his own blighted sense of honor that kept him from acting on his impulses.

She was his friend and he wasn't decimating that friendship with a long, slow ride on the back of a hay wagon.

He forced his features into a more affable countenance. "Sure. I'm ready." He grabbed the small bag he'd used to store her dinner and gestured for her to take it. "Eat this in the car."

"What is that?"

"Your dinner. A sandwich, some carrots, nothing fancy," he added when she looked confused.

"You made it? For me?"

"I may not be Wolf, but even I can throw together a sandwich."

She shook her head as if to clear it and then took the bag from his hand. "Thank you. I . . . that was really thoughtful of you."

He shrugged off her appreciation.

She didn't say anything else, but grabbed her backpack on the way out the door.

They were driving and she'd eaten half of the sandwich when she spoke again. "You didn't put any meat on it."

"The point was to get you to eat."

"Well, yes, but I didn't realize you'd remember I was a vegetarian."

"I'm not exactly a doddering old man. I'm only thirty-four, Claire. My memory works just fine."

"Well, of course, but . . ." Her voice just trailed off.

"Why don't you eat meat?" He'd wondered about it ever since he realized she was a vegetarian. "Is it part of your whole pacifist belief system?" Gandhi was a vegetarian, he remembered.

"I'm not a pacifist."

"Yes, you are."

"Excuse me, but I'm not, and I ought to know, don't you think?"

"Well, *you* said you were."

"When?"

"You refuse to handle a gun and I've seen how you react to talk about killing."

"I don't handle weapons because I know nothing about them. That makes a gun in my hand a dangerous thing . . . both to myself and the people around me."

He agreed, but he'd never heard a civilian talk that way. Well . . . okay, there was published rhetoric on gun control, but most people thought they were smart enough not to hurt themselves with a weapon, no matter how deadly. "That's commendable."

"No, it's logical. As for me being uncomfortable talking about killing people, that makes most nonmilitary types nervous, or hadn't you noticed?"

He laughed at her acerbic tone. "I've noticed, but you've made it clear you have a problem with violence." Did she think he would be offended by her beliefs?

He wasn't. He just didn't understand them.

"Most people have a problem with violence."

"You know what I mean."

"Believing nonviolent conflict resolution should be one's primary reaction in a disagreement does not make me a pacifist."

"I hate to tell you this, but yes, it does."

"No, it does not. A pacifist is someone who believes that nonviolence is the *only* acceptable response to conflict. I don't agree with that . . . I merely believe it should come first."

"Sometimes there is no choice."

"I'm sure that's true, in theory."

"Screw theory. That's an observation made on sixteen years spent as a soldier."

"I didn't mean to offend you."

"Who said I was offended?"

"Um . . . no one. Maybe I'd just better eat my dinner."

"I still want to know why you don't eat meat."

"You'll laugh at me."

"No. I won't."

Her look said she didn't believe him.

"I won't."

She sighed, giving in with bad grace. "Fine, but if you do . . . you just may find out how far from a true pacifist I really am. I have too vivid an imagination. When I eat a hamburger, I see some poor cow with tragic brown eyes facing the slaughterhouse."

"That would put pretty much anyone off meat. So, why not think about something else?"

"I can't. Did you ever watch the movie *Chicken Run*?"

"Yes. I've got a couple of nephews who think it's their job in life to keep me educated on the animated movie industry."

"Well, even chicken nuggets make me think of Ginger. She was such a gutsy little thing."

"And you can't stand the thought of eating her."

"No."

"The movie is fantasy. Ginger isn't real."

She laughed. "I know that, but I can't help what my mind conjures up when I'm eating."

In a way, he understood. He couldn't help the images that his mind conjured up of her lying naked in his bed, either.

Chapter 3

Claire flipped off the call light for Lester's room before making her way down the silent hallway to see what he needed. It was late, almost three in the morning, and few Belmont Manor residents were awake. Perhaps Lester was even the only one.

She found him clad in a robe and pajamas, sitting up in a chair and thumbing through a composition book like the ones she used to take notes in her classes.

"Did you need something, Lester?"

He looked up, his dark eyes intimidating even in a weathered face attached to a body stooped by age. "Just a little company. You didn't work yesterday."

According to the nurses and other aides, he never called for late-night company on the nights she had off. Maybe they didn't listen with the same amount of tolerance to his sometimes confused ramblings. She'd had a lot of practice with her mom; Lester's dementia was less taxing to her patience than her mom's drunken discourse had been.

She smothered a yawn. "My best friend got married

today . . . or yesterday, rather." She smiled at the memory. Josette and Nitro were the perfect couple, and her friend deserved to be supremely happy; she was such a sweetheart. And Claire thought Nitro might actually turn out to be a man who could be counted on in the long run. "I took the night off to help her with last-minute preparations."

Lester frowned. "I never got married."

"I know."

"A hired killer doesn't make a good husband."

"I'm sure you're right," she said, humoring him.

He looked down at the book in his lap and then shut it. "I killed too many people. Couldn't bring myself to marry even after I retired. What if I talked in my sleep? I'd have had to kill my own wife."

She didn't know how much of what he said was truth, or how much was fantasy, but sometimes it sounded so real it was chilling. This was one of those times.

"I don't think you would have killed your own wife, Lester."

His gaze turned so cold it made her shiver. "You can't let your emotions get in the way of a kill when you are a professional. I was a professional. The best." Unmistakable pride laced his voice. "I would have done whatever I had to, but I didn't want to face that kind of circumstance . . . so I never got married."

"Were you lonely?" she asked, thinking of her own future stretching out years ahead of her.

Maybe putting up with sex was worth it to have a family, but then she'd have to deal with the vagaries of life and the risk that it could batter her kids the same way it had battered her. It didn't seem fair to have kids in a world like the one that existed today.

"Never got lonely. Life is too full of interesting things

to see and do. You appreciate that when you see a lot of death."

"I imagine you do."

"I like having you and Queenie around now, though. She's a firecracker." He smiled, his expression warming about twenty degrees. "If I had known I'd meet her in a place like this, I would have moved in sooner."

"The feeling is obviously mutual. Queenie thinks you are a king among men." Sweet and as bubbly as a bottle of soda pop, the other Belmont Manor resident had shown her preference for Lester from day one. Talk about opposites attracting.

"She's nuts. I told her about what I did, but she just thought it made me more mysterious. She even read my kill book. The working of a woman's brain is a mystifying thing."

Not in the least offended, Claire laughed. "I suppose it must seem that way to you."

"JFK's not as safe as he thinks he is," Lester said, slipping back into the past.

"I'm sure you're right."

"I tried to tell Marv at the agency, but he said presidential safety wasn't his detail. No one else in the government outside the agency knows I exist. They won't listen to me."

"Who is Marv?" she asked, curious in spite of herself.

"You know who he is. My contact with the agency. We were together in the war. He wasn't much of a sniper, but he sure understood logistics."

"World War I?"

"Yeah. You okay, Melba? You sure are asking some strange questions."

Every once in a while he called her Melba, and all she'd learned about the other woman was that she'd worked in some secretarial capacity for Lester a long time ago. His senility was growing steadily worse, but Claire still liked being around him. She didn't care if he made sense. He was an interesting man and knew more about odd trivia than she did.

She couldn't stay and visit too long tonight, though, no matter how much she might want to. A group of politicians was coming on Monday to tour the facility. Apparently it was some part of a report they were doing on the living conditions of the elderly in Oregon.

It was up to her and the rest of the junior staff to make sure the place shone with cleanliness and gave the appearance of a healthful environment. Not that it wasn't usually clean, but this was like spring cleaning at the end of summer.

Hotwire walked into his office and did a quick visual check of his equipment. A light flashed, indicating Claire's alarm had gone off. He swore, adrenaline pumping into his blood, an immediate sense of impotency sweeping over him. What could he do for Claire from his home in Montana?

Nothing. He didn't like knowing that. Not one bit.

Fortunately, the light was yellow, which meant she'd turned it off . . . or someone had.

He grabbed the phone and dialed Claire's number.

She picked up on the third ring, sounding breathless. "Hello?"

That breathy little hello instantly started him thinking of her writhing in the middle of an acre of silk sheets. The predictable effect of his imagination on his cock wasn't exactly comfortable. He grimaced. "It's Hotwire."

"Uh . . . hi."

"Is everything all right?"

"Sure. Um . . . is there some reason it shouldn't be?" She sounded guiltier than a kid caught sneaking out of her bedroom window after curfew.

"Your alarm went off."

"Did you give the police instructions to call you if it did?" Her voice vibrated with outrage. "Don't you think that's a bit excessive? I do not need a baby-sitter. Seriously. What were you thinking? Don't tell me this was Josette's idea. Sheesh, I don't know what you thought you could do about it, in any case."

He'd noticed before that she talked fast and furiously when she was concerned about somebody else, angry, or feeling self-conscious. He wondered which one she was at the moment. She sounded mad, but there was something in her voice that hinted at embarrassment, too.

"Tell me about the alarm, Claire."

A big, heavy sigh came across the phone line. "Classes are over in another week and a half."

"So?"

"Well, my final project in my Unix programming class is due. There's a glitch in the program and I've been trying to figure it out."

"What does that have to do with the alarm going off?"

"I forgot to use the remote code on my laptop to disarm it when I got home."

"There's a keypad inside as well."

"I wasn't thinking about the alarm. I told you, I was trying to figure out my program . . . I didn't think about the alarm at all." That was definite chagrin in her voice. "Not until it went off, anyway."

"Did the police come?"

"You know they did."

In fact, he hadn't. "Good."

"It wasn't *good*. It was awful. I was a nervous wreck trying to explain the alarm to the police. What if they'd thought I was the one breaking in? After all, the house doesn't belong to me."

"That's highly unlikely."

She grunted, the sound one of pure disgust. "I was mortified. The neighbors came out and gawked. One of them even came over to make sure I was all right."

"How long did the alarm go off before you noticed it?" he asked, trying to control the amusement in his voice.

"I don't know." She sounded petulant and he'd never heard her sounding that way.

It made him horny. Heck, just about everything she did made him want her.

"I'm surprised your neighbor came to check on you."

"He's ex-military. A retired SEAL or something. You guys are all alike . . . interfering."

He laughed.

She made a sound like steam escaping a teakettle, and he bit off his laughter.

"That alarm is a big pain." Something in her tone alerted him and he started running a diagnostic on the system from his computer.

"No strange phone calls, or anything?" he asked, just to keep her talking while the system ran its check.

"Other than this one? No."

"There's nothing odd about one friend calling to check on another."

"I thought you were Josette's friend."

"Is there anything that says I can't be yours as well?"

"Um . . . no."

"Good." Then his computer beeped and he glared at

the screen, wanting to bite something. "Why did you disable the alarm, Claire?"

There were probably only a handful of people in the country that could have done it without the code, which he had not given *her* on purpose. And according to the stats he was now looking at, she'd done it a lot faster than even she should have been able to.

"How do you know I did?"

"I ran a diagnostic."

"Oh. You mean you have my security system hooked up to your computer?"

"Yes."

"That's how you knew it had gone off?"

"Uh-huh. I didn't leave instructions for the cops to call, but maybe I should fix that."

"Don't you dare. This was humiliating enough as it is."

"The alarm can't do you any good turned off."

"I'm not having the police out here every other day because I accidentally set it off. That's just not okay, Hotwire."

"So don't set it off."

She was silent on the other end of the line.

"Come on, sugar. I know you struggle with focusing on the world around you sometimes, but you can train yourself to remember the alarm."

"Why do you call me sugar? I'm not a piece of candy."

"You taste as sweet as one."

"Yeah, right."

"Trust me. I'd rather suck on your tongue than a peppermint stick any day of the week."

"You're flirting with me," she said accusingly.

"And I bet you're blushing." She acted tough, but

she reacted to the attraction between them with more vulnerability than he was sure she wanted to admit to.

She sighed, the soft sound shivering through him. "Maybe."

"You're awfully innocent for a woman of twenty-eight."

"Innocent is one thing I'm not." The cynicism in her tone was absolute. "And how did you know how old I am? Did you hack into my identity records?"

"No. I found out the old-fashioned way. I asked Josie."

"Oh."

"You're not going to sidetrack me from the issue at hand."

"I wasn't trying to sidetrack you."

No, it probably hadn't been on purpose. She just had a tendency to jump from one subject to another. "I'm turning the alarm back on and this time I want you to leave it that way."

"If it goes off again, I'm cutting the wires."

"You'll do no such thing."

"Watch me."

"You do not have authorization to dismantle the alarm."

"This is not the military. I don't need authorization. I'm the one living here. If I don't want an alarm disrupting my life, I don't have to have one."

"Then move out, but as her renter, you have no right to circumvent measures Josie has put in place to protect her property. The alarm and the house it safeguards belong to her, not you." The words were harsh, but he had no choice.

He couldn't force her to keep the alarm enabled from several hundred miles away, and he'd already used the argument about Claire's own safety to no avail. She refused to give credence to his concerns, but that didn't make them any less real. And he refused to dismiss them because she didn't want the inconvenience of remembering the alarm.

"You're right," Claire said, her voice subdued. "I'm just the renter. This isn't my home. I won't disconnect the alarm again. If that was all you needed . . ."

Josie was going to kill him. He'd hurt Claire's feelings and he wasn't all that happy about it himself. "Claire—"

"Thank you for calling to check on m . . . the house. As I said, everything is fine."

"Sugar—"

"I'll try not to inconvenience you again. Good-bye."

The phone went dead in his ear and he swore pungently, glad his mama wasn't there to hear him. His army drill sergeant had never intimidated him like her five-feet-nothing of southern belle charm.

He hadn't meant to hurt Claire, and he had not called to check on the damn house. His jaw ached from clenching it as he reset the alarm. He checked his messages and e-mail, but couldn't get the hurt tone of Claire's voice out of his head. Finally, he gave in and called her again.

She didn't pick up, and he checked her schedule only to realize she had a class and would be working later that night. He left a message telling her he had re-armed the system, but didn't know what to say to undo the damage he'd done to her feelings, or even if it was a good idea to try.

Choking back tears, Claire unlocked her front door.

Lester was dead. She couldn't believe it. He'd been at Belmont Manor practically since she started working there three years ago. There had been other deaths over that time. How could there not be, with the average age of the residents seventy-five years? But Lester was different. Lester was special. She'd loved him like family.

For a woman who had known as little family as she had, that meant something.

Just the night before, they had sat talking for over two hours and he had been mostly lucid. He'd told her more about his life as a paid assassin and she was convinced now that most of what he told her was real. He'd only started telling her about it this last year, since his senility had worsened, so it had taken a while to sort truth from hallucination. Unless he hallucinated the same things consistently, the stuff about his dark alter ego was real.

She'd told him she was surprised he'd lived so long, considering what he did, but he said he'd kept his real identity a strict secret. The government and clients for his private jobs had only known him by the name Arwan . . . Celtic god of the dead. It was fitting for what he had done.

Only she didn't care what he'd been in his past; he had been an important part of her life now and it hurt so much that he was gone. He was the closest thing she'd ever known to a father figure she could respect, which was pretty darn pathetic, but there it was.

She shut the door as the tears started to fall. She swiped at them and belatedly remembered the alarm. Saying a word she rarely used, she rushed across the room to its hidden keypad and coded in her entry before it went off again. She made it just in time and disarmed the system through the veil of moisture blurring her vision.

It was a good thing she really did plan to move, because she hated having to remember the alarm. She would miss this house, but just like everywhere she had ever lived . . . it wasn't her home. It wasn't permanent. She was just a renter.

She'd lived a lot of places in her life, some of them scarier than others, but they'd all had one thing in common . . . they had been temporary stops, and this house was, too.

She wasn't hungry and she couldn't face studying. She was exhausted from grief over Lester and working after almost no sleep for the second weekend in a row. She stumbled down the hall to her bedroom, stopping along the way to reset the alarm.

That should make Hotwire happy.

Claire was dreaming. She was sleeping in the front seat of the old Buick she and her mom had called home for a few months when she was twelve. Part of her knew it was a dream, that she was a grown-up woman now, living in a house, not a car, but everything felt so real. She could even smell the must of the perpetually wet floor carpets.

She could hear her mom's slow breathing from where she slept in the backseat and she could hear a siren's wail. It was really close. The cops were coming . . . they would arrest her mom and put her in jail, too. Or maybe juvenile hall. Wasn't it illegal to live in someone else's abandoned car? She didn't want to go to jail.

She started to whimper, fear clawing through her insides like an angry cat. Something came flying over the seat and landed against her face. Her mom's pillow? Why had she thrown it? Claire tried to push it away, but it wouldn't budge.

She struggled, desperation choking her.

She came awake with a jolt. She couldn't breathe. There was something against her face and she could still hear the siren's wail from her dream.

It was the alarm.

Someone had broken in. Someone who was holding a pillow over her face.

She opened her mouth to scream, but the pillow blocked it.

She thrashed, but couldn't get any leverage.

The person was saying something. Counting. Her hands flailed and her right one hit a hard object. Then she remembered.

Hotwire had made her put a can of mace at the head of her bed. Weak from lack of oxygen, she grappled for it. There . . . got it. She fumbled with the safety, terrified she wouldn't get it undone in time. Then, she directed it above the pillow over her face and pressed the button. And kept pressing while she waved it back and forth.

Vicious swearing. No more weight against the pillow. She pushed it up and sucked in air while terror-induced adrenaline caused her body to buck under her assailant. She managed to knock him sideways. She rolled off the other side of the bed and hit the hardwood floor with a thump.

The phone was ringing, but she couldn't move to answer it. She was too busy trying to breathe. She pushed up onto her knees and sucked in one shuddering, noisy breath and then another. Her lungs were still starving, but she had to get out of there.

Her assailant lurched to his feet and lunged for her with a clumsy movement. She brought the mace up and sprayed again, this time aiming directly for the eye holes in his dark ski mask. He reared back, screaming. She ran for the door, but her oxygen-deprived body was clumsy.

She made it to the hallway, the house alarm screaming around her. Disoriented, it took her a fraction of a second to decide which way to go. She rushed for the front door, but she was only halfway across the living room when something grabbed her hair and yanked. She went backward and landed with a painful jarring flat on her back.

She saw the foot coming toward her head, but couldn't do more than try to roll out of the way. She didn't make it. Pain exploded in the back of her head and then everything went black.

Her head hurt like someone had used it for hitting practice with a brick bat. She groaned.

"Miss Sharp, can you hear me?"

"Yes," came out a husky slur.

"Can you open your eyes?"

"Can try . . ." She willed her eyelids to peel back and winced when they did. "Too bright." She shut them again.

"Please, Miss Sharp, I need you to open your eyes and keep them open."

"Hurts . . ."

"I'm sorry." The voice was kind.

She would try to do what it wanted.

She opened her eyes again, this time blinking at the brightness and trying to let her vision adjust. A light flicked in her left eye and then her right. She flinched from it. "No."

"I won't do it again."

"Okay. Thank . . . you . . ." Her voice trailed off when she found it impossible to finish the thought.

He touched her head all over and her neck, asking questions. She tried to answer, but she cried out in pain when he probed the back of her skull.

"You've got a nasty bump here."

Memories were flooding back. "Kicked me."

The man made a disgusted sound and then asked, "You remember what happened?"

"Yes."

"That's good news."

"Really?" She didn't particularly enjoy remembering those terrifying moments.

"A concussion is usually accompanied by retrograde amnesia, the inability to remember what happened just prior to passing out."

"Don't have a concussion?" she asked, confused.

"I'm not sure, but your ability to remember is a good sign that if you do have one, it is not severe."

"Who did this to you?" Another voice. Male.

She turned her head toward the voice and tears sprang into her eyes when excruciating pain shot through her head.

The voice belonged to a uniformed policeman.

Old conditioning died hard, and she cringed at the sight of the blue-clad officer standing so close. "Don't know," she croaked. "Wore a mask."

"I'd like to finish my examination before you interview her." The first voice belonged to a white-coated doctor, she now realized.

The policeman nodded.

She looked around her without moving her head. She was in an emergency room cubicle. How long had she been out? She didn't remember leaving her home.

"How did I . . ."

"How did you get here?"

"Yes," she sighed.

"A neighbor came to check on your alarm. He saw you lying on the floor of your living room through the open drapes. He called 911."

"I know the neighbor . . . used to be a SEAL."

"Yes, I believe the older gentleman is former military," the policeman said.

"Not so bad . . . guess."

The officer laughed, but she didn't know why.

A nurse joined the doctor and they gently examined her, checking her reflexes and responses, asking lots of questions.

Finally, the doctor sent the nurse out of the cubicle for a pain reliever and he straightened to stand beside her bed. "I'd like you to have an MRI, but from my initial examination, you appear to be a very lucky young woman. You appear to have no more than a mild concussion. It could have been a lot worse."

She blinked. "Yeah. I think he wanted to kill me."

"Why do you say that?" the policeman asked.

That began the interrogation.

Chapter 4

It was hard to focus, and she just wanted to go to sleep, not to mention that talking to the authorities always made her tense. She had no good memories connected with the police. A state policeman had come to tell her and her mom that her dad was dead. After that, her encounters with the police had always been full of fear . . . both hers and her mother's. Unless Mom had been too drunk to be afraid. Then she'd been belligerent and that had only increased Claire's fear.

It had been years since Claire had had a negative run-in with a cop, but old habits died hard. No matter how irrational they were. But she tried to answer the officer's questions the best she could. Finally, when her words were slurring, the doctor shooed the officer out of her cubicle.

"Can I go home now?" she asked the doctor.

"I would still like to do an MRI."

She shuddered inwardly at what that kind of test would cost. "No."

"You need it."

"You said . . . concussion not so bad." It was hard to concentrate after answering so many questions for the officer. She was so tired and her head still hurt.

"I would like to confirm that diagnosis with the test."

"Not good enough reason . . ." She drew in a shallow breath. "I want to go home now."

"Do you live alone?"

"Yes."

"You aren't going to like hearing this, but in that case, with your symptoms, I would rather keep you overnight for observation than send you home."

"No." She didn't have medical insurance. No way was she going to stay overnight in the hospital. The bill from the ambulance and her emergency room visit would be high enough.

"You will be taking an unnecessary risk with your health."

"But not a big risk." And it was necessary, even if he couldn't see it.

"That depends on how you look at it," he said.

"Not staying."

The doctor nodded his head curtly, as if he could tell it would be useless to argue further.

"You'll need to call someone. You cannot go home alone, and you'll have to sign a release form saying you are denying the prescribed medical treatment."

"I'll sign the form." But there was no one she could call.

When she told him that, he would try again to insist she stay overnight.

She opened her mouth, prepared to argue her case despite her aching head and weakened state. The doctor got called to another patient before she could start, and she breathed a sigh of relief. If she could get up and get dressed before he got back, she would have a stronger case for discharging herself.

She gingerly slid her legs over the side of the bed and pulled herself into a sitting position with the handbar on the bed. Then she stayed where she was until her head stopped spinning. Slowly, moving her head as little as possible, she stood up and then shuffled, one slow step at a time, to the cupboard where she figured they had stored her clothes.

She searched it gingerly, careful not to jar her head with her movements. She hit pay dirt on the third drawer. She couldn't stifle a groan of frustration when she realized what she was looking at. She'd been brought in to the hospital in her pajamas.

A spaghetti strap tank top and white cotton bikini panties were hardly appropriate for her trip home. Especially on public transport. Maybe she could wear a hospital gown over them and splurge on a taxi. It would cost less than staying the night in the hospital.

It took forever to get her clothes on. She was sliding the gown back on like a robe when the curtain swept back with a series of metallic clicks.

"What are you doing out of bed?"

She looked up and stared, not able to comprehend the vision before her. It was Hotwire, and his eyes were blazing blue fire at her.

"I'm getting dressed." She paused and took a deep breath, then let it out. "So I can go home."

"Have you lost your mind?"

"It feels like it got knocked out of my head," she admitted.

"Claire, damn it to hell."

She'd never heard Hotwire swear. It sounded strange and gave the impression he was really rattled. He didn't stop with one word, either, but let out a string of obscenities that would have made any dockworker proud.

He bit off a final four-letter utterance and glared at

her. "You were going to go back to the house where you were attacked . . . *by yourself . . . in this condition?*"

"I can't afford a night in the hospital."

"Can you afford to die?"

She didn't answer. There was nothing to say to that. He wouldn't understand the mentality that came from going where you had to when you knew you had no options. Most people took their personal safety for granted, assuming it was theirs by right. She knew it was a luxury a person could not always afford.

For no reason she could understand, her eyes filled with tears. And it made her mad. She never cried, darn it. Tears were for the weak and she was not weak. Not like her parents. She'd proven that time and again. And she'd keep proving it until she believed it.

He said something under his breath and then strong hands gently helped her pull the gown on. He tugged it close and tied the dangling strings to keep it that way.

When he was done, he carefully lifted her into his arms. "It'll be okay, sugar."

The doctor came back in. He took in the sight of Hotwire standing there, holding her in his arms like a small child, though even in her awful condition she felt one hundred percent female, being held like this.

He smiled wryly. "I take it she'll be going home with you."

"Why isn't she staying for overnight observation?"

"She refused. She also refused the MRI I recommended." Evidently, the doctor believed he'd found an ally in Hotwire.

Hotwire looked down at her. "Why not?"

"I don't have medical insurance."

His jaw tightened, but he didn't blast her like she expected. "I'll take her home with me."

She smiled, relieved. "Thank you."

"After the MRI," he said grimly.

Now it was the doctor's turn to smile.

Claire was almost asleep when they got to Hotwire's hotel, and she let him pick her up out of the car and carry her to the elevator without so much as a murmur.

Once inside, she stirred in his arms. "Are you sure you won't get in trouble for having an extra person in your room?"

"It's not a problem."

She sighed. "I'm surprised no one said anything when you carried me through the lobby. The desk clerk sure looked hard."

"I'm positive he's seen stranger."

"Than a guest dressed like a hospital patient reject?"

"Sure. This is downtown Portland, not Mayberry. I've been here less than a week and I've seen no less than a dozen heavily pierced punk rockers, a group of Goth vampire wannabes, and a woman who was at least sixty wearing a pair of pink satin hot pants and a studded black leather jacket."

Claire's head snuggled trustingly against his shoulder. "If you say so."

He let them into his room and carried her through to the bedroom. It was hard to force himself to lay her down on the bed when they got there, but he did it.

He pulled back the covers and then moved her under them. "I'll get you something to drink."

When he came back with a glass of juice from the minibar, she was fighting to keep her eyes open. "I don't have any clothes."

"I'll go to the house and get some for you."

"Thanks . . ." She sighed. "Need my backpack, too," she slurred.

If she thought he was going to let her study in this condition, she was nuts, but he could get the backpack and even her laptop if having them with her made her feel better.

"I'll get it."

She picked fretfully at the hospital gown. "Don't like this."

Neither did he, not nearly as much as what was underneath, but he didn't relish helping her take it off, either. Seeing her practically naked wasn't going to do much for his self-control. The only thing saving them both was her obvious physical frailty. Stifling a sigh and making it a point not to look at her body, he helped her untie the gown and pull it off.

She rolled onto her side facing him, her pretty mouth turned down at the edges. "It hurts, Hotwire."

"I'm sorry." She'd already had pain meds in the hospital and couldn't have another dose for a couple of hours.

"Try to sleep."

"Yes." Her eyes slid shut, but the tension of pain was stamped on her features.

He sat down at the end of the bed and turned the covers back so he could take her foot in his hand. He massaged it and put pressure on the points he'd learned to from a Chinese doctor on a mission a few years back.

"Feels nice," she said without opening her eyes.

"Good." He kept it up and eventually her body relaxed into sleep.

He made himself let go of her so he could leave to get her things before she woke up again.

When he got back into the room, she was still sleeping. Her red hair was a wild mass of curls on the pillow, surrounding a pale face marred by the exhaustion of pain. He'd had injuries like that and knew how much they hurt. Claire wasn't a merc—she wasn't even a soldier. She should never have to know that kind of pain. And feeling as weak as she was, she had still planned to go back to the house and take care of herself.

He shook his head.

She'd even admitted in the car that she had no intention of going to Belmont Manor so someone there could look over her. It was her place of employment, not her personal nursing staff, she'd said acerbically.

His mouth twisted. She was too stubborn for her own good. Too independent. Though she hadn't demurred even once when he said he was going to help her. Did that mean she didn't mind depending on him, or that she knew arguing would do her no good? She was far from stupid, after all.

The next twenty-four hours were hell on them both. She just wanted to sleep and hide from the pain in her head. However, he had to keep waking her up to check her responses, make her eat, and keep her hydrated with juice and water. Neither of them enjoyed the process.

But finally, he allowed her to fall into a deep sleep, knowing the worst of the danger had passed. He took a shower, put on a pair of jockey shorts, and climbed into the bed to go to sleep himself.

He woke up six hours later, instantly alert, but confused all the same. Soft, feminine warmth was draped across his chest, and Claire's face rested right over his heart.

How had she gotten there? From her boneless, well settled condition he figured she'd been there a while. Why hadn't he woken up? No one had gotten the drop on him during sleep since his first year in the army when Nitro played a typical nighttime prank on a fellow recruit. It had only taken one time, and Hotwire had learned to sleep with a subconscious awareness of what was going on around him. So, how had he slept through Claire not only invading his personal space, but draping herself over him like a soft, warm, and very pleasant blanket?

One of his arms was wrapped around her back and his other hand rested on the silky smoothness of her thigh. His morning boner tightened to the point of pain. This was bad.

Carefully, with no intention of waking her, he began to extricate himself from her embrace before his libido convinced him to do something that would embarrass them both. However, the second he started to slide out from under her warmth, she woke up, jolting upward with a jerk and bringing her knee into painful contact with his balls.

"Aaagh, Claire!"

"Hotwire?" She stared at him like she'd never seen a man before. "What are you doing under me?"

"Getting my nads decimated," he ground out.

Her brown eyes widened and she gasped. Then the offending knee moved back.

When she went to sit up all the way, she ended up straddling his thigh and wincing with pain as she grabbed her head. "Oh, gosh . . . that hurts."

He couldn't stand the pain in her eyes. "Lie back down."

She shook her head and then cried out. "Oh, that was stupid."

"Claire."

"I can't lie back down. I'm on top of you."

"Apparently you slept there."

"I did?" she asked, sounding supremely shocked. "That's not possible."

"I promise you, it is."

"But I've never slept on top of someone before." Her

eyes looked wild. "It must have been the painkillers. I'm not used to taking drugs of any kind." She bit her lip. "I have to get off you, but if I move again, it's going to hurt."

He reached out and holding her by the waist, lifted her off of him. Then, changing his hold on her, one hand on her waist and the other cradling her head, he lowered her to her back. "Is that better?"

"Yes, thank you," she replied primly and then bit her lip, her face contorting again.

"What is it?"

"I have to go to the bathroom. Badly."

He didn't say anything, just picked her up and carried her to the en suite. His stealth movement training came in handy, allowing him to move quickly without jostling her. The way she held her thighs tightly together said it all.

He stood her beside the commode. "Can you handle it from here?"

She blushed, a fiery red. "Yes."

He left the door open, but absented himself so she would have a measure of privacy. His head was still reeling from the fact she'd managed to ensconce herself on top of him during the night without him noticing.

She came out of the bathroom wearing the hotel robe over her little top and cotton panties, moving about an inch at a time. He swiftly crossed the room and picked her up to carry her back to the bed.

"You're really strong." She didn't say it like a come-on and he didn't take it as such.

"Comes with the territory."

Her small hand rested against his chest, sending totally inappropriate messages to his libido despite his brain's warning that that wasn't a come-on, either. "Thank you for taking care of me."

"My pleasure." And as depraved as it made him feel

to acknowledge it, because she was weak and wounded, he had to admit it really was pure pleasure to be carrying Claire like this.

When they reached the bed, she clung to his neck instead of letting him lower her to the mattress. "I don't want to lie down again."

"You need your rest."

"I've been in bed *forever.*"

"Only about thirty hours, actually."

"That *is* forever. No one should have to stay in bed that long."

He just smiled, enjoying her crankiness.

She pouted, her lower lip protruding in an expression both endearing and sexy. "I'm hungry."

"We'll have to fix that, then." He settled her on the suite's sofa in the main room. "We can order lunch from room service."

She leaned against the sofa arm, looking pale but determined to remain upright. "Okay."

He grabbed the menu and skimmed it for something vegetarian for her. "Any preferences?"

"I'm not a picky eater."

"Except the no-meat thing," he said with a teasing smile.

"That's not being picky."

"What is it, then?"

"Self-protection."

Considering what she'd told him about why she chose not to eat meat, he had to agree.

He called down an order for them both before sitting in the armchair near Claire. "Why don't we go over what happened Sunday morning?"

Claire breathed a sigh of relief when the room-service waiter knocked on the suite's door. She was impressed with Hotwire's interrogation style, but it was exhausting. She'd thought the police officer was thorough, but she and Hotwire had only been talking about thirty minutes and she felt like he already knew more about what had happened than she did.

He rolled the food trolley over to her, having dismissed the waiter at the door. He hadn't bothered to dress, though he had pulled a pair of jeans on before room service arrived. The top snap was undone, though. He had an incredible body, all sculpted muscle and golden skin.

It was all she could do not to fan herself with her hand.

Luckily, the food grabbed the attention of her senses and she sniffed the air appreciatively. "It smells delicious."

"The food here is pretty good."

Her tummy rumbled. "I don't know if it would matter."

"You haven't eaten much in the last thirty hours."

Some of that time was hazy in her memory, as she had slipped in and out of restorative sleep. "You kept feeding me dry toast."

"I didn't want you getting nauseous and puking. The last thing your poor head needed was for your body to start heaving."

"Well, it worked." She smiled and pulled the silver warming lid off her plate.

He'd ordered her a tofu and vegetable stir-fry over rice. She could smell the Chinese spices and soy sauce and it made her mouth water.

She looked up when he said, "Excuse me for a minute."

She nodded and he disappeared into the bedroom. He returned shortly, wearing a t-shirt that hugged the rugged contours of his chest, and the snap on his jeans had been closed. He'd even pulled on socks and shoes.

"You got cold?" she asked, disappointed at the loss of such a fine view.

"My mama would string me up by my toes if I came to the table half-dressed to eat with a lady."

"Your mother sounds like she ruled with an iron fist."

"Wrapped in the velvet glove of southern gentility."

"You love her." It was in the tone of his voice every time he mentioned the other woman, that and a deep, abiding respect.

"Doesn't everybody love their mother?"

"I don't know." She wasn't sure *love* described the feelings she'd had for Norene when she died.

Pity, anger, confusion, despair . . . they'd all been there, but love? Claire couldn't remember feeling much liking for her mom, not since her dad's death and the subsequent reversal of roles between her and her surviving parent. Norene had done too much to make Claire's life miserable for her to feel the kind of abiding affection Hotwire obviously had for his mom.

He lowered his tall frame into the armchair again, and then uncovered his plate. With shock, she realized he'd ordered an identical meal to hers for himself.

At her inquiring look, he smiled. "It occurred to me that watching other people eat meat couldn't be pleasant for you, considering your imagination's tendency to wander in less than appetizing paths."

"I didn't mean to make it uncomfortable for you to eat what you prefer."

"Right now, I prefer a vegetable stir-fry."

"You're a very nice man, Hotwire." But she couldn't let him think she needed that kind of consideration. "But don't worry about me. I mean it. What you eat is not a problem for me."

He frowned at her. "You're not used to people showing you consideration, are you?"

He made it sound like she was deprived. "Josette's very considerate. So are Les and Queenie."

She had people in her life. Maybe not many, but some.

He just shook his head. The interrogation continued over lunch until Hotwire was finally content that he knew everything. Then, they finished their meal in silence, the expression on his face thoughtful. When they were done, he rolled the trolley out into the hall.

She curled up in the corner of the couch, tucking her feet under her. "Any amazing insights?" she asked as he rejoined her.

He frowned, his blue eyes dark with unnamable emotion. "Nothing amazing at all. To tell you the truth, I'm pretty stumped."

"You said you thought one of the terrorists might decide to get even with Josette."

"Yes. We tried to keep her name out of the official investigation, but under the circumstances, it wasn't easy."

"We?"

"Me and my friends in the FBI."

"Oh. It must be nice to have such well-connected contacts."

"It can be."

"So, whoever saw her there must have told others. Somebody came after her, then mistook me for her because I'm the only woman currently living in her house." She sighed. "That's the only thing that makes sense because there would be no reason for anyone to want to kill *me*."

"We don't know your assailant was trying to kill you."

She snorted. "Yeah, right. He had a pillow over my face. He was smothering me. What would you call it?"

"He may have only intended to knock you out, or maybe disorient you . . ."

"To what purpose?"

Hotwire's mouth flattened grimly. "He might have wanted to rape you, or kidnap you, or tie you up so he could burglarize your home without the threat of you calling the cops."

"But the alarm was going off."

"Okay, so the burglary scenario doesn't fit, but either of the other two still does."

"You really think a rapist would stick around to do the deed while a house alarm was going off?"

"Criminals ignore alarms all the time, because in many cases, so does everyone else. Most alarms are not set up to alert local law enforcement and even those that are set up that way are limited by the response time of the local police."

"Josette's house alarm is designed to dial 911 with an automated message." She'd never forget the stress or embarrassment of having to explain to the officers who answered the call how she had forgotten to code her entry into the alarm and hadn't noticed it was going off for several minutes.

"Yes."

"But the officer at the emergency room told me my neighbor called it in."

"He told me the same thing. I looked into that while you were sleeping. Apparently, the automated call went unanswered because of simple human error. The 911 operator put the call on hold and then disconnected it by accident."

"That's convenient for the bozo who broke in and tried to smother me."

"Just as there is no such thing as a totally fail-safe security system, there is no such thing as a perfect person."

She sighed. "I know, but it's not exactly reassuring to think that but for the can of mace you insisted I keep in my bedroom, I could be dead."

"If the assailant had been a professional, that wouldn't have made any difference."

"What do you mean?"

"What color were your assailant's eyes?"

"It was dark, but I think they were a light color, like gray or pale blue."

"Right. A professional would have worn night goggles, which would have, one, given him better vision; two, protected his identity; and three, prevented the mace from blinding him."

"So, you think whoever broke in isn't used to doing things like that?"

"I'd say so, yes."

"Just because he forgot his goggles?"

"There's more."

"Tell me."

"Well, he broke into the house like an amateur."

"What does that mean?"

"He broke a window instead of picking the lock."

"What window? Wouldn't I have heard something?"

"Probably not. He broke the window on the door from the garage to the backyard. It was a simple matter of reaching in and unlocking the dead bolt with the key dangling from the nail beside the door."

She felt herself blushing. "I didn't want to lose it."

"And you didn't really believe you were in danger."

"Well, no, I didn't. I've been attacked and almost smothered to death, and I'm still having trouble wrapping my mind around that little bit of reality."

"There was no sign of forced entry to the door from the garage to the kitchen."

She bit her lip, feeling foolish. "Josette and I never locked that door."

"If I'd known that, I would have insisted on replacing

the door to the outside with a solid steel one. I wanted to anyway, but Wolf and I ran out of time."

"I'm sorry. I feel so stupid. I might as well have put a sign in my window inviting him in."

Hotwire shook his head. "Don't apologize. A determined criminal will find a way in. You did not invite anything. Do you hear me?"

She swallowed at the vehemence in his voice. "Yes, I hear you. I'm not the bad guy, just an idiotic house renter."

"You are in no way an idiot. Your only crime, if it is one, is that you were too trusting in the safety of your surroundings."

No doubt. She'd learned early in life to assess her level of personal safety. Josette's house had always been at the top of the charts, so incredibly different from the places she'd lived in after her dad died. "I'm also not hot on revenge, so I find it difficult to imagine anyone wanting vengeance against Josette enough to try to kill me thinking I was her."

"We can't be sure the assailant was after Josie."

"But it's the only thing that makes sense," she reiterated.

"Nevertheless, when investigating a crime, it's good to remember that just because a chicken has wings, doesn't mean it can fly."

"In other not-so-colorful words, appearances can be deceptive."

"Yes."

"Um . . . Hotwire, you're a former mercenary, turned security specialist. How do you know so much about investigating a crime?"

Chapter 5

He relaxed in the chair, stretching his long legs out in front of him. "It's a hobby of mine. I've done some freelance work for the government between missions."

"But how . . ."

"I trained in covert ops in the Rangers. I learned how to be a spy—duty first, people second, and the mission supreme." His words were bitter, and she wondered at the story behind them.

But right now it was hard enough to keep her mind focused on the problem at hand, much less try to figure out his complex mind. She was growing tired again, though not as sleepy as before, and the pain in her head was overwhelming.

"Back to your assailant."

"What about him?"

"You said that he stayed, holding the pillow over your face, despite the fact that the alarm was going off."

"Yes. He was counting."

"He was tracking the time on the alarm and your time without air. The mark of a professional."

"But I thought you said he was an amateur?"

"I'm having trouble classifying him, to tell the truth."

"Why does it matter if the person who came after me was 'in the business' or not?" she asked, using a phrase she'd learned from Lester.

"One thing about that terrorist group we took down . . . they were well trained. Too much about this attack does not jive with that."

"But nothing else makes sense." If she kept saying it, maybe he would get it. "No one could want to kill *me*."

"Are you sure about that?"

She couldn't believe he had to ask. Maybe she was naïve, but she didn't think most people spent a lot of time worrying about getting knocked off. "I'm positive."

"Then I guess we're going with the theory that it's Josie they are after. For now, anyway."

For forever, as far as she was concerned. "That means she's in danger."

"Not hardly, if the people going after her are all as untrained as your assailant, but I already contacted Nitro to alert him to the situation."

"Good. I hope they are having a great time."

"According to Nitro, it's heaven on earth."

She couldn't imagine the taciturn man saying anything that effusive, but he must have implied his version of the equivalent. And that did not surprise her. Nitro and Josette had found something that Claire thought was extremely rare . . . honest, reciprocal, and unconditional love between two people who could genuinely count on each other.

Hotwire paused. "He and Josie want me to stay with you until they return."

"I . . ."

"If you say it's not necessary, I'm going to get irritated."

"I wasn't going to say that. It *is* necessary. Even I can see that. I don't want to end up a corpse in my own bed, but I don't know how it's going to work out for you."

"What do you mean?"

"What about your business?"

"I've been working remotely from this suite for the last few days already."

He'd said something when he first brought her to the hotel about having been in Portland a few days. It hadn't computed at the time, but now it made sense. Sort of. "That explains how you got to the hospital so fast, but I don't understand why you were here. Are you on an assignment?"

"Not unless you count watching over you."

"You came for me?"

"Yes."

"But why? I mean, I know Josette asked you to keep an eye out for me, but I think she meant make the occasional phone call, not keep a watching brief."

He shrugged. "I didn't like being so far away when your alarm went off the first time. There was nothing I could do from Montana. So, I decided to take care of that."

This man took his promises to his friends very seriously. "So, why didn't you come and stay at the house?"

He grimaced, his gaze filled with self-censure. "I should have. None of this would have happened if I'd been there."

Her own eyes widened. "You can't believe that. It's not your fault. You can't be sure your presence would have made any difference."

"Can't I?"

That actually made her smile, despite the fact that her head was pounding. "Your arrogance is showing again."

"Again?"

"You're pretty impressed with your effect on women, too."

"I prefer to think of it as justifiably confident. There's a reason roosters strut, you know."

She laughed and then had to smother a groan at the pain it brought. "I still don't understand why you didn't come to the house." Was it the bash she'd received to the head that made everything so confusing, or was this situation as surreal as it felt to her? "Surely you don't think I would have minded?"

He shook his head, his expression primitive and just slightly predatory. "I checked into the hotel because I knew that if I stayed with you, I'd be sleeping in your bed and not because I kicked you out of it."

"Oh." She licked her unaccountably dry lips. "And that would be bad."

He merely looked at her and let her draw her own conclusions. Of course it would be bad; no matter how good that kiss at the wedding was, she knew sex wasn't all it was cracked up to be. Not even close, and sex between them would ruin what there was of a friendship between them.

It always did.

She didn't ask him what he planned to do now since the decision to stay together had been taken out of both their hands.

Hotwire watched as Claire tried to stifle yet another yawn. She'd insisted on staying out of bed and watching television after lunch. She'd wanted to study for her finals, but he'd bullied her into resting. It hadn't been that hard after he explained he'd already been in touch with the university and she was scheduled to take them all a week late.

Graduating midyear had a lot of advantages, one of them being that she wasn't under a graduation ceremony deadline. He was glad, because he got the impression that no amount of bullying or logic would have held her back if putting off taking the finals meant waiting to graduate.

Unlike Josette, who had been content to take her education at a slower pace, Claire was driven to finish *now*. It could be because of finances, but he got the feeling there was more to it than that. He'd like to know what, and now that they were forced to be in one another's company, he intended to live dangerously and indulge his curiosity about her.

He stood and stretched. He'd been working on a security plan for a large computer manufacturer while surreptitiously watching Claire lose her battle with exhaustion.

He walked over to her. "I think it's time you went back to bed."

"It's still the middle of the day."

He bent down and lifted her, noting with some concern that she didn't complain at all. "If you want to get well enough to study for your finals, you need to rest so you can resume normal activities," he said as he carried her through to the bedroom.

She grimaced in pain as he tucked her into bed.

"I'll get you your meds. You haven't had any since you got up earlier."

"No, thank you. I don't need anything." But her pain-dulled eyes denied her claim.

"You don't have to put on a tough front for my benefit. You need the pain medication and you're taking it."

"It's not a front." Her all-too-kissable mouth flattened into an intractable line. "No meds."

"Why not?"

"I don't like drugs. Of any kind."

"It's pain medication, sugar. You're not shooting up heroin."

"No."

"You need it."

"No."

His teeth gritted with frustration. "You are being stupidly stubborn."

"Maybe you can do that thing you did last night with my feet?" she asked, like she was offering a concession. "It helped."

He shook his head, whether against his own urges or her denial, he wasn't sure. "I know you're into health food and all that, but a few doses of pain medication are not going to permanently damage your body."

"No."

"Don't you know any other words?"

"I'm sorry. I don't mean to be an irritant, but I really don't want to take any more pills. If you don't want to do the thing with my feet, that's okay. I'll be fine. Really."

"You're a lousy liar." He reached out and brushed her hair from her temple. "I'll do the acupressure massage, but you have to promise to take the pain meds if it doesn't help enough."

She said nothing and he knew he didn't have her agreement.

He would have to do a very thorough job with the massage. Uncovering her feet, he took one into his hand. He was thorough, using every bit of skill he had learned. Her eyes slid shut and her facial muscles relaxed slightly, telling him he was having an effect.

He massaged up her calves, using a combination of

kneading and acupressure to decrease the pain and leave her muscles pliant. When he reached her knees, he didn't test his self-control by going any further. Instead, he moved to her hands, enjoying the feel of her soft skin more than he should as he tried to take away her pain.

No matter what his reason for touching her, it was having a predictable effect on his body. As his kneading fingers moved up her arms to her shoulders, the covers slipped, revealing nipples as hard as his aching cock.

He couldn't help it—he groaned.

Her eyes fluttered open. "Are you okay? If you're tired of doing it, you can stop."

Was she really that naïve? Maybe her hurting head was clouding her reasoning. "I'm not tired of touching you."

"Oh." Her eyes slid shut again and he continued the massage, his gaze sliding to those hard little nips over and over again.

He wanted to see them without the barrier of her shirt. Would they be pink or a dusky brown? Sure as certain, right now they were flushed red with arousal.

He continued the massage up her neck, and pressed gently against a series of acupressure points right up to the matching pair on top of her head and between her eyes. Unable to stop himself, he moved his fingers down her temples, her neck, and over her collarbone until he stilled with his fingertips on the upper swells of her breasts.

She moaned, a soft, sexy sound. Her eyes opened again, this time the arousal in their brown depths unmistakable. "Hotwire?"

"There is another natural pain reliever that's even more effective than acupressure massage."

She licked her lips. "What?"

"Pleasure. A long, extended climax will release chemicals into your bloodstream that obliterate pain."

"I . . ."

He let his hands slide down just far enough to cup her generous breasts, playing his thumbs over the hard peaks. "If you won't let me give you pain meds, sugar, let me give you pleasure."

"There's something wrong with that reasoning, but I can't quite work out what," she said in a breathy voice.

"Don't try too hard. It'll make your head ache worse."

Her lips tilted in a small smile. "Heaven forbid."

"Will you let me pleasure you, Claire?"

"You can try."

"Is that a dare?"

"No . . . I'm just not very responsive."

"Your body says otherwise."

Her brows drew together. "Yes, it's really weird. I wonder if the concussion has something to do with it."

He shook his head at that bit of nonsense. "So, I have your permission to touch you intimately?"

"Yes." Then she hissed as he pinched her nipples and just as quickly released them.

"Okay, there are a few rules for this kind of pleasuring."

"Rules?"

"Number one, you need to stay relaxed. At all times."

"That's not possible. I don't feel relaxed right now."

"Maybe we need to fix that before the pleasure starts. Can I pull the covers back?" he asked, his fingers poised to do so.

"If you're sure you want to do this." She sounded like she honestly could not understand why he'd want to. "You know I can't . . ."

"I know." What did she think, he was some kind of

selfish adolescent who would demand sex in payment for helping her feel better? "I don't expect you to and I wouldn't let you even if you were offering, which I'm intelligent and mature enough to realize you aren't. Okay?"

"Okay."

He pulled the blankets back, teasing himself by revealing her sexy curves one tiny bit at a time. When he had the blankets at the bottom of the bed and her entire body was exposed to his hot gaze, he just stopped and stared at her. She had the perfect woman's figure. Full breasts, a small waist and narrow hips, but not so narrow that she could ever be mistaken for a boy. He knew her butt was heart-shaped, but he'd give about anything to examine it in detail.

He wasn't going to. It was hard enough on him to be doing this. How he was going to keep his hands off of her after giving her a climax he had no idea, but he'd do it.

He'd faced harder challenges . . . somewhere in his past, even if he couldn't remember them.

"Is something the matter?" she asked.

"No. You are just so beautiful, it about takes my breath."

"You like my body?"

Was she serious? "What's not to like? You're the stuff adolescent boys' wet dreams are made of."

She frowned in distaste. "I don't want to star in anyone's *wet dreams.*"

"Not even mine?"

Her eyes widened and then filled with reluctant interest. "Do you dream about me?"

Instead of answering her, he started touching her feet again. If they started talking about his dreams, he was going to want to live them out, and his current level of arousal was painful enough. She made a purring sound as he kneaded her arches and he smiled.

Giving her even this level of pleasure was a major delight for him. He could grow addicted to that sound.

He worked his way up her legs, reveling in the freedom to touch her, this time with no intention of stopping at her knees. Masseuses did this all the time without getting boners, but day-am . . . he was so hard he could have drilled for oil in a rock canyon with his penis.

He didn't mind one bit, though.

The sexual discomfort was worth it because she was relaxing and her eyes had closed again. The frown of pain smoothed from her pale features, to be replaced by an expression of bliss that made him feel as arrogant as she'd accused him of being.

He was doing that to her and he loved it.

He was careful not to touch any blatantly erogenous zones at first as he massaged her body into total liquid compliance to his touch. So when he caressed her breasts again through the shirt, she didn't even moan. He massaged them as carefully as he had the rest of her body.

When he zeroed in on her nipples, he brought them to rigidity slowly so that her body remained pliant. But once he began to play with them in earnest, she moaned and arched upward.

He pressed down on her breastbone. "Relax, baby. Think boneless, liquid thoughts."

"Okay," she sighed out, relaxing once again against the bed.

He played with her, letting one hand slide down her stomach and back up again until the scent of her arousal filled the air around them. Every time she started to stiffen, he stopped touching her or massaged a less erogenous area until she relaxed again. He was shaking with his own need by the time he let his fingertips slide underneath the waistband of her panties.

He almost lost it at the feel of the damp, silky curls covering her mound. She cried out when his finger dipped between her humid, swollen outer labia. He stopped moving his hand and reminded her to relax.

"I can't. It's too much."

"You can do it, Claire. It will be worth it. Trust me."

"I'll try," she said on a pant.

"Breathe slowly, sugar."

She took a deep breath and did as he said. He started touching her again. She felt so good, so silky and wet and hot.

He dipped into her, barely trespassing her opening. "You are amazingly tight."

She mumbled something he couldn't catch and he smiled despite the pain of his acute arousal.

He circled her wetness, brushing upward to contact with her clitoris. The small nub was swollen and hard against his fingertip.

He touched it, telling her how beautiful she was, how good she felt to him, but stopping every time she tensed in any way. He brought her to the edge of release again and again while her breathing ruptured. He wanted to keep her from spending until she was so ready to go over, he could blow on her and she would come.

When they got to that point and she reached her ultimate pleasure, her orgasm lasted as long as most men spent in foreplay. It was the most beautiful thing he had ever seen. She arched, crying softly and then moaning out her pleasure.

When her body fell back against the bed in total abandon, he slid his hand from her warmth and then cupped her from the outside of her panties until her breathing pattern indicated she had fallen asleep.

He covered her up and headed for the shower to take care of the boner that had been tenting his jeans for the last hour, or more.

Claire woke up to the sound of a steady thumping. It wasn't an unpleasant sound, like someone hammering. More like those heartbeat recordings played to calm crying babies. She'd read about it on the Internet and then listened to the wave files that accompanied the article. She had easily understood why the sound soothed babies. It was nice. Comforting.

So was the warmth against her cheek and sense of security she felt, from being held.

Oh, gosh, she was being held. That heartbeat was Hotwire's and he was underneath her, just like earlier. How had she gotten here?

Had she rolled over on top of him? She couldn't see him pulling her into his arms, but then she would never have imagined him touching her the way he had before she slept, either. And not expecting recompense in her body. Men just were not that generous.

But he had been.

He had asked if he could give her pleasure to take away the pain. She'd agreed, but been totally unprepared for what he meant by pleasure. She'd never experienced anything like it, which was not so surprising. She'd be willing to bet few women had, but she'd never read about anything like it, either. And she read a lot.

It had worked, too. The dull ache in her head was now nothing like the sharp, slicing pain she'd experienced earlier.

But that still didn't explain how she had ended up on top of him. She'd been a light sleeper for as long as she could remember. Claire simply could not see how

Hotwire could have pulled her into his arms or how she could have rolled on top of him without her waking up.

Not only had she slept very soundly, but she had slept for *hours*. She could see the bedside clock from where she lay on top of Hotwire. Unbelievably, it was just a little after five A.M. And other than the almost negligible throb of pain in the back of her head, she felt great.

Ready for anything. If normal sex did this for a person, celibacy would be just a word, not her way of life by choice. What if sex with Hotwire was that good?

It was an interesting thought, but not one she wanted to explore at the moment. Even if maybe he was a guy who could make her feel things she had thought were pure fantasy before last night. He was still totally commitment-phobic.

The thought of trusting someone intimately who didn't do the "C" word was just plain stupid.

"You awake, Claire?"

"Yes."

"I thought so."

"How did you know?" She hadn't moved.

"You're tense and your breathing changed."

"Oh."

"You're on top of me again."

"I noticed."

"It's starting to become a habit."

"I'm sorry."

"Why? Did I say I didn't like it?"

"It can't be comfortable to sleep with a woman draped across you like a dead weight."

"Comfortable? No, I wouldn't call the way I feel right now comfortable . . ."

She tried to move, but the arms he had wrapped around her tightened.

"Hotwire?"

"Uncomfortable isn't the same as unpleasant. In fact, there are times I find it distinctly pleasurable to be uncomfortable."

She shifted, trying to move, and felt an unfamiliar hardness against her thigh. She stilled, shocked by the heat pulsing off of it and awed by its dimensions. Those dimensions were all too evident to her, because there was nothing between her thigh and his erection.

"You're naked," she gasped.

Chapter 6

"I always sleep in the buff."

"You were wearing jockey shorts before."

"A concession to your modesty."

She leaned up, propping her hands on his hard chest and doing her best to look into his eyes. However, he was little more than a vague shape in the darkness, though she could certainly feel him.

She was careful not to move her lower body against the blatant evidence of his arousal. "You don't think I'm modest anymore because I let you touch me yesterday?"

It was a logical conclusion, but she didn't like it.

"Does my nudity offend you?" he asked instead of answering her.

Did it? His nakedness titillated her. It intrigued her. It even scared her a little because it made her feel stuff she didn't want to, but it didn't offend her. "No."

She could sense his smile, even though she couldn't quite see it. "You allowing me to touch you had nothing to do with a lack of modesty and everything to do with trust. I'm honored you trusted me with your body."

Coming on the heel of her earlier thoughts, she wasn't sure she liked that conclusion any more than her first one. But it made even more sense. She did trust him. To a point, anyway. As he'd pointed out, she *had* trusted him to help her with her pain and not to push for what she'd been in no position to give. She also trusted him to keep her from harm.

"You are hero material through and through," she mused, trying to work it out in her own mind. "A woman would have to be brain-dead not to realize you can be trusted on some level."

He went rigid beneath her, an inexplicable sense of tension emanating off of him. "I am no hero, Claire. I'm a mercenary . . . a soldier for hire, a man who puts duty to the mission above everything else."

"You are an ex-mercenary, as you are so fond of pointing out, and you can't tell me you don't care about the people you help. I trust you with my safety." Why did she feel the need to keep saying it? It wasn't like she enjoyed trusting a man to that extent and wasn't entirely sure she was using all her smarts in doing so, no matter how heroic he was.

"Since keeping you safe is my current mission, that's an okay bet to take, but don't romanticize me, Claire. I'm no hero in a white hat."

She laughed out loud at that. "I'm the last woman to do that . . . for any man. Believe me. But I don't get why you're so adamant about it. I would think that in your line of work, you would like being seen as the man in the white hat."

"It's an old story and not one I want to get into right now. Probably not ever."

"Okay."

He let out a startled sigh. "That's it? No inquisition?"

"You said you didn't want to talk about it. I respect that. There are things in my past I wish I could forget, things which cannot be changed that define who I am. I guess I'll just be grateful that you see it as your duty to keep me safe and leave it at that."

"Thanks."

"For what, not badgering you?"

"For not moving," he corrected dryly, but she wasn't sure he wasn't thanking her for the other, too. "I don't relish another knee in my nuts."

She accepted the topic change with grace. Like she'd said, she understood. "I'm sorry about that. I hope I didn't do you any real harm."

"I survived."

"Barely."

"Please. I'm not that fragile."

"A man's testicles are his most vulnerable spot."

"Did you read that on the Internet?"

"Josette told me—well, all of us—during the self-defense classes she taught at the shelter."

"What else did she teach you?" he asked, sounding genuinely interested.

"Some basic hold-breaking techniques. The concept of using your opponent's size against him. That sort of thing."

"She's real good at that last one. I've seen her kick butt on men twice her size." The blatant admiration in his voice for her friend stirred uneasy feelings in Claire that she tried her best to ignore.

She had absolutely no reason or right to be jealous.

"Josette's good at a lot of things," Claire said with a smile she didn't have to force.

"Yeah. Nitro's a lucky dickhead."

She gasped and then laughed. "Do you call all your friends such nice nicknames?"

"Sure. You should hear the one I have for you."

"What is it?" she demanded, instantly curious.

"Terabyte. Because that's how much information I figure you've got stored in your head from all the reading you do on-line and otherwise."

"Oh. Does Josette know you call me that?"

"Sure. They all do. They think it fits, too."

"Oh," she said again, not sure how she felt about that. Being a walking computer wasn't such a bad thing, was it? It was better than being terminally stupid, naïve, or a lush.

"Does she know you call Nitro a lucky dickhead?" Claire asked, tongue in cheek.

"No, because I don't usually. You going to tell her?"

"Nope, but if I ever meet your mother, watch out," she teased. "I bet she would classify *dickhead* with the other words you aren't supposed to say around a female."

He groaned theatrically and she smiled. "This is really strange, us having a conversation in the dark with me on top of you."

"That's not the word I'd use for it."

She choked on a giggle, surprising herself. She *never* giggled. "Maybe it would be better if I moved."

"No doubt. We are definitely playing with fire here." The heat emanating from his skin said he wasn't kidding.

"So, I should move."

"But I like this, don't you?" He ran his hands down and over her backside, making her breath catch in her throat. They settled on her thighs, just below her panty line, a warm and tantalizing presence.

"Uh, yes . . . I like it, too."

"Besides, I've never been a man to shrink from a challenge."

She'd certainly gotten that impression so far. "I see."

"Do you?"

"Actually, not very well. It's pretty dark in here."

"That's probably best. If I could see you, too, I don't think I could control my baser urges."

Honestly, she wasn't sure she wanted him to. What she really wanted was for him to slide his hands over her bare bottom. Which was really stupid. It was one thing to let a guy make you feel good and another to offer your body and the emotions that went along with doing that.

She wished she could believe that sex was as much of a no-brainer as the sexual revolutionaries of decades past had preached it was. But it wasn't. Not for her, anyway. Even when it had been dismal, and that pretty much summed up all her experiences with the opposite sex, she had still felt emotional connections she would have been happier never experiencing.

"What's your name?" she asked, to get her mind off of the feel of his hands on her thighs.

"What?"

"I want to know your name."

"Last time I checked, it was Hotwire," he said as if speaking to a woman severely hampered by a head injury . . . as opposed to one only slightly hampered.

She glared at him through the darkness. "I mean your real name, dufus."

"Dufus?"

"Uh-huh. Just think of it as another friendly nickname."

He was silent for so long, she didn't think he was going to tell her, and then he sighed. "Folks back home call me Brett."

"I like that."

"Why?"

"Because it fits you."

"I mean, why did you want to know?"

"We're friends."

"Josie's my friend, too, but she calls me Hotwire."

"Are you saying she doesn't know your real name?"

"No."

"Are you bothered I do now?"

"No."

For some reason, that made her feel good. "I'm glad." She felt him twitch against her and realized that no amount of subject-changing was going to diminish the risk of their position. "I think I'd better move to the couch."

"We've had this discussion before."

She remembered. When he'd come to help Josette and Nitro on their last mission, Claire had offered Brett her bed, but he'd refused to put her out. Even though, at her size, she was infinitely more suited to sleeping on the sofa than he was. He'd made a pallet on the hard-wood floor and refused to be budged.

The sofa in the suite was even smaller than the one at the house. "Your feet would hang off the end. Heck, probably half your legs would. You are not short."

"I've slept in worse places." He'd said that the time before, too.

"But the point is, I'll fit better on the sofa."

"No, the point is you have a concussion, and no way in hell am I letting you leave this bed."

"You are not my boss."

"I might as well be, because you are in no physical condition to defy me."

"I could just move back to my side of the bed."

"Won't work. We'd just end up like this again, and that would play hell with my self-control."

"And that would bother you, wouldn't it?"

"I'm no masochist."

Neither was she. Usually. If Norene had taught her anything, it was that men could not be relied on, but here Claire was, relying on him to keep her safe. Of course, her dad had done a fair job of teaching her that lesson as well. So, why did she feel so darn protected? Secure, even?

Must be her brain was still scrambled from the concussion. Because physical safety was not security, and that was all that he was offering her.

"Claire?"

"Huh?"

"I think you should move so I can get out of here." His strained voice told its own story, and she didn't think it had anything to do with her being too heavy for him.

"Oh, sorry. You're right, Brett."

He sucked in air. "I prefer Hotwire."

"I like Brett better."

"Only my family calls me Brett."

"You don't want me to use your real name?"

Hotwire sighed, knowing he was going to give in and wishing he wasn't. But damn it, she sounded wounded and he didn't like hurting any woman, but he positively hated doing it to Claire. "Go ahead. I'm used to Hotwire. That's all."

"Thank you."

"It's no big deal."

"Yes, it is."

"Fine. You're welcome." But she was right. It was a big deal.

The only woman besides family to use that name since he was eighteen and joined the army had been Elena. He had asked her to use it, wanting to hear his name on her tongue when she came under him.

He hadn't even had sex with Claire, and yet he felt closer to her than he wanted to be. Damn it to hell, anyway.

Unwilling to wait another second for her to move of her own volition, he lifted her off of him. He was careful not to jostle her and relieved when she made no sounds indicating pain.

He rolled out of bed and headed for the living room. He doubted he was going to sleep any more anyway, so where he lay down really didn't matter.

"Brett."

He stopped at the door. "What?"

"I want to get up and take a shower. I feel a lot better."

"How's your head?"

"It hardly hurts at all."

"Okay."

"Don't say it like you're giving me permission. I would have done it anyway. I don't want you getting the impression you can boss me around, bigger and stronger or not."

"No doubt. You are one determined woman, Claire Sharp."

She came into the living room half an hour later. Her hair was still wet and hung around her head in dark red ringlets. She'd dressed, but the additional clothes did little to hide her feminine beauty. Which was probably his fault. When he'd packed for her, he had rebelled at bringing the oversized t-shirts she wore so often. He found a few tank tops in a drawer and grabbed the pairs of jeans in her dresser and a handful of underwear.

She'd chosen a pale yellow tank top that fit like a glove, and hugged her generous breasts lovingly. He could even see the shadow of her nipples. His sex came to life with a vengeance, going hard and aching in three seconds flat. He spent so much of his time around Claire like that that he was almost used to it. Almost . . .

"You look edible," he growled, bluntly declaring the first thought that popped into his head.

And holy Hannah, she did.

"Thanks. I usually wear this particular top under another shirt, but you didn't bring it. I um . . . noticed there weren't any bras, either."

"I packed quickly." It was a lame excuse, but the truth was that leaving her bra behind had *not* been on purpose. "I'm sorry I forgot."

She smiled and shrugged lightly. "It's okay. I don't mind dressing this way around you . . . I mean, as long as I'm just hanging around a hotel room, it doesn't really matter."

Need exploded inside him, hot and urgent, at her slip of the tongue. She hadn't meant her words as an invitation, but that didn't stop his libido from taking them that way. It took every ounce of his formidable self-control to keep him in his chair.

"But I'd really appreciate it if you would take me to the house."

His brain was still grappling with the near-debilitating desire she sparked in him, and it took a couple of seconds to make sense of what she said. "So you can get a bra?"

"Definitely. There's a reason women my size wear a bra, and it isn't all about looking perky on top."

"It's uncomfortable to go without, huh?"

"Yes, but I also want to get my other books. The one I need to study for my first final is on the dining table along with the printout of the notes I have to turn in with my final Unix project."

"No problem. Let's get some breakfast and then we'll go."

"Room service?"

"It isn't serving yet. I thought we could stop at a pancake house on the way."

She looked down at herself, her lips tipped down in a frown. She definitely wasn't one of those women who ran around showing lots of skin and who was comfortable in clothes that showcased jiggling breasts when she walked.

More's the pity.

"You can borrow one of my shirts to wear over that one. It'll be too big, but you'll be covered."

Her brown eyes glowed. "Great. Thanks."

Even with the stop at the restaurant, it was still early when they arrived at the house.

Claire unlocked the door. "I don't suppose you left off setting the alarm when you came to get my clothes?"

Brett pushed the door open and herded her inside. "I had no choice. The police had to cut the wire because no one knew the deactivation code and you were out cold. I didn't want to leave you alone any longer than I had to, so I didn't take time to fix it."

She heard what he was saying, but she was incapable of responding. Her mind was too busy trying to grapple with what she was seeing. The living room and dining room beyond were a mess. Every drawer had been opened, stuff was all over the place, and even the cushions on the couch had been thrown on the floor.

"Did the police do this?" she asked in disbelief. And if they had, why would they?

Hotwire said a word she'd never heard him use. "No. Someone searched the place after I came to get your clothes."

She rushed for her bedroom, her heart in her throat. What if her locket was gone again?

"Claire, where do you think you're going?"

She ignored Brett's demand and ran into her bedroom. It looked even worse than the living room. Her bedding was everywhere, her clothes ripped out of drawers and strewn across the floor in messy piles. Even her mattress and box springs had been shoved off the bed frame and leaned drunkenly against the far side.

She took it all in with a quick glance before diving for the drawer in her nightstand where she'd taken to keeping the precious necklace.

She fumbled around inside, but it wasn't long before she discovered the necklace was gone. "No," she moaned.

Brett's hands settled on her shoulders. "It's not gone. I put it in the outside pocket of your suitcase when I got your clothes. I'm surprised you didn't notice."

She spun to face Brett, dislodging his hold on her. "How did you know?"

"I *didn't* know that your place was going to get broken into."

She waved her hand dismissively. "I didn't mean that. How did you know to take my necklace?"

"Claire, it's no secret how important it is to you. I just figured you'd want it with you while you were at the hotel."

"Because you didn't intend to bring me back here to stay?"

"Well, no. Not right away, anyway, but that's not important right now."

"It's not?"

"No. You can't go running off half-cocked like you did, coming in here in a situation like this. What if the perp were still in the house?"

She never even considered the possibility. "It's daylight. I guess I just thought he'd be long gone . . . that this kind of stuff happens at night. Sorry."

"Don't worry about it, but I'm going to finish securing the premises. I want you to lock yourself in here until I tell you to open the door—don't touch anything."

"I'd rather go with you."

He just looked at her, and as stubborn as she could sometimes be, even she could see that this was his sort of thing, not hers.

"All right. I'll wait like a good girl."

He gave her a wicked smile. "Don't be too good, sugar. That's no fun at all."

Her heart beat so fast she could feel it from the message in his glittering blue eyes as she locked the door behind him. The man was darn good at the flirting thing. He'd said not to touch anything, so she stood in the middle of the room, hugging herself, realizing that flirting aside . . . she was so cold from shock, she was shivering.

When he returned a few minutes later, she unlocked the door with trembling fingers she felt were a betrayal of the strength she knew inhabited her insides. She hid her hands behind her back. "Did you find anything?"

"Whoever it was broke in the same way they did the night your assailant tried to smother you with the pillow, but there's no sign of him now."

"Him?"

"Foot imprints outside the side door in the garage are those of a man."

"Oh. So my assailant was a guy, too?" She'd been almost sure he had been.

"Yes, and from the shape of the footprints, both break-ins were by the same person."

"Well, that's good to know."

He looked quizzically at her.

"One enemy is preferable over two," she explained. She looked around her. "Why did he do this?"

"It's clear he was looking for something, but this is definitely the job of an amateur."

They were back to that again. "Care to tell me why?" she asked, curious in spite of herself.

"He used way too much energy, there's no pattern to the search, and he left the place in total disarray. Professionals don't leave evidence they've been somewhere unless they have no choice, they want to leave an unspoken message behind, or they are confident they won't be caught."

"Maybe he was in a hurry."

Brett shook his head. "Whoever did this does not realize how much easier it is to track a disorganized criminal rather than an organized one. He left clues to his intentions all over the place."

What kind of clues could Brett see in this mess? "Like what?"

"Like the size of the object he was looking for. It's bigger than a CD because he left all hiding places that small alone."

"You figured that out in the short time you were gone securing the premises?"

"What can I say? I'm good."

Chapter 7

She rolled her eyes at this new bout of his *justified confidence,* as he called it. "And so modest."

"Modesty is for wimps."

She shook her head and smiled.

"Knowing that it is bigger than a CD, unfortunately, does not tell us what exactly it is the perp was looking for. He doesn't appear to have looked in the toilet tanks because your little froufrou decorations are still on them. So, either he's looking for something he didn't expect to be hidden in water, or he didn't think of it."

"So, that really doesn't tell us anything, does it?"

"No. Sometimes, amateurs can be blasted annoying."

She laughed at that.

He scowled. "If you can leave off your hilarity for a moment, maybe you can tell me what you think he was looking for."

"I have no idea." She stared around at the disaster that was her bedroom. "This all seems so unreal. I don't have anything that anyone would want."

"Just like there is no reason anyone would want to attack you?"

"Right."

Brett looked at her, his expression unreadable. "I asked Josie about you and she knows almost nothing about your background."

"She never asked." Not directly, anyway, and Claire had become very adept at sidestepping discussions that could lead to revelations about her past.

It wasn't something she liked to talk about. Although she had a feeling Josette knew more than she'd told Brett, because she could remember a couple of conversations that had bordered on painfully frank.

"Well, I'm asking now."

"What exactly do you want to know?"

"Who, if anyone, from your past might be after you now?"

"There is no one. I told you."

"I know what you told me and I know what I see. The terrorist group we brought down might want to hurt Josie, but they'd have no reason for searching her house. Not now that the FBI has copies of all her files."

"But I don't have anything anyone would want, either."

He said nothing, but she felt a distance opening between them, like he was cutting himself off from her. Suddenly, he wasn't the man who'd given her the most sensual experience of her life. He was an aloof stranger, his eyes assessing her with cold implacability.

"If you did and they didn't find it, it sure as certain wasn't from lack of effort," was all he said, however.

Then he turned and left the room.

She followed him, wanting to see the devastation to the rest of the house and trying to think of some way to bridge the mental barrier he had erected. He obviously didn't believe her.

For three days, he'd given her a steady stream of unstinting and even *compassionate* support. Having it abruptly cease made her realize how much she had come to depend on it. That scared her more than the man who'd tried to smother her with a pillow.

Josette's bedroom wasn't nearly as messy as Claire's, but that was because she had already moved her things to Nitro's house. The bed had been torn apart and empty drawers had been left open, but that was about it.

She found Brett in the kitchen, apparently going back over the room for further clues to the intentions of the person who had attacked her. At least that's what she assumed his careful scrutiny of every inch of the room meant.

"Find anything?" she asked.

He shrugged, his silence screaming along her nerve endings.

She didn't bother to follow him out to the garage, but stayed inside and started tidying things in the living room. She really didn't want to look in his face and keep seeing that blank, I-don't-know-you expression.

He walked in after she'd put the cushions back on the sofa and had started to organize the entertainment center.

"What are you doing?" he asked, his voice accusing.

"Cleaning up." If she sounded like she was talking to a dull-witted ex-merc, she could be forgiven.

It had to be obvious what she was doing.

"I told you not to touch anything. We need to call the authorities and report the break-in."

Have the police involved . . . again? She stifled the shudder the thought gave her. "So they can come and make an even bigger mess with fingerprinting powder all over the place? No, thank you."

"Don't you want the perp caught?" Suspicion laced his voice and vibrated off of him in waves.

She glared at him. "Geez . . . you're not overly paranoid, are you? Of course I want the perp caught."

"Then why no cops?"

She was feeling exposed enough without voicing her irrational fear of the police. She knew it made no sense, but years of conditioning were hard to get rid of. She went on the offensive rather than deal with that reality. "If you wanted to bring in the police, why didn't you call them as soon as we arrived and discovered the house had been broken into?"

"I wanted to look things over first." His arrogance again.

"If you're so good at what you do, then why do we need to call it in at all?"

"Because our chances of finding the culprit increase if we bring in more manpower. Besides, there are records the police have easy access to that I don't."

"Like what?"

"Fingerprint records."

"It would take an absolute idiot to search my house like this and not wear gloves."

"So, maybe he's an idiot." The look he gave her said he thought she was hiding something and he was just waiting for her to confirm that suspicion by arguing again.

Her mouth snapped shut, having been open and ready to do just that. She sighed. He was right, anyway. No matter how much she hated the thought of calling the police, it made sense to do so. Forcing herself to react like the grown-up she was and not the child she'd been, she stopped cleaning.

"Fine, call the cops. I'm taking my books in the back-yard and studying."

The pile she had left on the table was still there, but her notebooks had been scattered all over the floor. She went to pick them up, but was pulled backward by a hand on her shoulder.

"What part of 'do not touch *anything*' did you not understand?"

She moved away from his touch, unable to bear the warmth of his body when his tone was so cold. "What am I supposed to do, stand around and twiddle my thumbs while we wait for the police to come? The break-in isn't exactly an acute situation; it could be hours or even tomorrow before they make it over here."

"So, we wait."

She huffed out an impatient sigh and turned to glare at him. "What difference can it possibly make if I pick up my books and notes?"

That suspicious look was back in his blue eyes and it was all she could do to not stamp her foot.

She gritted out, "I'm not hiding anything, darn it."

"Then why are you being so uncooperative?"

"I'm not. I'm being realistic. I know just how easy it is to evade the law." She sighed, knowing it was useless to argue.

Worse, it would probably nourish his belief she was trying to cover something up. She clamped her mouth closed again.

"What's that supposed to mean?" he asked, the suspicion in his voice magnified.

"Nothing. I didn't mean anything. Call the cops already."

"No. You said you knew how easy it was to evade the law. You want to explain that to me first?"

"Fine," she snapped, pushed beyond endurance.

"Let's say whoever broke in and searched Josette's house didn't wear gloves, no matter how unlikely that scenario is. You said it yourself—he's an amateur, which means this could be his first crime and his fingerprints won't be on file."

"Fingerprints are evidence against him later, not just a way of identifying who he is."

"He has to be caught first and just how is that going to happen? What are the cops going to find that you haven't?"

"I don't know, but you can't rule out the possibility his prints are on file and he may have left them here somewhere."

"Even if he's a criminal, the chances his fingerprints are on file with the local authorities are pretty dismal. And as quickly as many law offices and the FBI are going to centralized computer records, they aren't all there yet. Not by a long shot."

"A small chance is better than no chance."

"Right, only even if they are on file and he has a record, he's probably not gainfully employed and therefore easily traceable—if traceable at all. Do you have any idea how many crimes like this go unsolved every year?"

"Did you read about that on the Internet, too?" The sarcasm in his tone hit her on the raw.

"No. *I lived it.*"

He smiled grimly. "Now we're getting somewhere."

When she realized he'd taken her words as proof that she had something in her past she'd been hiding, she wanted to groan at her own stupidity. Instead she crossed her arms and glowered at him with all the frustration she felt.

Unfazed by her anger, he said, "I'm going to call this in, and then, while we're waiting for the police, you're going to explain what you just said and tell me how I'm supposed to believe a woman with a criminal past doesn't have any enemies."

"I didn't say I had a criminal past." But she knew her denial was useless.

He had a thought stuck in his head, and until she told him the truth, it was going to stay stuck. Maybe even then.

Unsurprisingly, his only reply to her assertion was to turn away and make the call on his cell phone.

When he was done, he turned back to face her. "Someone will be by in an hour or so."

"Great, here's hoping it's not too much *or so*."

"Let's go for a walk in the park. Maybe the fresh air will improve your mood."

"I'll still be with you, won't I?"

He clenched his jaw, his blue eyes narrowed. "Yes."

"Then I doubt my mood will improve."

He didn't say another word until they'd walked half the circumference of the park. "Explain."

"What, the theory behind nanotechnology? Or did you want me to put quantum physics in easy-to-use terms?"

"Neither, smart mouth." For just a second he sounded exasperated rather than distant, but then he drew his cold demeanor around him like a force field again. "You know exactly what I want here."

"An explanation of why I know so much about the fallibilities of the system?"

"Yes."

"When we weren't on the street, which only happened twice and didn't last all that long," she hastened to add . . . she hated pity and she didn't want Brett going all *sympathetic* on her, "after my dad's death, my mom and I lived in low-rent housing. People's places got broken into all the time in our neighborhood. Ours included."

And they'd never once called the cops. Mom had been too sloshed and Claire hadn't wanted the interference. Besides, they'd had nothing of any real value worth stealing. She'd been pretty sure the cops wouldn't have even made a personal visit off the call.

Brett said nothing.

She sighed. "Look, I know how hard it is for the average citizen living in middle-class America to accept, but the cops aren't all guys in white hats and even the ones who are heroic can't fix society's ills. They help, but there's only so much they can do."

"That doesn't mean they can't do anything."

"I know that, but a call to 911 can only help when there's something left to fix."

"Explain what you mean by that."

She bit back a sigh. "My dad committed suicide when I was eleven. He got laid off . . . you know how dynamic the computer industry is. Well, his job got phased out and he and my mom had been living on the edge of financial disaster since before I was born. We were in debt up to our eyebrows because they both had to have the best of everything. New cars every couple of years, a huge house . . . I was in private school. The works, but when he couldn't get another high-paying job right away, the house of cards started to fold."

"And he killed himself rather than deal with bill collectors?" Brett asked in disbelief.

"Yes. It devastated my mom. She found him . . . he shot himself. That sounds like a trite story told on the six o'clock news, but I lived it. She ran around screaming, 'Call 911, call 911!' Only there was nothing anyone could do. Dad was dead, we were in bankruptcy, and even her designer clothes got repoed to pay the bills."

"You have a thing against the police because they couldn't save your dad?"

"No. I don't have a thing against police."

He made a sound that effectively said, "Yeah, right."

"Okay, so I have a thing . . . but it's not against them. I just have a hard time dealing with them. Mom started drinking after Dad died, and she wasn't an easy drunk. She didn't just go to sleep on the sofa and snore the National Anthem. She brought men home, she had screaming rages and fights with her boyfriends. The cops would be called. They'd come and they'd threaten to take me away. Mom would get hysterical and I had to calm her down. She said if she lost me, too, that she'd do what my dad did."

"Kill herself?"

"Yes."

"And you believed her."

"Why wouldn't I? She was weak. Just like my dad. Neither of them could deal with reality. She hid from it in a bottle. He hid from it in death."

"And they both left you to pick up the pieces."

"Yes."

"You said your mom died."

"After a protracted bout of liver cancer. Yes. I took care of her."

"That's why you're twenty-eight and just finishing your degree?"

"Bingo. I couldn't leave her alone to attend classes. I finished my senior year as a homeschooled student."

"Let me guess . . . you taught yourself."

"Of course." She sighed, pushing the old memories away. "So now you know why I can't be the target of whoever broke in here."

He stopped, pulling her around to face him. "How do you figure that?"

She let their eyes make contact and a craven relief she wished she didn't feel surged through her. He didn't look condemning or disbelieving any longer.

"I may have made a new life for myself, but I don't have anything anyone would want to steal. And I don't have a criminal record." It still rankled that he'd accused her of having a larcenous past. "There is no one in my past or present that could have any reason for doing the break-in."

"You can't be sure of that."

"Yes, I can. I don't make friends easily. The people closest to me are Josette and the residents at Belmont Manor. Tell me, how could my connection to a bunch of elderly people make me the target for what's been happening?"

"I don't know, but it all points to you, Claire."

"I don't see how. The whole house was torn up, not just my bedroom. The guy who attacked me could have thought I was Josette."

"That scenario doesn't feel right. It never did, but nothing else made sense."

"It still doesn't."

"Are you sure you're telling me everything?" He was no longer so cold, but neither was he looking at her with the combination of sexy desire and warm concern she'd grown addicted to so pitifully fast. "I want to help you, Claire, but I can't do that if you hide stuff from me."

Betrayal sliced through her. "I just told you things I've never shared with another person and you still think I'm holding back? Do you think I like admitting that my dad killed himself rather than stick it out with my mom and me, or that my mom killed herself, too—just more slowly—with her drinking?"

"I'm sorry about that, sugar, I really am—"

"I don't want your pity," she said fiercely, cutting him off. "I just want you to see that there is nothing in my life that could make me the target of all of this. All right?"

"I understand your doubts, but you could be forgetting something, or not thinking in terms that would make a threat a threat. I know this sounds confusing, but this isn't about me not believing you. It's about my gut, and it's telling me you are dead center in the middle of this mess."

"Well, your gut is wrong." She spun on her heel and started back to the house.

His hand landed on her shoulder, big and warm and impeding her progress.

She slowed down, but didn't stop. "Take your hand off of me." She couldn't stand him touching her right then.

"Where do you think you are going?"

"Where I go and what I do is none of your darn business." She didn't care if she was being irrational. She was mad and she wanted to get away from him. The fact that his instincts told him that she was in the middle felt like he was judging her somehow, like he had to see something wrong in her to feel that way.

"I made it my business when I promised Josie I would keep an eye out for you."

The blatant reminder that Josette was the only reason he was there did nothing to improve her mood. "I release you from your promise." Knowing the words were stupid made her even madder, and she tried to tug away from him so she could walk faster, but he wouldn't let go.

He pulled and she found herself wrapped up next to him, his scent and heat taunting her. They stopped again and he tilted her chin up with his hand so her gaze had nowhere to go but his face. "It doesn't work that way. I didn't make the commitment to you, and I keep my promises."

"You made it *about* me and I don't want you held to it anymore," she insisted, her voice sharp, her heart beating too fast.

"That's too bad, sugar, because I'm not going anywhere."

Unable to stand the contact, she shoved with desperate strength, breaking his hold, and stepped back. "I don't need you watching over me and I don't want you around me."

"You need me, all right," he retorted harshly. "Someone is after you."

"So you say."

He made a noise that sounded suspiciously like a bear growling. "Whether it's you or Josie they are after, you can't stay in the house by yourself."

"I'm not staying in the house at all."

Whatever was going on, Josette's house wasn't safe. Claire didn't know what she was going to do, except that she had to leave. She needed to go someplace that got her away from the danger of staying around Brett as well as far away from the man who had tried to smother her.

"Where do you plan to go?" The question was innocuous, but his body language said she wasn't going *anywhere* if he had anything to say about it.

"That's not your problem. As long as I'm out of Josette's house, I'm out of your hair. Your responsibility to me ends."

"Like hell."

"Leave it alone, Brett. We're done here."

Suddenly the air shimmering between them changed, and the sense of antagonism coming off of him disappeared, leaving her disoriented. So when he moved into her personal space and cupped her shoulders, she just stood there, incapable of objecting, though she didn't know why.

"I didn't mean to hurt your feelings." He sounded contrite, like he really cared.

But she shook her head. Other people rarely *meant* to hurt you, but they did it all the same, and she'd let herself feel too much for this man. "It doesn't matter."

"It does matter, sugar. You're wanting to go off half-cocked because of me. I can't let you do that. You'd end up hurt and it would be my fault."

"You are not responsible for my safety—or my feelings, for that matter. I wouldn't give you that much power over me."

Hotwire wasn't sure why Claire was so pissed off, but he knew he had to fix it. He was not letting her walk away from him, not when her life was so obviously in danger.

Maybe she was offended because she thought he didn't believe her. "You said you don't know why these things are happening, and I trust you. I really do." He looked into her doe-brown eyes and willed *her* to believe *him*. "It's just that my gut is saying you are at the center of whatever is going on, and I've learned to trust my instincts."

"But I don't know how I could be," she said vehemently, looking not in the least appeased.

"I learned a long time ago, the bad guys don't always make sense."

"I don't understand why your instincts latched on to me, Brett. I really don't."

The sound of his name on her lips gave him a twinge like it always did. Like it or not, this woman was under his skin and she wasn't going anywhere for a while. "I don't either, sugar, but they have. You're my friend and I don't want you hurt."

She dropped her head so all he could see was the top of her wild mop of red curls. "Do friends distrust each other?"

She was still bothered that he'd accused her of having a criminal record. Talk about getting the wrong end of the stick. "Sometimes. People aren't perfect, Claire, but that doesn't mean they don't care."

"But why should you care? I'm nothing to you."

Did she really believe that?

"You are my *friend*," he repeated, emphasizing the word. "That means something to me."

He'd slept with a lot of women, but few had been called *friend* in his life.

"To me, too," she whispered.

"Does that mean you forgive me?"

She nodded, but she wouldn't meet his eyes.

He tipped her head up so she had no choice. "Really?"

She closed her eyes, blocking him out.

He leaned down until their lips almost touched, knowing he was taking unfair advantage of her physical attraction to him, but willing to use anything to re-establish rapport with her. He was done trying to make the words work for him.

"Claire?" he whispered against her lips, his mouth brushing oh so lightly against hers.

She sighed into his mouth. "What?"

"Open your eyes and tell me you forgive me."

Her eyes fluttered open, their brown depths hazy with the passion that flared instantly between them. "I forgive you."

He groaned, forgetting what they were talking about, and closed the minuscule distance between their mouths.

He kissed her until she melted against him and his body shook with the need to take her.

A dog barked, breaking into his concentration, and he remembered where they were. Exposed to danger in a public park. He was acting with less competence than a rookie. What if Claire was hurt because he was so busy kissing her, he let someone sneak up on them?

He pulled away reluctantly, despite the strict self-criticism. "The cops should be here soon."

"Yes."

"We should get back to the house."

"Uh-huh," she said vaguely.

He smiled, pleased by his effect on her, and led her back across the park.

Since there was nothing else to do while waiting for the police to arrive, they settled onto the couch and flipped on the television. Hotwire put his arm over Claire's shoulder and didn't realize he'd done it until she snuggled into his side.

It felt good, so he didn't let himself worry about the strange compulsion he had to touch her all the time.

He was skimming through the channels when Claire stopped him. "Wait, I know her."

"Who?"

"Go back to the public access cable channel."

He clicked back to the image of an elderly woman talking to a young man.

"They don't spring for much in the way of sets, do they?"

The two people were sitting on folding chairs in the middle of a bare room.

Claire shook her head impatiently, as if his small joke annoyed her. "That's Queenie! What in the world is she doing on television?"

"Who's Queenie?"

"She's one of the residents at Belmont Manor. One of my friends."

The woman with fluffy white hair and pale green eyes had to be seventy if she was a day. Claire really did have a bunch of geriatrics for friends. He wasn't surprised. She was a kind person and the elderly people she worked with would no doubt enjoy her undemanding company.

"What's she talking about?" he asked Claire. "What government conspiracy?"

"I don't know. Shh . . . listen." She grabbed the remote and turned up the TV.

Queenie hardly looked like the proverbial sweet old lady. Her eyes were red-rimmed and glittering with anger. "I'm absolutely convinced it is a government conspiracy. Lester had information that could make the powers that be look very bad in the eyes of the public."

Chapter 8

"Once again, we are talking with local resident Queenie Gunther, close friend to the recently deceased Lester Wilson," the reporter said, his face toward the camera. Then he turned back to Queenie. "You suspect foul play in the death of your friend?"

"News must be slow today," Hotwire said as Queenie answered an affirmative to her interviewer.

"It's one of those pay-by-the-hour public access channels. Queenie used to host a local talk show on one of them. She's still got contacts in the industry."

"My poor Lester. It's my fault he's dead," Queenie said, sounding genuinely distressed. "I wrote the exposé, and two weeks later, poof . . . he's gone."

"Do you mind sharing the gist of that exposé with our viewing public?"

Hotwire couldn't help wondering just how big that audience was. He didn't imagine many viewers tuned in to watch this kind of programming. Reality TV it was not.

"I discovered that my dear friend had been an assassin in his younger days," she said, even now, in the face of her grief, her eyes glowing with excitement. "He worked for the government mostly, but did a few private jobs."

"And you believe the government iced him to keep him quiet?"

"Iced him?" Hotwire snorted. "Who writes this guy's dialogue?"

Claire hushed him again with a small frown.

Queenie was nodding vehemently. "Yes."

"It's been a long time since he was a young man—surely no one cares enough about something that happened forty years ago to act on it now."

Queenie glared at the young man. Clearly his comment hadn't been part of the planned program. "I *saw* his kill book. The last job he took on was in the early eighties."

Hotwire tensed as the interviewer shifted nervously in his seat. "Still, that was two decades ago."

"Young man, my Lester had connections with the government, connections that would be embarrassing if revealed."

"Where is the kill book now?"

"It's missing." She said it like the fact proved her theory the old man had been murdered.

"Are you sure about that? Maybe it was moved after his death?"

"It disappeared the night before he died. He told me. He was worried about it. I searched his room with him and then again after his heart attack. It's definitely gone."

The interview ended soon after that, and an infomercial on weight loss came on. Hotwire flipped off the television.

"Poor Queenie—she's blaming herself," Claire said sadly.

He looked down at her, his mind whirling with possibilities. "Why?"

"She wrote an article for the *Senior Gazette* lambasting the government for ever having a paid assassin on their payroll."

"The exposé she mentioned at the beginning of the interview? It was published in the *Senior Gazette*?"

"Yes."

"How many people could have seen it?"

"Actually, the circulation is bigger than you would expect. It's delivered to all the residents at Belmont Manor as well as three other facilities associated with it, a group of politicians with an agenda on care for the elderly, and several individuals who have requested copies. If their bills are being paid by a family member, the resident's family will be mailed a copy as well."

More people had probably read that article than had watched the interview. "Did she mention seeing the kill book in the article as well?"

"She hinted strongly at it."

Hotwire's gut was going nuts. "The assassin, Lester . . . was he another resident of Belmont Manor?"

"Yes."

"Was he your friend, too?"

"Yes, we were very close." Her eyes filled with tears and this time she didn't try to blink them away. "He died the night before my attack. I miss him," she said forlornly.

The urge to comfort battled with his need to gather more information. The need for info won. Her safety was paramount, and they were finally getting somewhere in terms of discovering a motive for Claire's attack. He could deal with her hurt later.

"Did you spend a lot of time with him?"

"More than I did with anyone else, even Queenie. He

would call for me at night when I worked. We would talk."

"Did he tell you about his days as an assassin?"

"Yes, but at first I thought he was fantasizing. It was just recently I decided he was recounting real events from his past."

"He told you who he killed?"

"Some of them, but the names didn't mean anything to me. Like the interviewer said, most of that stuff happened forty years ago."

"What was his name?"

"I told you, Lester Wilson."

"I mean his professional name."

"How did you know he had one?"

"He lived long enough to move into a retirement community . . . he had to have worked under the anonymity of a pseudonym."

"It was Arwan."

"Celtic god of the dead."

"Exactly," she said, sounding surprised he knew.

He raised his brow mockingly. "You're not the only one who reads."

She smiled at him, her eyes glinting mischievously and making it hard for him to keep his focus on the conversation at hand. "Touché."

"How many people besides you and Queenie did he share his secrets with?"

"None that I know of. Senility was setting in and he may have told others without me knowing about it, but he acted like it was still a big secret. And the rest of the residents and staff reacted with disbelief when Queenie published her article."

"Who did he work for?"

"He never told me, but he let Queenie see his kill book."

That's what the woman had said in the interview, and if Hotwire's suspicions were justified, she'd put herself in danger admitting it so publicly. "Shit."

Claire gasped.

"Pardon my language," he said automatically and let out a long breath. "I hate to say it, but she might have something."

"But Lester was an old man. He wasn't hurting anyone."

"He was a freelancer—that means he worked for civs. They tend to go nuts about being exposed."

"Civs?"

"Civilians."

"I see . . . is that mercenary speak?"

"Soldier speak, but my point is that Lester's clients aren't all necessarily dead or too old to care that their secrets may be exposed."

Her eyes widened. "You're serious."

"Yes, I am."

"Wow."

"How did he die?"

"Heart attack."

"He had a weak heart?"

Claire bit her lip, her gaze filling with horror. "Actually, no. Do you think the government had him killed?"

"No."

"Thank goodness."

"I think it's very possible a civ is involved and that Queenie could be in danger as well."

Claire jumped up and grabbed Hotwire's arm. "We've got to go to her. We've got to make sure she's okay."

"We're waiting for the police, remember?"

"Unlock the door and leave a note. They don't need us here to dust for prints."

"They do to file a report. We can't just leave."

"Yes, we can. Queenie's life is more important than filing a police report."

Hotwire gave in to Claire's urgency. He called the police station on their way to Belmont Manor and told the dispatcher that he and Claire were going out and would call when they returned.

Claire rushed into Belmont Manor, her heart in her throat. Queenie lived in the more self-sufficient apartment level and that's where Claire headed, with Brett right behind her.

She stopped in front of the elegant white door and knocked. Everything at Belmont Manor was elegant, from the white wainscoting in the communal dining room to the understated pattern in the wall-to-wall burgundy carpeting in all the hallways and community areas.

When Queenie didn't answer a second knock, Claire bit her lip. "Maybe she's still down at breakfast."

"Let's go find out."

They had to pass the lounge on the way to the dining room, and Claire's knees almost buckled with relief when she heard Queenie's trilling laugh.

She grabbed Brett's elbow. "She's in here."

He stopped her outside the door. "Now that we know she's okay, what is your plan?"

"We have to watch over her."

"Stay here twenty-four-seven?"

"If that's what it takes." But she knew she wasn't being realistic, and Brett's expression agreed with that assessment.

"Come on, sugar. You have to stop reacting. We need to deal with this situation logically. First, do we tell Queenie we think her life is in danger?"

Claire shook her head vehemently. "She'd probably take an ad out in *The Times*. She came by her name naturally. She's the quintessential drama queen."

"So, what do we tell her?"

"I don't know."

Brett sighed. "I can have her watched, but a secret bodyguard can only be so effective. It might be easier to control her need for melodrama than it would be to keep her safe without her knowledge."

"We can't even be sure she's in danger. I mean, Lester could have died from a heart attack like everyone thinks."

"Yes, but it's too damn suspicious that you were attacked and your house was ransacked after one of your very few close friends is revealed to be a former assassin."

She had to agree. "What are we going to do?"

"What if we sent her to stay with Josie's dad?"

"How would we get her to go? She's going to want to stay where the action is."

"Tough." The ruthless determination in that one word left no doubt in Claire's mind who would win a contest of wills between her elderly friend and Brett. "We'll tell her Tyler will help her look into the government conspiracy surrounding Lester. That ought to interest her."

"Do you think it's a good idea to feed both of their delusions?"

"I think it will keep her safe and they can theorize harmlessly to their heart's content together. His new wife should keep them on the sane side of paranoid."

"Queenie won't leave until after the memorial service. I think I should stay with her."

"No."

"Brett—"

"You are just as much at risk as she is. More so, for all we know, because an attempt has already been made on you."

"But we can't just leave her here."

Brett frowned. "Then we tell her about our suspicions now and get her to come to the hotel with us for the night."

"Claire, my dear, what are you doing here? I thought you had finals today." Queenie stood not far from the entrance to the lounge, her wrinkled face creased in a smile of welcome, but her usually merry green eyes dim.

Claire didn't think about it—she just stepped forward and pulled the other woman into a hug.

Queenie hugged her back, her frail body trembling. "I killed him, Claire. I did it. I don't know if I can stand it."

Claire briefly tightened her hold on Queenie and then stepped back, shaking her head. "You didn't kill him."

"Don't tell me you believe that taradiddle about a heart attack."

"No, I'm not saying that."

Queenie nodded approvingly, but then her face crumpled. "Then you know it was my fault."

"No. It wasn't." The refrain was so like the words she'd spoken over and over again to her mom and to herself, even after her dad's death, that they hurt in a way she didn't even want to deal with. "You aren't responsible for the actions of—"

Brett cut her off. "Let's talk about this upstairs."

Queenie wiped her eyes with a lace-edged handkerchief, her expression speculative. "Who is this, Claire, your new boyfriend?"

Since Claire had never had a boyfriend that Queenie

had met, the "new" was a kind euphemism on the older woman's part.

"Actually, he's one of Josette's friends."

As she knew it would do, the information brought a spark of interest to Queenie's eyes and she gave Brett an avid once-over. "You're a mercenary?"

Brett put out his arm for Queenie to take and slipped his other around Claire's waist. "Why don't we discuss that upstairs as well?"

When they got to the apartment, Queenie insisted on making them tea and Claire jumped up to help her. Anything to get away from Brett's touch. It was driving her insane.

The kitchen was really nothing more than a small nook in the living area, so Queenie began her interrogation of Brett while setting up the tea tray.

"Why did you become a mercenary? I assume you were some sort of special forces military, not one of those silly boys who take a six-week course and think they can battle evil in the four corners of the world because they know how to shoot an Uzi."

"No, ma'am, I wasn't one of those boys."

She nodded approvingly. "You look far too sensible and intimidating."

"Intimidating?" Brett drew out his drawl, giving Queenie a lazy smile. "That's not the word most women use."

"You're a charming devil, I'll give you that, but it's in the eyes. The same as in Lester's. You can try to hide it behind an amiable façade, but I see the truth."

Brett just raised his brows at her.

"And which branch of the Special Forces were you in?"

"I was an Army Ranger."

Queenie's eyes lit with interest. "Lester was one of

the first to volunteer for that designation during World War II." Brett had obviously risen several notches in her estimation. "Now, tell me why you left such an honorable career and moved to something as disreputable as selling your gun arm to the highest bidder."

"Queenie!" Claire admonished, sure Brett would be offended.

"I left behind one too many comrades on the order of my superiors."

"The Rangers have a credo—never leave a comrade behind to be taken by the enemy."

"Not all comrades and casualties are Rangers, especially in covert ops."

"Your superiors did not allow you to protect others with the same dedication as your fellow Rangers?"

A flicker of pain passed through Brett's blue gaze. "Exactly. As an independent operator, I never abandoned the people who depended on me."

"That is commendable."

Brett shrugged.

"Brett and the other two mercenaries in his company didn't sell their gun arms to the highest bidder, either, Queenie. They specialized in extractions and now they run a security provision and consulting company."

"I see. I'm glad to hear that. It was one thing for an old bird like me to take on Lester with his background, but Claire has a lot of good years left in her life. She doesn't need them marred by a man too scarred by killing to have a fully developed conscience."

Claire was tempted to place her hand over Queenie's mouth to silence her.

Brett just smiled with enough southern-boy charm to make Queenie glow. "No, ma'am. She doesn't."

"I am assuming your conscience is still intact, then, young man?"

"Yes, ma'am. And any holes that need filling in have my mama and sister to see to them."

Queenie's lips quirked and she shook her head. "Claire is going to have her hands full with you—I can see that right now."

"I have no intention of putting my hands on him," Claire gritted out.

Brett gave her a mocking look and his blue eyes challenged her ability to make that claim.

And darned if she didn't blush. "Can we get back to the matter at hand?" she demanded vexedly.

"You mean Lester's murder?" Queenie asked.

Claire felt compelled to say, "We can't be certain it was a murder. Lester was eighty-five. His heart could have given out without warning."

"Other than the way his mind would wander, he was one of the healthiest men I knew," Queenie said with asperity. "He could have been sixty-five, considering how spry he was."

Claire felt an immediate need to smooth the older woman's clearly ruffled feathers. "Of course, you're right."

Queenie was still frowning. "And you do think murder is a possibility?"

"Unfortunately, yes," Brett said, his eyes hard and his manner all business. "I would go so far as to say a probability."

"I don't suppose you have any connections in the government that would help us find his killer?" Queenie asked Brett.

"I do have connections, but I think you're barking up the wrong tree by assuming the government is responsible."

"I have seen things in my life, young man, things that have left me a very cynical woman where the government is concerned. Lester's a prime example. He worked for the government, *killing people.*" As tough as Queenie tried to sound, her shock at that reality exposed her naiveté.

"Regardless of who is at fault," Brett said, "the fact is that after the broadcast of your interview today, you could be at risk, too."

"You admitted reading the kill book," Claire added. "Even though it's now missing, whoever doesn't want its secrets revealed might decide you're too big a liability to have around."

Queenie's eyes snapped. "Good. Let them come after me. I dare them."

Brett shook his head. "Queenie, they got to Lester, and he was a professional. Don't underestimate them."

The militant gleam faded from her eyes as they filled with tears. "Yes, they got to my Lester."

"I don't want them to get to you, too," Claire said.

"But wouldn't I be good bait to draw them out?" Queenie asked with a glow of budding excitement. Claire's stomach lurched with fear.

Brett laid his hand on Queenie's. "You care about Claire, don't you?"

"Of course. I love her like family."

"Lester's death hit her hard because in a lot of ways, her friends here at Belmont Manor are her family. If anything happened to you, she would be devastated. I don't want that to happen, and I'm arrogant enough to believe I can catch the bad guys without using either you or Claire as bait."

"Why Claire?" Queenie immediately demanded.

"It's well known she spent a lot of time with Lester, too."

"Oh, of course. I should have thought of that. What do you suggest, then?"

"I have a friend in Nevada. He's recently married, but his wife's a nice woman and wouldn't mind some female company, I'm sure. I'd like you to go stay with them."

"In Nevada? That's so far away."

"Yes. It's someplace you'll be safe. You have no link to Tyler Graham, so no one will look for you there. If you went to stay with family or friends, you could be putting them at risk. And Tyler is an expert on government conspiracies. You two will have a lot to talk about."

"He is?"

"Yes."

"What about him and his wife, are you sure they'll be safe, with me coming to stay? I could be bringing danger. What if I'm followed?" she asked with hushed excitement.

Brett did not so much as blink at Queenie's dramatics. "You'll be traveling with one of my operatives who will make sure that doesn't happen. And in any case, Tyler is a former mercenary just like me."

"I see. And you don't think his wife would mind me coming?"

"No. Tyler told me her sister recently moved to the east coast to be closer to her grandchildren and she misses her. Having your company would be good for her."

"I've always wanted to visit the desert, but I never quite got around to it. I can't leave until after the memorial service tomorrow."

"Of course not," Claire said, relieved Queenie was cooperating so easily, "but I would feel better if you would come to stay the night at the hotel with Brett and me."

"You're staying in a hotel? What's the matter with your house?"

"I want to keep her close by," Brett said before Claire could answer, "and the hotel offers anonymity."

"Yes, I suppose it would." Queenie gave another one of her approving nods. "You're a thorough man. I like that."

Brett took them back to the hotel and settled her and Queenie into the room. They'd just finished lunch when Brett got a call on his cell phone from the police and he left to meet them at Josette's house.

He and Claire didn't get a chance to discuss his meeting with the police when he got back because of Queenie's presence. Claire assumed Brett didn't want to give an elderly woman with a flair for melodrama and journalistic whistle-blowing more information than was absolutely necessary.

It was decided Claire and Queenie would share the bedroom while they had a rollaway delivered for Brett to use to sleep in the living area. It was a surprisingly enjoyable evening spent playing Scrabble and gin rummy. Queenie beat the pants off both Claire and Brett in both games. There was definitely something to be said for experience.

Claire wasn't surprised at how much she enjoyed her time with Queenie. She had always loved elderly people, Queenie and Lester especially. They were safer than her peers, whom she could rarely identify with. What surprised her was how much Brett appeared to enjoy the older woman's company and how easily he managed her.

"Thank you for being so good with her," she said to Brett while Queenie was preparing for bed in the bathroom.

"She's a nice lady."

"But a lot of people are impatient with the elderly. I like the way you treat her."

"I have a grandmother—two, in fact. Treating older women respectfully comes with the territory."

She smiled, thinking how nice it must be to have a big family like he did.

"Why don't you live near your family?" she asked before she thought.

He shrugged. "I don't know. I guess I just figure we all get along better with a little distance between us."

"But you love them."

"And they love me."

"So, why don't you get along?"

"We do get along."

"But you said . . ."

"I just don't fit in with the rest of the clan."

"Why not? I can't imagine you not fitting in anywhere."

He smiled at that. "Thanks, but everyone in my family is a major overachiever, and then there was me."

"You don't consider yourself an overachiever?"

"My sister is a judge and my older brother is a professor of law at his and my father's alma mater."

"And you were Special Forces in the army, spent the better part of a decade rescuing people from dangerous situations while dabbling in government work, and now you're running a security consulting firm that specializes in situations no one else wants to touch. I'd say you fit right in."

Brett's gaze grew hot, his smile pure predatory male this time. "Thank you, sugar. It's nice to know you're appreciated."

Embarrassed by how much she had revealed of her admiration for him in that impassioned speech, Claire took a hasty step backward. "Well, um, good night."

"Just one more thing."

"What?"

"This." He pulled her to him until their bodies barely touched and his lips hovered over her own.

Her heart sped up and she opened her mouth, but couldn't think what to say. He didn't move, just stared down at her, the heat in his blue gaze searing her insides until it felt like warm honey ran through her veins. She could no more move away than stop breathing. In fact, that might be easier.

Something moved in his eyes, and then he closed the gap and kissed her.

As she let herself press intimately against him, the inevitability of what they were doing washed over her. She'd been wanting his mouth against hers since he broke the bone-melting lip lock in the park that morning. This kiss was different, though, not a scorch-her-socks-off encounter like the one he'd given her earlier. Instead, his mouth was gentle against hers, his lips staking a claim in a wholly different way that made her toes curl into the carpet all the same.

His arousal teased her, letting her know he wanted more than a kiss and, heaven help her, she wanted that, too.

When he let her go, she stumbled back a step and he steadied her. "To be continued."

"What?" she asked vaguely, her focus on the lips that had been giving her so much pleasure.

"Queenie is out of the bathroom."

"Oh." Oh, goodness. Claire had been thinking about making love with Brett when Queenie was in the other room.

Brett smiled. "I want it, too. Good night, sugar."

She stumbled back toward the safety of the room she would share with Queenie. "Good night, Brett."

* * *

The memorial service for Lester drained Claire. She missed the old man already and the service brought home to her that he was gone for good. Blinking back tears, she listened to Queenie give the eulogy, her love for the deceased man vibrating in every word.

Claire's tears escaped and a warm arm settled around her shoulder while a tissue held by a masculine hand appeared in front of her. She took it and wiped at the moisture on her face, ashamed of her loss of control, but hurting too much to do anything about it.

"It's going to be all right, Claire," Brett whispered in her ear.

It was a standard phrase of comfort—meaningless, really—but she felt inexplicably better. And his arm around her gave warm comfort. She didn't feel alone in her grief as she had been the times before when she'd lost people she loved. Even her dad. Her mom had been too wrapped up in her own disillusionment to comfort her daughter.

And when Mom had died . . . there'd been no one.

Claire turned into Brett's strength, allowing herself to rely on him for just this little while. She could go back to being her own little island later. Right now, she needed what he was offering.

Hotwire ushered Claire and Queenie out of the funeral home into the warm Oregon sunshine. It was late afternoon, but the long days of summer meant the sun shone hot and bright on them.

"Excuse me?" A man's smooth Texas drawl came from behind them. "Aren't you Queenie Gunther?"

Queenie stopped and turned. "Yes, that's me."

"Your eulogy for my uncle was really moving."

Chapter 9

Hotwire and Claire had stopped when Queenie did. He now shifted so he could see the speaker. A sandy-haired man with green eyes, in his late twenties to early thirties, stood opposite Queenie. He was dressed in a gray suit, but his black t-shirt and cowboy boots said he was not the typical conservative businessman.

"Your uncle?" Queenie asked with patent hope.

"Yes, ma'am."

"You're a little young to be Lester's nephew," Hotwire inserted, his instincts on instant alert.

The man shrugged, the gesture confident and easy. "If you want to get technical, I'm his great-nephew. He never had kids, but his sister, my grandmother, had four."

"*His sister?* Is she still alive?" Queenie asked.

The younger man shook his head. "She died years ago. So did my grandfather and my other great-uncle, Charles, and his wife. The rest of the family is still around, though."

"Lester had more family?" This time it was Claire sounding hopeful.

Lester's nephew grinned at her, his green eyes a little too interested for Hotwire's comfort as they assessed Claire. "A passel of us, miss. He was the middle child in a family of five children."

Hotwire put his arm around Claire's waist and felt like smiling when she made no move to pull away.

"Yet, you're the only one that came to the funeral?" she asked, her tone asking for an explanation.

The nephew nodded and frowned. "He wrote the family off decades ago, not long after he returned from the war. No one else had heard a word from him in years."

"How did you know about his death?" Hotwire asked.

"I've been keeping tabs on him."

"He never said anything about meeting you," Claire said.

"We only met a handful of times and just once since he moved into Belmont. Right after he went there to live. I wish now I'd made more effort. He was an interesting man."

"Yes, he was," Queenie said.

"I get the *Senior Gazette* y'all put out. After reading the article you did on him, Miz Gunther, I understood Uncle Lester a whole lot better. He had his reasons for staying away. If he was anything like the other men in our family, they had to do with keeping the rest of us safe."

"Yes, I'm sure they did," Queenie affirmed with strong conviction. "This is just amazing. I had no idea Lester had any family left."

"I'd like to swap stories with you, ma'am. I could tell you about his family and you could tell me about him. Seems you knew him better than anyone else did."

Queenie smiled, her eyes going misty. "Oh, my, yes . . . except maybe for Claire. She was like a daughter to him."

"He was a dear friend," Claire said.

The nephew turned to her with an intent look. "I'd be obliged if you would let me take you to dinner so we could talk about my uncle."

"I—"

Hotwire squeezed her, cutting her off. "Maybe we can arrange something later."

The expression in the other man's eyes said he understood that Hotwire had staked a claim, but the cajoling smile he gave Claire indicated he wasn't intimidated by it. "I'm only in town for a couple of days. I would really appreciate it if you and Miz Gunther would join me for dinner tonight."

This time Hotwire didn't give either woman a chance to answer. "That won't be possible. Queenie has other plans and Claire needs to study for her finals."

"I can study tomorrow," Claire disagreed.

"Surely I could put off—" Queenie started to say, but Hotwire shook his head and let her know with a frown he didn't want her mentioning her upcoming trip.

Both women frowned at him, but they didn't argue further.

"You can get together with . . ." He let his voice trail off, waiting for the nephew to identify himself.

"Oh, excuse me." The sandy-haired man put his hand out to Queenie. "Ethan Crane."

"It's truly a pleasure to meet you, Ethan. I feel as if a little part of my Lester has been given back to me."

"You do me an honor, ma'am."

"Please call me Queenie."

Ethan nodded.

"You sound Texan," Hotwire said.

Ethan's brows rose as if he knew exactly what Hotwire was doing . . . fishing for information. "My family hails from East Texas."

"You live there now?"

"No. I'm a little like my uncle. I found the bosom of my family stifling. I've lived in D.C. for the last few years, but I still go home for holidays."

Claire stiffened as if the comment was a slight against Lester, who obviously hadn't made such a concession. "The war changed your uncle. He never felt having a close family would be a good idea. That's why he never married."

"Considering his career choice, that certainly made sense. He told me he was a salesman when I met him."

"Did you believe him?" Hotwire asked.

"No," Ethan replied without hesitation, "there was something in his eyes."

Something Ethan no doubt recognized from his own background.

"What branch of the government do *you* work for?" Hotwire asked casually.

He found himself on the other end of a meticulous sizing-up. Then Ethan spoke. "Officially? The state department."

"And unofficially?"

"That would be telling."

Hotwire nodded. The man might be lying through his teeth about who he worked for, but Ethan Crane was undoubtedly a professional.

"You're in town through tomorrow night?" Hotwire asked.

"Until Friday, actually."

"Tell me where you're staying and I'll call later to make arrangements for Claire and me to meet with you."

"Not Queenie?"

"She's got other plans."

"That's no surprise with such a charming lady."

Queenie preened under the compliment, but she also looked ready to argue for putting off her trip to Nevada.

Hotwire frowned. "Your plans are set, Queenie."

"But surely with Ethan's arrival . . ."

Claire turned to face Hotwire, her expression set in familiar stubborn lines. "After everything she's been through, it wouldn't be right to prevent Queenie from spending time with Lester's nephew."

If the man was the former assassin's nephew. Hotwire wouldn't be able to confirm that until he got back to his hotel room and could use both the phone and his computer in privacy.

"We can discuss this later." He took both women by the arm again and started tugging them toward the car. "Where are you staying?" he asked Ethan as the other man followed them.

"At the Phoenix Inn on Highway 26."

"We'll be in touch."

When they got back to the hotel room, Hotwire short-circuited any argument by telling the women he would arrange for Queenie to leave Friday instead of that evening.

The elderly woman seemed to wilt after thanking him, and Claire insisted she lie down for a nap.

She disappeared into the bedroom with Queenie, but came out, shutting the door behind her, fifteen minutes later. "Thank you for rearranging your plans so Queenie could spend some time with Lester's nephew. It's important to her."

"I had that figured out," he said with a smile that faded before his next words came out, "but we need to confirm he is the old man's nephew before either of you spends any time in his company."

"Confirm it?" Claire's doe-brown eyes widened in shock. "But you heard him . . . his whole family is from Texas."

"For all we know, his family is from Texas, but that doesn't make it Lester's family, too. Or Lester's family may very well live there, but Ethan isn't necessarily the long-lost nephew he claims to be. He gave us enough information that verifying his story shouldn't be too hard, and having met him, we should be able to make a visual I.D. on Lester's nephew, if he exists. If he works for the suits in Washington, my contacts with the FBI should be able to confirm that, too."

She sighed, her shoulders slumping. "Oh. I almost forgot about the investigation. It didn't occur to me that Ethan could be one of the bad guys."

"Maybe he's not. He's certainly better at hiding his status than the other MIBs at the memorial service."

"MIBs?"

"The men in black . . . government agents who like to keep a low profile and do a good job of cleaning up messes other agents or agencies make."

"I didn't see anyone like that." She sounded af-fronted—whether it was with herself or the government agents, he couldn't tell.

"I wouldn't expect you to recognize them, but I'd be embarrassed if I didn't after the years I spent freelancing for the FBI."

Claire dropped into the armchair and then pulled her legs up so she could wrap her arms around her knees. She'd changed from the dark clothes she'd worn to the funeral and now wore a brightly colored tank top and shorts.

The view of her bare legs was damned disturbing. He tried focusing on her face, but her lips looked way too kissable.

Figuring it didn't matter which part of her he looked at—he was going to end up horny, anyway—he sat down on the edge of the coffee table facing her. "We didn't get a chance to talk last night, but we need to."

She turned her head sideways and rested her cheek on her knee. "What about?"

He picked up the remote and turned on the television to mask their voices in case Queenie hadn't fallen asleep yet. "Josie's house was searched."

"I know that."

"Again."

"Again? You've got to be kidding!" Claire sat straight up, the shock coming off of her in palpable waves. "How could you possibly tell? It was a mess when we left yesterday."

"I set some security measures in place when we took off for Belmont Manor yesterday. They got tripped."

She leaned forward. "Are you sure?"

"Yes, but other than those measures, nothing was out of place and I would have noticed, no matter how messy the place was."

"You spent a long time in each room. You weren't just trying to find clues about what he was looking for, were you?"

"No."

"You expected another search."

"I thought it was a distinct possibility, yes. The searchers were professional this time."

"The men in black?"

"Probably. Queenie mentioned the kill book in the article and on television. It wouldn't take much investigation to find out you were the other person who spent the most time with Lester."

Claire paled. "This is getting scary."

Hotwire shook his head, a smile creasing his mouth. "Scary was finding out some maniac tried to smother you. *This* is interesting."

Claire shut her book and rubbed her eyes. She'd been studying for over two hours while Queenie slept in the other room and Brett had been busy at his computer. He'd brought her books and notes from the house and she actually felt like she might be ready for her first final.

She stood up and stretched, bones popping and cramped muscles aching with relief. "I really need a run."

Brett looked up from his computer screen. "Are you done studying?"

"For now."

"Ethan's story pans out. I managed to obtain a picture of the nephew and he's who he says he is."

"I'm glad for Queenie's sake."

"I couldn't get any information on him from my contacts with the FBI, but they could confirm he is employed by the State Department."

"Isn't that odd?"

"Not if he's one of the MIB."

Shock coursed through her. "Lester's nephew?"

"Why not? By his own admission, he hadn't seen much of his great-uncle. What better cover to come into a situation than as legitimate family?"

She shivered. "That's positively Machiavellian."

"Not to mention smart." Brett sounded like he was genuinely impressed.

"That, too, I guess."

"I hit another dead end with the government. My contacts have no idea who wants Lester's kill book, but they're keeping their ears to the ground for me."

Disappointment settled like a lead weight in her stomach. "I was really hoping we could find something out that way."

"I think Ethan is a better bet for that."

"You think he'll tell us what he knows?"

"Why not? The guy who tried to smother you has an agenda and we don't know what it is, but from past experience we can guess what the government's is."

"To hush the whole thing up."

"In a word, yes. It's in Ethan's best interest to solve the mystery of Lester's death and get the kill book back."

"But who took it? Do you think there's a third party involved?"

"We can't rule out the possibility." He stood and stretched. "I could do with a workout, too. There's a facility on the first floor, along with a pool and sauna."

It sounded like heaven, but she had to clear her suddenly parched throat to talk. Watching Brett's muscles undulate had to be right up there with seeing the Sistine Chapel in nirvana-like experiences.

"What about Queenie?"

"I'll call my operative in to keep an eye on her."

"He's staying here in the hotel?"

"Yes."

"Why didn't you introduce us?"

Brett looked confused. "You wanted to meet the operative?"

"Why not?"

"Why would you?"

"To be friendly?"

"I don't want you friendly with my operatives." He sounded so fierce, she was taken aback. "Collins is here to do a job, not make new friends."

"Queenie isn't going to like that. She lives by the Will Rogers motto . . . you know, she's never met a stranger. She'll be hurt if he's cold with her."

Brett let out what sounded like an exasperated breath. "He won't be cold."

"So, it's okay for Queenie to be his friend, but not me?" This conversation was getting very strange.

"Yes."

"Why not me?"

"Because."

"Because why?"

"Because you are *my* friend."

"So is Josette, but you don't seem to have a problem with her having other friends."

"That's different." In all the time she'd known Brett, she'd never seen him look uncomfortable with a conversation or situation, but he looked it now.

In fact, his expression had a lot in common with how she pictured a man being tortured with thumb screws would look.

"How is it different?"

"I don't want Josie, but I want you."

"What's that got to do with me being friends with this Collins person?"

"He's a man."

"So was Lester."

"Collins is young. His face doesn't break mirrors and he's got a reputation with women." He said the last like it was the coup de grace in his argument.

"So do you," she reminded him, humor filling her as she got the picture.

He was feeling territorial. It was the male instinct at work and didn't mean that Brett felt anything special for her, but like he said . . . he wanted her. The male of the species thought that gave them some level of possession; no doubt his was abetted by the fact that she wanted him, too, and that he'd brought her the ultimate pleasure.

Never mind the fact that he was anti-commitment and she didn't *want* to want him.

One second he was talking to her from the other side of the room and the next he was inches from her, his powerful body vibrating with primal tension. "You're mine, Claire."

"I most certainly am not."

His hands cupped her face and his gaze trapped hers, his so intense, she could barely breathe. "Yes. You are."

"Wanting me doesn't mean you own me," she said very carefully as she stepped away from that warm and insidiously seductive touch.

Brett sighed and ran his hand over his face. "I don't want to own you."

"Then I can't be *yours*."

"Yes, you can. Oh, hell . . . pardon me for cursing . . . I don't really want to stop you making friends with other men, but the way I feel around you is primitive."

"That bothers you?"

"Yes. It shouldn't matter to me if you meet Collins."

"But it does."

"Yes. This thing between us doesn't have room for other people to get in the way."

"There is no *thing* between us."

He shook his head. "You're lying to yourself if you

believe that. We started something the night before last and it won't go away or give either of us rest until we finish it."

"Sex is not that consuming."

His mouth quirked below his knowing blue gaze. "Tell me that after we make love the first time."

"We're veering from the subject."

"Which is?"

"Me being friends with anyone I want to."

"If you want to meet Collins, I'll introduce you, okay?"

"You don't sound happy about it."

"I'm fine." But his glare belied his words. "I'm not a possessive man."

"Um . . . define possessive."

He shook his head as if trying to clear it. "This is crazy. Why are we arguing? You aren't going to want Collins. You want me and you're not the kind of woman to play with two men at once."

"I don't want to play with anyone."

"Not true. You want to play with me."

She opened her mouth to deny it, but he didn't give her a chance. He kissed her instead, his lips molding hers, his tongue exploring her lips and the interior of her mouth with a thoroughness that made her tremble.

When he lifted his mouth, they were both breathing hard.

Chapter 10

Collins turned out to be a taciturn man who reminded Claire a lot of Nitro, but surprisingly, his ways did not put Queenie off. She was happy to stay in the hotel suite with him while Brett and Claire went to work out.

Warm-up had a whole new meaning when she had to watch Brett stretching his well-developed muscles. *Overheated* might be a better term. He'd changed into a snug-fitting tank top and athletic shorts for the workout. The sheer mass of sculpted perfection on display overwhelmed her senses and it was all she could do to remember to move from one stretching routine to another. His body was simply incredible. She couldn't seem to keep her eyes off its delectably honed contours.

"If you keep looking like that, the workout you get is not going to be on one of these machines." His promise-filled drawl rasped along her nerve endings, taking her body temperature to tropical levels.

She swallowed and forced her gaze to slide away from him. "Sorry."

"Don't be. Just be prepared for the consequences."

Her gaze flew back to his and her heart stuttered at the look of naked desire on his face. "We can't do anything. Not with Queenie in the room."

"This is a hotel. We can rent another room."

"You'd rent a second room just so we could . . ."

Blue sparks of devilment glittered in his eyes. "So we could make love? In a heartbeat. So don't push it. I'm primed and ready."

She looked where he indicated and couldn't stifle a gasp. He was intimidatingly big and she didn't think it was the fit of his shorts that made him look that way.

He smiled at her, his expression full of masculine humor. "Like I said, sugar, primed and ready."

"Would it be? Making love, I mean. How could it be? We don't love each other."

"Call it whatever you want, but when it happens, it's going to blow your image of sex to kingdom come."

The dark promise in his voice made her shiver, but she couldn't help saying, "I think you are being a little ambitious."

"I don't think so. You've made it clear you don't think much of sex. I'm going to show you that it can be every bit as consuming as I've said it can be."

But for how long? She'd given up on the whole sex thing because it hadn't been anywhere near mind-blowing, but also because men saw it as something so much less intimate than it was. It required letting someone inside her body . . . giving part of herself to that person whether they wanted it or not. She didn't know if it was that way for other women. She'd never asked, but it was definitely that way for her.

And she didn't like those consequences one bit.

"Why are you so against marriage?" The question just

popped out. She hadn't meant to ask it, wasn't even sure she wanted the answer, but now she'd get it.

He abruptly stood up and moved to the universal weight machine and started adjusting pulleys. "I was engaged once."

She stopped stretching and stared at his back as he settled onto the machine and started doing a reverse butterfly lift. She couldn't believe what she had just heard.

"You were engaged? Mr. No-commitment?"

"It was a long time ago, before I made that rule."

"Is she the reason you won't commit now?" Claire asked.

"You could say that."

Her stomach knotted in a pain that she didn't understand.

Marriage was not on her list of things she most wanted to do before turning sixty, either. She'd seen enough relationships break up and couples cause each other so much pain, her parents included, that she'd never wanted to follow that path.

But it still hurt to hear him confirm his lack of desire for a commitment after experiencing the sexual desire he'd sparked in her.

Claire rose to her feet and moved across the room to step onto the glide machine. Next to running, it was her favorite way to exercise. She'd discovered it while living in her first apartment after Fanny died. The complex had had a small workout facility. It had been hard to leave, but with her school schedule, she'd had to cut back her work hours and couldn't afford an apartment on her own. She'd ended up living with Josette and certainly did not regret that.

"What happened?" she asked after adjusting the tension to where she liked it.

Brett did several repetitions on the weight machine and she wasn't sure he was going to answer.

When he did speak, his voice came out low and even, no emotion evident at all. "I met her when I was on a covert ops mission for the Rangers. She was a civilian contact for us, working for the current regime. But she didn't believe in their ideology . . . she wanted something better, more stable, for her country. She was willing to risk her life to see that happen."

He went silent again and Claire wasn't sure if she should say anything or just wait. In the end, she couldn't think of anything to say, so she waited and wondered.

Brett got up and changed his position to do a different muscle group. "I knew I shouldn't get involved with a local, but neither of us could help ourselves. The attraction was instantaneous."

Like it had been with Claire and Brett, but obviously there had been a lot more on his side than a desire for sex with the other woman because they'd ended up engaged.

"We fell in love and I asked her to marry me. She agreed, but said we had to wait until after the mission."

"She put the good of her country above her personal happiness," Claire said.

"Yes. It was one of the things I really admired about her. She was from a wealthy family who had prospered under the regime she was so dedicated to bringing down. She was a visionary who saw beyond her own comfort."

"I bet she was a good contact to have, considering her position in society."

"She was." He went silent again, switching to another lifting set. Then he said, "Things went FUBAR just when we thought we would complete the mission. We were ordered to pull out. I had another assignment waiting for me."

Claire knew what was coming, but wished she could be wrong. "You had to leave her behind."

His fiancée had been the reason that Brett had left the military. She was sure of it.

"I didn't want to, but my superiors thought if she left right then, too many other positions would be compromised. I asked her to come with me anyway. She wanted to wait until I came back from my new mission. It lasted longer than it was supposed to. I knew I should go back for her, but I had orders and I obeyed them. She was betrayed to her government and killed two weeks before I returned to my base. I didn't find out until I got there."

"You felt like you failed her." Now she understood all that rhetoric about duty first.

"I did."

"I don't believe that. She knew the risks she was taking by staying, and you said she had connections. She could have gotten herself out of the country if she'd wanted to."

"She was trying when she got betrayed."

"That's not your fault."

"I don't see it that way."

"You aren't omniscient, Brett. You had no way of knowing she would be betrayed before your mission was over."

"The risks were there."

"And she knew about them and made her decisions accordingly."

"It was my job to protect her."

"You tried."

"Not hard enough."

Claire shook her head, wishing she could help him, knowing his belief in his own culpability was set.

"I'm sorry," she said, meaning so much more than just regret over the other woman's death.

"I was, too. She was a special woman. So smart, she left me for dust sometimes."

Claire could not imagine. Brett was the most intelligent person she'd ever known.

"She sounds amazing," she forced out past a throat choked by inexplicable tears.

"She was. She deserves to be remembered."

Suddenly it all made sense—his leaving the military, his rule against marriage, or even a majorly committed relationship.

"Your refusal to ever marry is your way of remembering her, isn't it?"

"Yes."

He'd set himself up as a living memorial to a dead woman.

It sounded like his deceased fiancée deserved the kind of devotion Brett was determined to give to her, but that didn't stop the pain piercing Claire's heart.

She would never be more to him than a friend for whom he felt passion. Even if his mind wasn't set on remaining true to his lost love, there was little chance Claire could even hope to live up to the perfection of the other woman. His lost fiancée had been everything Brett admired and he had loved her. He wanted Claire for sex and that wasn't the same thing at all.

Was it enough? No, she knew it wouldn't be, but what she didn't know was whether she had the strength to turn away from the passion. She'd never felt anything like it, and even knowing it would mean more pain for her down the road, she had this horrible aching need to give in to it.

"What was her name?"

"Elena."

"It's a beautiful name."

"She was a beautiful woman."

Of course she was. Apparently, Elena had been everything a man could want. Beautiful, smart, and self-sacrificing.

No normal woman could compete.

*   *   *

Brett arranged with Ethan to meet for lunch at a small Italian restaurant on the west side. Its quiet ambiance and ample spacing between tables guaranteed the privacy Brett needed for the discussion he planned to have with the other man.

Queenie told stories about Lester through the main course while Ethan interspersed with information about Lester's estranged family.

"Were his sisters and brothers very hurt when he cut off communication?" Claire asked, her brown eyes warm with compassion for people she'd never met.

"By the time I was born, I think they'd learned to accept it. I don't remember him ever being referred to in a negative light. In fact, he always figured as this mysterious war hero my cousins and I made up stories about."

Queenie smiled. "Lester would have loved knowing that. He never wanted his family to know about his vocation."

"Yet he didn't mind you writing the article?"

Queenie's eyes filled with anguished guilt. "He said it was all right, but I knew he was going senile." Her voice broke and she had to collect herself before going on. "I wanted to expose the government's perfidy, but it cost Lester his life. I wasn't ready for him to go."

Hotwire watched as Ethan's eyes narrowed with interest. "What do you mean, the article cost him his life?"

"I killed him. I killed my Lester." Her voice trembled and tears filled her eyes, spilling onto her gently wrinkled face.

Claire's hand covered Queenie's, her own expression tormented. "Don't say that. It isn't true."

"But he wouldn't be dead if I hadn't written that article."

"You don't know that was what triggered the killer. You can't know. We weren't the only people who saw Lester frequently. Nurses, orderlies, and even doctors could have known about his past. He'd gotten to a point where he rambled about it frequently."

"He told others?" Ethan asked, his voice having changed subtly, though Brett doubted the women would notice.

But he knew that tone. It was the voice of an experienced interrogator.

Claire looked at him, her touch still comforting the elderly woman. "Yes. There's no way of knowing how many people or even who they were, really. Anyone who came into contact with him toward the end could have learned his secrets."

"But it was the government who murdered him," Queenie said with fatalistic conviction.

"You think the government is responsible for my great-uncle's death?"

Queenie nodded vigorously despite the wetness tracking down her cheeks and the sadness that had settled on her like a mantle. "They didn't want their secrets exposed."

"But I thought you had already exposed them."

"I didn't give the kind of details Lester could have. He asked me not to." Her mouth wobbled, but she took a deep breath and went on. "Then there was the kill book."

Ethan's eyes narrowed. "You have his kill book?"

"Goodness, no. If I did, you can bet your bottom dollar I would publish it and shame the devil." She sighed with obvious regret. "It was stolen. I'm sure that was the government's doing as well."

"I work for the state department, Miz Gunther. I can

assure you, we don't make a habit of murdering civilians or stealing their property."

The elderly woman gave Ethan a pitying look. "Queenie, please . . . and I'm sure your part of the government doesn't, dear boy, but Lester's kill book says that some agencies do that very thing."

"There were organizations that operated during the Cold War that had a great deal of autonomy and operated in utter secrecy."

"You don't think those sorts of organizations exist today?"

"Perhaps," Ethan allowed noncommittally, "but a relationship with the government that ended decades ago would hardly be a threat to national security today."

"Are you saying you don't think the government is interested in the kill book?"

"No, but I don't think they stole it, either. Uncle Lester was a war vet. If the government wanted to bury his kill book, they would have tried appealing to his sense of patriotism first."

"Well, you are entitled to your opinion, of course." But her tone and expression made it very clear she didn't share it.

Hotwire couldn't help smiling at the snippy response. The old woman was a firecracker for sure.

But his smile disappeared when Ethan turned to him, his gaze watchful. "Do you think Lester was murdered?"

"I think it's a strong possibility. The government wasn't his only client."

"No autopsy was done."

"Heart failure is an acceptable cause of death to most coroners when the deceased was in his eighties."

"But you don't buy it."

"No."

"Uncle Lester was cremated—there's no way of checking."

"Even if we could, there are too many untraceable ways to bring on a fatal heart attack to assume the killer was stupid enough to use a drug that would show in a blood analysis."

"That's true." Ethan leaned back in his chair, never taking his eyes off Hotwire. "Do *you* think it's the government?"

"I wasn't on the scene after the death, but I have ample reason to suspect a civ is involved somewhere, and it has been my experience that civilians are the ones most likely to go off half-cocked and kill a man before they check to see if something as important as his kill book is missing."

"How do you know Uncle Lester's killer didn't take the book the night it disappeared?" Ethan asked.

Hotwire saw no reason to keep news of the second break-in from Queenie or Ethan now. Soon, the elderly woman would be in Nevada where her dramatics could not affect his investigation or get her killed. And if Ethan was any kind of agent at all, he'd do a routine check on police records pertaining to the people he knew were involved with Lester's life and find out for himself.

"Because he searched Claire's house trying to find it and if the government already had it, the second search the next day would not have taken place."

"You can't be sure that was the government," Claire said.

Hotwire reached across the table and tucked a wayward curl behind Claire's ear. "No, I can't, but even if another professional is involved, I think the kill book disappeared before anyone got to it."

"But how?"

"Maybe Lester hid it."

"But he had Queenie looking for it the next night."

"He was senile, sweetheart. Just because he hid it doesn't mean he would remember doing so."

"So you think it's still out there, waiting to be found?" Ethan asked.

"Yes. Now answer a question for me," he said, focusing on Ethan. "Are you on assignment right now?"

Ethan grinned. "If I were, I wouldn't tell you. I might even lie and say I wasn't, but for what it's worth, no, I'm not, and I don't know what branch employed the suits that were at the memorial service. I will say they sparked my curiosity, and Queenie's suspicions clarify several things for me."

"Like you said, you could be lying."

"I'm not."

But Hotwire had learned a long time ago not to take a man's word for anything until he knew him well enough to know if he could be trusted. Very few people, male or female, made it into that category for him.

"You thought Ethan was one of the government agents?" Queenie exclaimed, her eyes wide.

"He *is* a government agent."

"But I'm not working on this case."

"It sure sounds like you're working."

"The man was family. If he was murdered, I want to bring down whoever did it."

Queenie gasped suddenly as if just now realizing something. "Your house was searched, Claire?"

"Yes. He tore it apart."

"He?" Ethan prompted.

"Ask Brett. He's the expert on these matters."

"Are you?" Ethan asked.

"Yes," Hotwire replied shortly.

"What exactly do you do?"

"You mean you didn't check me out?"

"If you work for the government, you are buried deep."

"Freelance."

Ethan nodded slowly. "That explains it."

Claire jumped in with an explanation of the security consulting company he and his friends had started. He listened to her with bemusement as she made him sound like a fricken hero. He shook his head. The woman saw life through some very rose-colored glasses.

"So, do you know what department is looking for the book?" Ethan asked him.

"No. My contacts haven't heard even a murmur of interest in Lester Wilson or the assassin, Arwan."

"Oh my, I had no idea you'd done so much investigating already," Queenie said.

Hotwire shrugged. "It hasn't done us much good. Do you remember the name of the agency that hired Arwan for his jobs?"

"It wasn't in the kill book, just a contact name. Now, let me think." She silently tapped one finger against her chin and then made a sound of triumph. "Alvin Thorpe. His name was Alvin Thorpe. Lester told me they were in the war together."

Brett smiled with grim satisfaction. A name was something concrete to go on, which was more than he'd had so far.

"I can find out who Thorpe worked for," Ethan said.

"Fine." Though Hotwire had every intention of finding out for himself as well. He still wasn't sure he could trust the other man even that far.

"We can compare notes," Ethan said, telling Hotwire he knew exactly what he was thinking.

"That would be wonderful." Claire smiled for the first

time since the discussion about Lester's possible murder began. "I think having another investigator would make this situation more manageable."

"You don't trust me to take care of it?" Hotwire asked her.

She rolled her eyes. "Please. You are always saying that backup on a mission is a good thing."

"And you see this as a mission?"

"Don't you?"

"No. I see it as personal." He gave her a meaningful look she couldn't misinterpret. "Very personal."

Her pretty brown eyes went wide with confusion and damned if she didn't blush. "Oh."

He wanted to lean across the table and kiss the lips she had pursed so enticingly in her disconcertment. One more night on the rollaway loomed ahead of him, and he cursed his soft thinking that had made him agree to allow Queenie to postpone her trip to Nevada until the following day.

He spent the rest of lunch in a state of semi-arousal, despite the fact that they did nothing but discuss the case.

He exchanged contact information with Ethan before taking the women back to the hotel.

"It's too bad he's going back to D.C.," Queenie lamented in the car on the way.

"He has to get back to his job," Claire said.

"Perhaps he will come out and visit again."

"I don't see how he could stay away. You're his last link to the uncle he never knew, but was always curious about," Claire consoled the other woman.

"I suppose you're right," Queenie said, brightening. And then she shot a sideways look at Hotwire. "Why didn't the two of you tell me about the break-in at Claire's place?"

"We didn't want to worry you," Claire said before he could reply.

"And the less you know, the safer you are," Hotwire said, knowing Queenie would not take it the way he meant it. Which was that she had a tendency to expose what she knew and dramatize.

"Oh, I see," she said. "I can't be forced to say what I don't know."

"Something like that."

Claire shifted nervously in the car seat. Brett had been giving her hot looks all morning, but they'd gone sulfuric since they saw Queenie off at the airport with the taciturn Collins.

She licked her lips. "Um . . . what's the plan for today? I thought maybe you could drop me at the library to study."

He looked at her incredulously. "I'm not leaving you anywhere alone right now."

"The bad guys don't know where I am, and I seriously doubt anyone's staking out the library watching for me."

"If you need to study—"

"I do," she interrupted.

"Then you can do so in the hotel."

"That's not working very well." Since the first bout of studying she'd done, she had had abysmal luck at focusing on her work in his much-too-disturbing presence.

"Why not?"

"It's too distracting."

"It's a hotel room."

"But you're in it."

Chapter 11

"Do I distract you, Claire?"

"Yes, and I can't afford to let you," she said bluntly. "I've worked really hard to graduate this term. I'm not missing out because I flunked all my finals."

"That's not going to happen."

"Not if I study, no."

"You're really worried about this?" he asked, sounding shocked.

"I guess it's hard for you to understand."

"Considering how smart you are, yeah."

"That's not the point."

"What is the point?"

"I'm not going to end up like my mom. She fell apart when my dad died and it wasn't just because he killed himself. She had no marketable skills, no education to speak of. When we lost the house and everything, she drank instead of trying to make something better of our life. I never want to be like that."

"And you're succeeding admirably, sugar."

"That's just it. I want to *succeed*. Not eke by. I've kept

a 4.0 grade point average all through. It's important to me that I don't falter at the last hurdle."

"In other words, you need to focus all your energies on acing these exams?"

"Yes."

In the blink of an eye, he had the sexual fire in his eyes banked and he was wearing the expression he'd worn the few times she'd seen him in work mode. "I'll help you."

"But—"

"Trust me."

"I don't need help so much as a lack of distraction."

"You want me to accept Ethan's help on the investigation, right?" he asked, something in his tone telling her he wasn't exactly pleased about that.

"Yes."

"Why?"

She frowned, not understanding his need to ask the question. "Because it will increase your chance of success."

"I want to increase *your* chance of success, Claire."

"So?"

"Doing well on your final exams is important to you. That makes it important to me, and you've had a rough week, the kind guaranteed to wreak havoc with your ability to study and even remember what you've learned in the short term. Whether you see it or not, you could use my help."

"But you've got your own stuff to concentrate on. You can't take time to baby-sit me through my finals."

"It's not baby-sitting, it's helping a friend. And I'm not dropping you off at the library by yourself to study. So your choices are limited: study with me, or try to study on your own with me in the room. It's your call."

"You'd probably be bored," she grumbled.

He looked at her once and then back at the road, his features set in stubborn lines she'd learned to recognize. "Your choice," he repeated.

"I guess we could try it," she said doubtfully.

She didn't see how having him study with her would be an improvement in the distraction stakes.

But she was wrong. Brett turned out to be a great study partner. He knew as much or more about most of her subjects than she did. The only post-high school education he'd had was in the military, but he knew just how to drill her for an exam and help her remember important elements from a class. Even when her thoughts wanted to scatter to the four winds because of everything that had been going on.

He refrained completely from alluding to future intimacy between them and seemed to know just when she needed a break to eat or work out, or just watch television for an hour. He made her laugh and he gave her total quiet when she needed that, too.

He spent time at his computer and on the phone, chasing down leads about Lester. However, he refused to discuss them with her, telling her he wasn't giving her any food for thought to chew on related to anything other than her studies. When she aced her finals would be soon enough for him to brief her on what he'd learned.

She was grateful because he was right. She was able to put it all completely from her mind, knowing he was working on it. And the weekend flew by.

Claire finished writing and laid down her pencil. As of this moment, she was done with her finals. She'd taken one on Tuesday, two the day before, and this was her last test.

She looked at the clock and realized she'd finished in half the time allotted. She grinned. She'd only been working for forty-five minutes, but she was confident of her answers. Brett had drilled her until she knew this stuff inside and out.

She stood up, a feeling of accomplishment rushing through her that made her feel like shouting. *She'd done it.* Not only had she fulfilled her requirements to graduate, but she was sure she'd *aced* all of her final exams. No eking by . . . success all the way.

Not bad for the daughter of a man too weak to continue living in the face of financial failure and a woman who had hidden from every challenge at the bottom of a bottle. With a feeling of supreme triumph, Claire dropped her exam paper on her professor's desk. He looked up from what he was doing with a vague expression in his eyes.

The only thing that ever elicited sharp and focused interest from this man was his computer. "Done already?"

"Yes."

"Congratulations. I'm sure you did your usual exemplary work."

Claire smiled. "Thank you."

He waved his hand. "Don't thank me. Wasn't a compliment. Don't believe in them. Merely the truth."

She was grinning when she left the room in search of a bathroom. She'd had two cups of coffee and a large glass of juice at breakfast.

Brett wouldn't be back to pick her up for at least fifteen minutes. The last two days, he'd shown up half an hour early and waited for her each time. She'd chided him for it, but he'd said he didn't want her to be alone. She didn't think using the community ladies' room constituted being alone. The campus might be sparsely populated at the moment, but many of the professors, like hers, continued to keep office hours.

She had just finished in the bathroom and was zipping up her jeans when the lights went off and everything went pitch black around her.

Claire bit off a gasp of shock and stopped moving entirely. Was it a power failure, or something else? The chills racing down her spine said it was the latter.

Acting on instincts she hadn't known she possessed, she ducked down as quietly as she could and rolled under the divider into the next stall. It was the handicapped one and had more space, even if it was too dark to see it. She slowly and silently got onto all fours and then paused, listening for sounds in the room around her. She couldn't hear anything over the running water of the recently flushed toilet.

She sent up a quick prayer of thanks for the tank taking so long to fill.

She started making her way out of the stall, into the main area. She moved an inch at a time, not wanting to make noise and alert whoever was in the bathroom with her. She stayed close to the wall, both to keep her bearings and to minimize the chance she would run into him.

She was crawling along the wall under the sinks when the door to the stall she'd been in slammed open. She had no idea how it had been unlocked from the outside, but she wasn't sticking around to find out.

The toilet stopped running and in the silence she heard a rush of movement and then a stifled curse. He'd discovered she wasn't there. She had to get out of the bathroom.

"I know you are in here, Miss Sharp. You're not going to get away." The menacing male voice came from her right and the exit was to her left.

Hallelujah!

Without a second's hesitation, she leaped to her feet and dove for where she thought the door would be. She missed it on her first try, hitting a solid wall in the darkness, but she spread her arms out on both sides and reached for it. She found the door, but as she grabbed the handle to pull it open, he grabbed her. She screamed with ear-piercing intensity until a gloved hand clamped over her mouth.

"You shouldn't have done that."

She bit the hand through the glove and the man holding her swore viciously. Then she brought her elbow back with all her strength and hit his chest.

He grunted, but he didn't let her go. "Settle down. I don't want to hurt you."

She wasn't buying it. A man who didn't want to hurt her would not have accosted her in a dark bathroom. She struggled wildly against his hold and then thought of kicking the door. No sooner had she thought of it than she started to do it, making as much noise as she could.

He dragged her backward, but she could smell the fear on him, like a pungent, unpleasant odor. "I want the kill book."

She tried to bite him again, but he was holding her jaw shut, so she kicked backward with her feet.

His arm holding her squeezed painfully. "Tell me where the kill book is. I know you have it."

She nodded her head vigorously and he lifted his hand from her mouth. She screamed again, this time managing to evade his hand for a couple of seconds.

Someone had to have heard.

Her assailant must have thought the same thing because he roughly shoved her to the floor and she heard him run. The door swung open and a dark shape wearing a ski mask disappeared through it. She got up and ran after him, but when she got out into the hallway, it was completely deserted. There was a door leading outside nearby, several leading to offices, and one that led to another part of the building.

He could have gone anywhere, but her first instinct would be to run outside, so she headed for that door. She shoved it open, but no man in dark clothes was anywhere around. In fact, no one was around at all.

She scanned the area for telltale movement, but saw nothing. Darn it. She'd picked the wrong option and he was probably long gone now.

She went back inside, frustration and fear-based adrenaline pumping through her.

"Claire, what are you doing out of your professor's office?" It was Brett.

She spun toward his voice and winced when he used a word she'd never heard him say.

"What happened to you?" he demanded, striding forward until his hands were locked on her shoulders.

She told him as succinctly as possible.

He gave her terse instructions to return to the bathroom. "He won't look for you there again. He'll assume you ran."

She nodded.

"I want to see if I can catch sight of him."

She nodded again, her voice a little too wobbly to use to good effect, and then went back into the bathroom, turning the light on as she went. She doubted Brett would find him, but if anyone had a chance, it was the former mercenary.

She took the time to wash her hands and arms and face. Crawling along a bathroom floor was bound to leave behind major germs. She shuddered at the thought. Far from leaving her more tolerant about dirt, her experiences as a child living with her mom when she hadn't always had a choice about being clean had left Claire intolerant of even the thought of being dirty.

Brett was back in a couple of minutes, and he walked right into the ladies' room.

He was all business, his expression hard with concentration. "I didn't see anything. Let's go talk to the other people in this building and find out if anyone else did."

"Okay." She moved toward the door, but he stopped her.

He touched her face gently, concern softening his features. "Are you all right?"

"I'm getting to be an old hand at getting attacked in the dark." She gave him a shaky smile.

He shook his head, his lips quirking in response. "You're a real trooper, you know that?"

The praise warmed her chilled insides, and she followed him out the door. Fifteen minutes later, she knew why no one had come in answer to her scream. The building was virtually deserted, her professor being the only faculty member in his office, and he had been preoccupied with his research.

The campus was deserted as much as it could be, situated where it was in the middle of downtown, as well. The few people Brett and she found to talk to had not seen her attacker, or at least given the limited description she had of him.

They were in the car when Brett turned to her, his expression nowhere near pleased. "Why did you leave your professor's office?"

"I had finished my test and I had to go to the bathroom. I had no idea the building was as empty as it was," she said in her own defense. "Besides, how could I possibly guess the bad guys would know I was taking a final exam today?"

"It wasn't exactly a state secret. We both should have realized the potential for something like this."

"I thought you already had and that's why you insisted on driving me and picking me up."

"That was just routine precaution."

She bit her lips to keep from smiling. He wouldn't see the humor in his answer or the current situation. It was only her bent sense of the ridiculous that made it funny to her. But she found it amusing in a really sweet way that he hadn't expected trouble, but behaved as if he did and was still mad at himself for not expecting it.

Talk about being a perfectionist overachiever. Oh, yes, he fit in with his family just fine.

He started the car and pulled out of his parking spot into the city traffic.

He kept checking his rearview and side mirrors as he drove.

"Are we being followed?"

"Not that I can tell, but I'm not going straight back to the hotel, just to be on the safe side."

"Okay. Why don't we go out for an early lunch to celebrate me passing my last final?"

"You sure you passed?" he asked in a teasing voice.

"Thanks to your help, I'm sure I aced it." She turned her body so she could look at him straight-on. He had such a yummy profile, she almost forgot what she was going to say next. Oh, yes . . . "I really want to thank you for being so understanding these past few days, Brett."

"Hey, what are friends for?"

"According to you, making sure other friends succeed."

He grinned and slid her a sidelong glance. "Where do you want to go to eat?"

"There's a Vietnamese restaurant I like on the west side. If anyone's following us, we'll be leading them in the opposite direction of the hotel."

"I've got an even better idea. It's only an hour and a half to the beach. If you don't mind Chinese, there's a great restaurant in Lincoln City."

"That sounds like fun." And it did. It also represented a real break from the events surrounding Lester's death. "Do we get to go walking on the beach after we eat?"

"Sure. I'll even buy you a kite."

"Have you ever flown one?"

"No, but it can't be all that hard."

She just smiled. "There is a definite technique required. Lucky for you, I've got it down."

"You can teach me."

"It will be my pleasure."

"That's what I'm planning," he said in a sexy voice that made her thighs clench and insides melt and just that quick, the sexual tension between them came roaring back with even more force than before.

It felt like there were underlying messages in everything they said on the drive to the coast, even though they spent most of their time talking about her classes and how she thought she'd done on her finals.

Once they arrived in Lincoln City, the authentic Chinese food was worth the drive, even without the incentive of a walk on the beach afterward. They both ate with chopsticks and Brett laughed when her tofu kept slipping off hers before she could get it to her mouth.

Finally, he reached across the table with his own chopsticks and fed her a bite. It was intimate, and reinforced the shimmering atmosphere of sexual awareness surrounding them.

"You're pretty good with these," she said softly after he fed her yet another bite.

"I spent a lot of time in the Far East."

"As a Ranger or as a mercenary?"

"Both." His gaze caressed her as effectively as if he'd used his hands.

She tried to stifle a shiver in reaction and ducked her head to take a sip of her tea.

At some point along the way, Brett had to have decided that sex between them was inevitable despite the things he'd said at Josette's wedding. He'd been bad for her sense of self-preservation before, but now he was lethal to it.

"You're done with school now, right?" he asked in a velvet voice that caressed her insides.

"Um . . . yes."

"It's time, Claire."

And she knew exactly what he thought it was time for. When she looked up from her tea, he was watching her with the intensity of a wild tiger sizing up its prey.

And really, that was too much.

"Tell me about the investigation," she said in a moment of inspiration. "You promised you would, once my finals were finished."

His expression didn't change, but he leaned back in his chair. "All right, but you're not going to put me off forever. Ethan found out the name of the government agency Thorpe worked for, but it was disbanded twenty years ago."

"Then, why were the MIB at the memorial service?"

"Someone who knew about the defunct agency and Arwan's jobs for them must have heard about Queenie's accusations."

"You think they knew Lester as Arwan?"

"It's possible. He had a long career, not everyone in that agency would have been as old as he was when it disbanded. It's likely that some of them now work for other agencies in high-ranking positions they don't want compromised by scandal from the past."

"But who are they?"

"We still don't know."

"Do you think it was one of those men who accosted me in the bathroom? He didn't actually hurt me."

"I don't know that, either. It was a gutsy, professional move—or just plain stupid. Could you tell if it was the same guy who tried to smother you?"

"The build was right, but so is that of a good portion of the male population—you excluded, of course."

"Me excluded?"

"You have the body of a Greek god, and pretending you don't know that is about as convincing as the thought of you twirling a baton in a tutu."

He laughed and she grinned back at him.

"He was wearing a ski mask again, but I didn't see his face. I couldn't tell if his eyes were the same as the man who tried to smother me. This guy stank of fear, now that I think about it . . . the man who tried to smother me used an expensive aftershave. One of my professors uses it. This guy could have, too, but I couldn't smell anything over his sweat."

"What's the brand?"

"I don't know, but we could ask my professor."

"It's a long shot and the chances are it won't lead anywhere, but we have to try."

"Aren't *you* just Mr. Gloom and Doom?"

"I'm hitting a lot of dead ends. I wouldn't mind having the kill book, either."

"Why did the man in the bathroom think I had it? He already searched my house."

Brett shrugged. "I guess he's grasping at straws and doesn't know where else to look."

"He said he *knew* I had it and it sounded like he meant that literally."

"Are you sure you don't?"

She rolled her eyes. "Oh right, like I'm going to forget Lester giving me something of that magnitude. I've never even seen the thing." But then a memory assailed her. Lester laying a composition book down in his lap. "Do you think he would have used something as prosaic as a composition book to keep track of his jobs?"

Brett's blue eyes flashed with interest. "Why not? It would be a lot easier to hide than a leather bound volume. No one would expect it. Why are you asking? Do you think you might have seen it?"

"It's possible. He had a composition book open and facedown in his lap one night while we were talking. Now that I think about it, that was an odd thing for him to have, you know? But he still didn't give me anything like that."

"You're right. It isn't something you would have forgotten."

They finished their lunch, and then he took her to a kite shop as promised.

She'd been in a couple before, but Fanny had always bought kites for the children at discount department stores. So, the plethora of brightly colored kites, wind socks, and outdoor flags caught her immediate attention and imagination. Kites floated from the ceiling and decorated the walls like nylon wallpaper. A gruesome skeleton was right next to a box kite with cartoon characters all over it.

Just like life . . . bright happiness could come right alongside grief and pain.

"You look thoughtful," Brett said from beside her.

She shrugged. "I suppose this isn't exactly the place for a philosophical moment, is it?"

"I don't know. I've had them in stranger environments."

She grinned. "I bet you have."

The shop owner, a short, round woman with curly gray hair, approached them. "Can I help you find something?"

When she discovered Brett had never flown a kite, she tried to steer him and Claire toward the beginner models, but Brett was fascinated by the diamond-shaped fighter kites, particularly one with a lizard on it and an enormously long tail.

"The deltas and box kites are more reliable for lift, especially for a beginner," the middle-aged owner of the shop said.

"What about this?" Brett asked, pointing to a reproduction of the Wright Flyer.

Claire groaned and Brett looked at her. "You don't like it?"

"The idea is to relax. Not battle with a kite on the beach. That one will take so long to build, the sun will be set before we even get a chance to get it in the air."

"Then maybe we should spend the night and fly it in the morning."

She shook her head and picked up a delta kite that looked like a giant butterfuly with several tails. "I like this one."

"It's too girlie," Brett said with a curl of his lip.

"We're celebrating me acing my finals, right?"

"Yes," he said warily, obviously guessing where this was leading.

"I want girlie."

Brett grumbled, but he bought the pink-and-purple kite. He also insisted on buying the lizard fighter kite.

Chapter 12

In spite of the ever-present coastal wind that seemed always to increase as the day wore on, the sun beat down on Claire's head as she and Brett picked their way down to the beach. They'd driven outside of town for beach access because the municipal parking near the access had been full.

The path between jagged rocks and sand grass was narrow, and she was glad she'd left her shoes on because the sharply bladed grass grew across it in places. But when they hit the beach, she wasted no time divesting herself of her sandals and burrowing her bare toes in the warm sand.

Taking a deep breath of the salt-laden air, she closed her eyes and lifted her face to the sun . . . and listened. Gulls flew overhead, their song mixing with the symphonic roar of the ocean. In that moment, she could truly forget all the ugliness they had left behind in Portland.

This was peace. This was beauty. A timeless place that had extended comfort to weary souls longer than written history could account for.

"Like the beach, do you?" Brett asked, an odd note in his voice.

She opened her eyes and smiled at him. "Oh, yes. Mom used to bring me here, before she lost her license for driving while under the influence. It was her favorite place and she loved it best in summer, but there's a stark beauty in the winter I've always been drawn to as well."

"I've never been to the beach in winter."

"Georgia doesn't really have a winter, does it?"

"Not if you mean cold, no . . . but storms, yes. We didn't spend much time at the beach regardless when I was growing up. My parents preferred the mountains."

"You mean like Aspen every winter?"

"Exactly. My father bought a vacation home there for Mama the year before I born."

Their backgrounds were so different. She'd only been to Mt. Hood a couple of times and she'd never so much as bought a ticket for the ski lift. "I guess you can ski."

"Sure." He said it like, *didn't everyone?*

"I can't. Not even water ski, but I can fly a kite. Want to give it a try?"

"I'm not flying the butterfly."

"What's the matter? Afraid someone will think you're a sissy?" she said, fighting a smile.

He was the most masculine man she'd ever known. Even with his southern charm, he exuded an aura of menacing strength that was unmistakable. His overachieving tendencies might make him a good fit with his family, but his personality and intimidating presence made him fit right in with his equally intimidating mercenary friends.

He sauntered close, managing to suck the oxygen out of the vicinity even though they were outside. Warm hands cupped the sides of her face and sent electric shocks through her. She shivered in response.

His brows rose in acknowledgement of her reaction. "My sense of masculinity is not in question, sugar."

"How could it be? You've got more testosterone than a room full of Olympic-contender power-lifters."

"You think?" His grin tugged at her emotions while sending her sensory receptors on overload.

"I . . ." She had to clear her throat to finish the thought. "I do think."

She couldn't say anything more because his mouth was on hers. Smooth, firm lips molded her own and demanded a response she had no hope of holding back.

Her body moved of its own volition into contact with his and she felt the hard evidence of his arousal immediately. Even while her feminine instincts rejoiced at the proof of her effect on this incredible man, the small still-functioning portion of her brain reminded her that they were on a public beach.

She was trying to muster a response to that thought when he broke the kiss.

He put distance between their bodies and rested his forehead against hers. "Kite-flying is not what I want to do right now."

Her head bowed as it was, she could not miss how his erection strained against his pants in silent, irrefutable testament to his words. A responding throb in the moist, swollen place between her legs avowed that her body agreed with his. However, now that his mouth was no longer playing havoc with her mind, her common sense prevailed.

"It's all we can do on this beach without getting arrested for performing a lewd act in public," she said in a soft, teasing voice.

"We could get a hotel room."

She forced herself to step back from him and break the final contact of their bodies. Their eyes met and amusement warred with temptation inside her.

"That's the second time you've offered. Should I be flattered or worried you've got some kind of hotel-room fixation?"

"The only thing I'm fixated on is having absolute privacy for what I want to do with you. Since you're the *only* woman I want to do things with that are better left behind the seclusion of a locked door, it's your call whether or not you should feel flattered."

Her brain said she shouldn't. Physical desire wasn't exactly a higher-level emotion, but she couldn't help feeling that for a man like Brett to desire her as much as he did was extraordinary. He didn't want just any woman to alleviate his urges, he wanted *her* and that made her unique to him. *Special.*

It boggled her mind that he could crave *her* when the world was full of beautiful, sophisticated, and accomplished women who would know just how to please a man like him. And who would be more than willing to give it a try.

How long could his fixation with her possibly last?

"What are you thinking?" he asked, his blue gaze probing. "You're wearing an interesting look I can't quite place."

"I've decided to be flattered."

"That's good." He took a step toward her, his big body towering over her and emanating sexual intent.

She backed away, a teasing grin on her face even though her heart was beating so fast she should be running a relay. "I've also decided to teach you how to fly a kite."

"Claire," he groaned out.

She bent down and grabbed the butterfly kite and

her sandals before dancing farther out of reach. "Come on. The wind is perfect for flying."

"I know another way to take you flying, sweetheart, and the day is perfect for that, too."

She spun away from him, her heart light, and headed down the beach. "Has anyone ever told you that you have a one-track mind?"

"It may have been mentioned a time or two," he drawled.

"So, you're always this single-minded when you want sex?" There went her theory of being unique to him.

"No." The word came out forceful and intense.

She stopped to look back at him.

His eyes captured hers and refused to let go. "Things are different with you, Claire."

"Special?"

"Yes."

"You sound like that bothers you."

"It does."

"Why?"

"I can give you my body. I can't give you my future."

"I know." It already belonged to a dead woman, and that, more than anything, should be enough to bolster her defenses against his sexual charisma.

Unfortunately, what her head said and her body felt were miles apart and not even speaking the same language.

"I don't want you to get the wrong idea," he gritted out.

"That you want something more than sex from me because you want it so much? Don't worry." She turned and started walking again. It was easier to talk about this without making eye contact. "I know I'm not the kind of woman you would make a life with even if you hadn't made your rule against marrying."

"That's not true."

It was a kind lie, but she knew better. She wasn't her mom, who had been beautiful but weak. Claire might be strong, but she was no Cindy Crawford in the looks department. Men like Brett required both in the women they chose to share their lives with.

With average looks and the personality of a computer sometimes, she was *so* not in his league.

"It doesn't matter. My plans for the future don't include white picket fences and toddlers creating obstacle courses in my living room with their toys, either."

Hotwire heard the words that should have alleviated his concerns, and all he felt was annoyance. "Why don't you want to get married and have kids? You'd make a great mother."

"Yeah, right. Every child wants a mom who was trained in the job by a drunk and who relates better to computers than people on most days." She was still ahead of him, so he couldn't see her eyes, but her tone was dead serious.

Was she really that clueless about what she had to offer? She would make some very lucky man an incredible wife and any child would be blessed for her to be its mother. The thought of some faceless man laying claim to her heart and body made Hotwire angry, but he knew he shouldn't be feeling that way.

He should be encouraging her to go find that faceless man instead of trying to seduce her into his own bed, knowing he had nothing to offer her but a lot of pleasure.

Not going to happen.

He'd realized that somewhere between showing up at the hospital to find her bruised and hurting and when he gave her a mind-blowing orgasm to alleviate that pain. He might as well give up the whole noble consideration thing because all it was going to do was make him cranky.

That did not mean he didn't think she'd make a great mom someday. "You're selling yourself short, sugar."

Claire dropped to the ground and ripped open the plastic bag with her kite in it. "It doesn't really matter, does it?"

"Of course it matters."

She started fitting the frame pieces into the nylon casings. "Why? What I do with my future, or don't do with it, has nothing to do with you."

He lowered himself to the sand beside her and started in on his own kite. "We're friends."

"So, what . . . you want to be a pseudo uncle someday?"

"I'm already an uncle."

"So why should it matter if I have children or not?"

He didn't have a ready answer for her. It *shouldn't* matter. "I guess it doesn't. I just don't like you selling yourself short is all."

"I don't think I am. Now, can we drop the subject?"

He shrugged, though he had to force the casual gesture from muscles that were too tight. "Sure, but don't think I'm going to be so accommodating about making love. That's one subject I have no intention of setting aside."

She didn't say anything in response and that worried him. Was she determined to hold him off? Had she used her studying as an excuse to distract him? No. It had really been important to her to ace her exams.

And he knew she wanted him. So why was she so reticent?

There were no answers in the shiny red curls that hid her face as she bent over the butterfly kite. Though why he was looking so hard when he was the one who had told her he wasn't looking for a future with her, he didn't know. She was an intense person who didn't trust easily, and with her background, it was no wonder.

He'd offered her sex and none of the relationship trappings that go along with it. That made him a real prize . . . not. But that didn't mean he was giving up. He couldn't, and frankly, he didn't think Claire could, either.

Kite-flying turned out to be way more engrossing, not to mention challenging, than Hotwire had expected. He said as much to Claire, whose butterfly had made a nose-dive for the sand for something like the fifth time.

She laughed. "Why do you think they have world-wide competitions? It's another take on the theme of man against nature."

He walked with her as she reeled in her string so she could retrieve the kite. "Your butterfly is losing."

"While your lizard is staying high in the sky—I know."

"Too much wind for your kite." The shop owner had said strong winds could be detrimental to a low-flying delta.

"If I went really, really high, it would be okay," she said, confirming his suspicions, "but I'm not excited about holding one end of a string attached to a speck in the sky. I like the challenge of keeping it fairly close."

He could give her something to excite her, and the wind wouldn't impact it one little bit. "So, being challenged is more important than success to you?"

A determined glint lit her brown eyes. "I want both."

The intensity radiating off of her affected his libido like a shot of Viagra and he had to will his hands to stay occupied with his kite and off her body. "You're real sexy when you get that stubborn look on your face, you know that?"

She laughed like he was joking, but he wasn't, and if she took a peek at what was happening below his belt buckle, she'd know it.

She got the butterfly back up and their strings promptly tangled. She swore and then slapped her hand over her mouth in embarrassment.

It was his turn to laugh . . . until his kite's tail got in the tangle and the diamond shape started heading downward.

"I'll get it, don't worry." But in her effort to scoot around him and free her string, she tripped and fell backward.

He grabbed for her, but was still trying to keep his kite from dive-bombing and ended up falling with her.

They landed in the sand with a thump, their limbs tangled as badly as their kite strings.

She was laughing like a kid on a merry-go-round, and he smiled at the pleasure glowing in her eyes.

"I think Mother Nature won," she said drolly.

He couldn't control the urge to brush his fingers over her smiling face. "That's one way of putting it."

Looking past his shoulder, she grimaced. "Both kites are headed for the sand now."

He dipped his head forward and breathed in her scent. It was every bit as fresh as the sea air, but infinitely more seductive to him. "That's unfortunate."

"You don't sound sincere."

"You expect me to care right now?" He'd managed to retain his hold on the kite string, but at that moment the only thing that interested him was the feel of the woman under him.

"Why not?" Her eyes were all innocence, but her voice was breathless.

She knew exactly what was on his mind, and in case she didn't, he shifted so his hardened sex was pressing against the apex of her thighs. "You sure you don't know the answer to that?"

Her soft brown gaze went unfocussed. "Wh-what?"

She was so responsive, her body's reaction to him instantaneous. How could she deny this thing between them?

Claire couldn't think, not with Brett's hard body pressing into hers as intimately as a man could do with his clothes on. He'd asked her a question, but she couldn't remember what it was, much less formulate an answer. This wanting for him grew and grew and grew, until it was a living thing inside of her. She craved the sensation of his naked skin against her, the tenderness of his touch.

Memories of the first night in the hotel would not go away, and with him on top of her like this, they overwhelmed her senses, making her inner woman demand more of the same.

Blue eyes, darkened to indigo with desire, bore into hers. "You want me, Claire, admit it."

"Yes." She licked her lips.

His gaze narrowed. "I'm going to kiss you."

"Please . . ."

He did, his mouth devouring hers with the passion that exploded every time their lips met. His tongue tangled with hers and she sucked on it, shivering with desire at the masculine sound of need he made. The kiss went on and on and she lost herself in it, wanting more than his mouth, needing to touch his hot, smooth skin.

Her fingers scrabbled against his shirt to undo buttons, but a hard hand settled over hers, stopping her. She moaned in protest.

He abruptly broke the kiss and rolled onto his back, his chest heaving.

She turned her head toward him. "Brett?"

"Give me a minute, sugar. You came damn close to being nailed on a public beach."

She'd noticed he only swore when he was not in complete control. A secret thrill went through her that she could affect him like that, but she shuddered. The effect was entirely mutual. Two seconds ago she wouldn't have cared less where she was as long as he made love to her.

Brett sat up and she reluctantly did the same, her body thrumming with a level of desire she'd never experienced before meeting this man.

"I need you now."

"I can see that you do."

"Are you saying you don't feel the same?" he asked with masculine aggression.

"No. I'm not saying that," she replied softly.

"Then we get a hotel room."

"That sounds so cold-blooded."

He shook his head, clearly impatient. "The last thing either of us feels around the other is cold."

"But . . ."

"But nothing. Time is running out, Claire." A different kind of desperation laced his voice. One she didn't understand.

"Why?" What made right this second different from two days ago, or two days from now, for that matter? She asked that, too.

"My mom's birthday is on Saturday and I'm expected in Georgia sometime before the big party."

He'd be leaving her. Her heart contracted, but she tried to keep her disappointment off her face. "I'm sure your family will be glad to see you."

He waved her words away as if they were pesky flies. "If I didn't show, both Mama and my sister would have my guts for garters, but that's not what's got my dick tied in knots. I've been taking cold showers for longer than I want to admit because of you, and now we have one, maybe two nights before the trip to Georgia will put a moratorium on anything physical between us."

She opened her mouth to speak, but didn't get a single sound out before he fiercely added, "Don't say you don't want me, because we both know you do."

"But what we want and what is good for us isn't always the same thing."

"Not in this case, sweetheart. I'll make it very good for you. I promise. And you're going to make it incredibly good for me, too."

Her insides clenched and her feminine core throbbed. "I don't doubt you."

Though she wasn't so confident about her own performance. She couldn't help wondering if sex had always been so flat before because she wasn't very good at it. After all, Brett made no bones about how much he enjoyed it. She'd always believed that it was more hype than reality, though . . . only his touch made her question that conclusion.

Which could mean that she'd just had bad partners, too. It was a much more confidence-boosting scenario, but she couldn't entirely rid herself of the niggling doubt that she was the one with the problem. One of her boyfriends had said she had issues with trust.

No, duh . . . but had that really made her unresponsive to sex as he'd accused? Would she falter at the last hurdle with Brett, the act of making love?

She couldn't imagine doing so while her nipples tingled inside her bra and the throbbing between her legs increased. She really wanted this man, but did she want him enough to dismiss the future as unimportant . . . to accept her role as a temporary lover?

Claire could never hope to replace his dead fiancée

in his heart and that meant she could not hope to be a permanent fixture in his life. Not ever. There was no percentage in that kind of relationship for a woman, but did she have the strength or even the true desire to turn away from what he was offering?

"Claire?"

There was no cajolery in his voice, merely a question. What was she going to do?

She looked into his blue eyes, her heart beating too fast while her mind spun with questions and answers that left her more confused by the second. She could see his desire—feel it with unmistakable clarity—yet he didn't push. He wouldn't. He was her friend as well as the man who wanted to take her to bed.

He was so darn honorable . . . and tough . . . and sexy.

So much of everything she believed made a man strong, so different from her dad and the men who had paraded through her life since his death. Brett epitomized masculine perfection to her.

Oh, man.

She loved him.

It shouldn't come as such a surprise, except, well . . . that she thought romantic love was pretty much for fairy tales and make-believe. It was just sexual desire and she, like so many other women before her, was trying to wrap it up in an emotional package with a pretty little bow.

Hadn't she tried that before and been severely disappointed? To love someone, you had to be able to count on him, and she couldn't count on anyone but herself.

You've certainly been counting on Brett for a lot these past few days, a snarky voice in her head reminded her.

Which did not mean she was buying into the whole love and happily ever after bit. Especially not with a man who'd sworn off love himself. But if they made love, maybe this nearly debilitating sexual desire would wane some and she could gain control of her emotions again. Her vision would not be clouded by her physical needs and she would be able to see him with clearer eyes, not through a silly, love struck haze that would never survive in the real world of sex and the morning after.

Right. Sex was going to clear her head, not cloud it further. That made so much sense, the snarky inner voice drawled.

She sighed. Great. She was arguing with herself. Maybe unrequited lust led to insanity. "When are you flying to Georgia?"

"*We* are flying down on Friday."

"I'm not going . . . am I?"

There was no misreading the irritation in his eyes. "Of course you are. I can't leave you here by yourself."

"You could bring Collins in to watch over me, or I could go stay with Queenie." Getting away from Brett might actually give her a chance to shore up her shaky defenses and clear her head without the whole sex gambit.

"No."

"I don't want to horn in on your mother's birthday celebration. That sort of thing is for friends and family."

"You *are* my friend."

"But your mother doesn't know me from Adam and it's *her* birthday."

"She'll be thrilled to meet you. She's been begging me to bring a woman home to meet her for ages."

Even worse. "But I'm not a woman you're thinking about marrying."

"Doesn't matter. She's a southern lady with her heart set on more grandchildren. She'll have our wedding planned by the end of the weekend." He said it like the thought was an amusing one, rather than horrific.

"But I don't *want* her thinking we've got a relationship like that. It's deceitful."

"I didn't say I'd tell her we were serious, but even if I tell her you're a friend in trouble, she'll draw her own conclusions."

"That's an even bigger reason for me not to go. I can't possibly go with you to Georgia. It would be terribly awkward for both of us, but I would think for you especially."

Chapter 13

"Why me especially?" he asked with a frown.

"You *can't* want your family thinking you're planning to marry me. After I leave Georgia, I'll probably never see them again, but you have to live with the consequences. Your mother is going to be upset when she realizes nothing will ever come of our friendship."

"I can't control what my family thinks, but I'm not responsible for it, either. I stopped worrying about my mother's plans for my life the year I joined the army instead of attending my father and older brother's alma mater."

She sighed at his intractability. "You're being stubborn and there's no need."

"You are going with me if I have to hogtie you and lock you in the bedroom on the jet for the flight." He said it so reasonably that she didn't compute the threat at first.

When she did, she glared. "That is so not going to happen."

"Are you sure about that?"

"Yes, but I find it interesting that you have a private jet." More like *intimidating*, but who was keeping track? "Isn't that a little decadent?"

"Not really. Wolf got one and I liked it so much I decided to get one of my own. It makes certain jobs I do for the government a lot easier."

"Mercenary work must pay well."

"You have no idea."

She was stunned into silence, but then her brain started working. "Have you ever heard of SAFE House, or the Portland Rescue Mission? They are in constant need of donations. Both organizations focus on finding solutions to the problems facing society today, not perpetuating them."

Brett threw his head back and laughed out loud.

She didn't think her suggestions were all that amusing and told him so, but he just shook his head, laughing harder.

When he finally calmed down he grinned at her. "Josie told me that would be your reaction when you found out I was wealthy. She said you never got dollar signs in your eyes on your own account but that you'd convinced her to donate to a lot of places she'd never even known about."

Claire ducked her head and bit her lip with worry that she'd pushed her friend unduly. "Josette didn't seem to mind at the time. I wasn't trying to take advantage of her good nature or our friendship."

He really sobered at that and reached out to take her hand. "She didn't. Trust me. She thinks you're pretty wonderful and the way you care about so many causes is admirable. So do I."

"Oh." Relief coursed through her. "Then you'll consider giving?"

"If you come to Georgia with me, I'll donate a fat check to three charities of your choosing."

"You're not serious?"

"I'd do it anyway eventually, I'm sure, but this way, I get to circumvent more arguing with you. You're darn stubborn when you want to be."

"You said you thought I was sexy when I was stubborn."

His eyes burned with primal hunger that stole her breath right out of her chest. "I do."

Oh, gosh . . . she was going to throw him back on the sand and ravish him if she didn't get herself under control. "We should untangle our kites and see if we can get them in the sky again."

Brett shook his head, his blue gaze intense. "No."

"But—"

"We'll reel them in and then we'll go."

"Back to Portland?"

"Is that what you want?"

And there it was . . . her confused desires and thoughts boiled down to one question. Did she want to go back to Portland, or did she want to stay and make love?

She could put it off until they got back, but that would be postponing the inevitable, not circumventing it.

At least if they stayed, there would be something special about their first time together, a memory she could cherish later that wouldn't be tarnished by the trouble waiting for her in Portland.

"I don't want to go back tonight."

Some of the tension emanating off of Brett faded away. "There's a resort hotel just south of Lincoln City. Will you let me take you there?"

"Yes."

His eyes narrowed. "Are you sure?"

"Yes."

"Good." That was all he said.

Then he started reeling in his kite. If she'd expected a bigger reaction to her agreement, she wasn't going to get one. She could see that pretty easily.

She followed his lead and they got the kites untangled and packed away without either of them breaking the silence. In fact, other than to remind her to buckle her seat belt, he didn't say another word to her. Not on the drive to the local pharmacy where he went in and came out only minutes later carrying a single bag. She had no problem guessing what was in it.

And he remained silent on the trip to the hotel, speaking only to the desk clerk during check-in. However, a powerful sense of purpose surrounded him, and Claire found she had no desire to make small talk, either.

Brett slid the hotel key card in the lock and opened the door to their suite. She looked at the suite's living area through the open doorway, but made no move to go inside.

He waited for her to go inside in silence.

Taking a deep breath, she moved forward, stepping into a nicely decorated suite. But it was the view through the wall of windows opposite the door that really impressed her.

The woman at the desk had said that all the rooms faced the ocean; what she hadn't said was that the view was so spectacular or that it was showcased by such a huge expanse of windows.

Brett shut the door and she watched in bemusement while he secured the room with things he pulled from a bag he'd brought from the car. He probably didn't even realize he was doing it, the security-conscious behavior was so second nature to him.

But one thing they did not have to worry about would be interruption at a key moment.

Then he turned to face her. "I want you, Claire. *Now.*"

She opened her mouth, but no sound came out. She licked her lips, took a breath, and tried again. "I want you, too."

The corner of his mouth tilted in a not-quite-there smile. "That's good."

Then he stepped forward and before she knew what was happening, she was in his arms, high against his chest and he was carrying her into the bedroom. It was cast in daytime shadows. He didn't bother to turn on a light—the only illumination came through the latte-colored lace panels covering the sliding glass doors and huge window to one side of them.

But she had no problem seeing the look of desire etched in fierce relief on his features. The intensity of it put a sharper edge on the need slicing through her.

Making love with this man was going to be incredible. If there was a tiny voice in her head warning her that it might cost more emotionally than she had to give, she was prepared to ignore it. She'd been dealing with painful emotions all her life.

Never before had anyone offered her the kind of pleasure she knew could be found in his arms.

She grabbed his face and kissed him with a hunger she was done trying to control.

He responded with his own voracious passion and soon she was trying to rip his clothes from his body while he did the same to her without dropping her. The bed was right there, but they didn't stop kissing long enough to get into it.

She couldn't stop. All she wanted was more and more and more . . . more of his lips, more of his naked body to touch, and more of his taste in her mouth. His shirt came off with popping buttons and finally she had her fingers against his bare chest. She skimmed the satin-smooth skin and silky chest hair with her fingertips while he shoved her top up and somehow managed to get her bra undone to expose her aching and swollen breasts.

A raw, earthy sound came from deep in her throat when he cupped and squeezed one generous mound. Then he took her nipple between his thumb and forefinger and played with it until she felt like exploding from that simple touch. The peak was so hard, the pleasure sensations arrowing out from it to the rest of her body almost hurt.

She ate at his lips, determined not to be a dud at this. If he could pleasure her, she could pleasure him, too, and she concentrated on giving as good as she got. Paying attention to every nuance of his reaction to her touching, she concentrated on repeating every successful foray.

He liked having the brown disks around his turgid nipples tickled with her fingernails, so she did that and other stuff . . . all the while her own body notching higher and higher toward a supernova of pleasure. He got her pants and underwear off and she wrapped her legs around his waist, rubbing herself against the muscular ridges of his naked belly.

The scent of her own musk teased her nostrils as she chafed her slick, swollen labia and clitoris against his hard torso.

It was all the stimulation she needed to go over the edge—star bursts went off with shattering devastation inside her while she moaned a litany of pleasure into his mouth. He didn't slow down in his touching at all, kneading her breasts with both hands now and dominating her mouth with hungry urgency. If anything, her climax drove him to a fever pitch and she found herself thrown back on the bed.

She didn't have to think about what came next. She just put her arms out, welcoming him to her.

With a hoarse sound, he ripped out of his jeans and shorts and then came down on top of her, driving into her with a single, merciless thrust.

She cried out against his mouth, her body stiffening with shock at his penetration. He was big and he stretched her sensitive flesh to the point of pain, but all her fevered mind recognized was the amazing pleasure of having him joined with her so intimately.

He broke his lips from hers. "It's all right, sugar. Relax."

She stared up at him, her mind not taking the words in while her body started climbing toward that ultimate peak again. She didn't know if she would survive another climax, but her intimate flesh wasn't reacting to that fear. It was pressing for her to do something . . . anything.

Only she wasn't moving.

He withdrew, pulling almost out and she gasped. "No! Don't leave me."

He laughed at that, the sound dark and not at all humorous. "I'm not going anywhere, but you need to relax or you aren't going to enjoy this as much as I am."

Was he serious? "If I enjoy it any more, it'll kill me," she croaked.

He pressed forward and finally the stasis on her limbs lifted. She arched up to meet him, welcoming him with voracious need into her body.

He grinned, the expression so feral it made her shiver. "That's right, sugar. Move for me."

She was only too happy to oblige him as she slammed her hips upward and ground her pelvis against his. He thrust into her, filling her completely and caressing every zinging nerve ending inside her channel with devastating intensity.

She grabbed his chest, kneading the hard muscles and reveling in the sensation of having this ultramasculine man so completely in tune with her.

He growled and increased his pace until she was shaking from the impact of his thrusts.

He looked down at her, his blue eyes burning with sexual need. "You are beautiful, Claire."

Beautiful? Oh, no . . . that one word and emotion crashed through her like a five-alarm fire in a forest of tinder. Her heart contracted and it wasn't from the primitive pleasure her body was wallowing in. He thought she was beautiful in her passion . . . not a computer geek, not a plain Jane . . . beautiful.

Oh, man, if what she was feeling inside wasn't love, she didn't want to know what emotion could power something else this profound. She wanted to make love until her body ached and his body gave out, but more than that . . . she wanted to look in his eyes, the windows to his soul, while she did it. And she wanted to hold him afterward, to be held by him.

While her heart wrestled with these new desires, strong masculine fingers locked onto her hips and she found herself held immobile while he pounded into her with driving force. Every surge of his hard penis felt so good that she gasped, and every time he pulled out, antithesis pleasure burst into shards through her most feminine flesh.

There was no warning . . . for either of them. The climax roared up and claimed them both in bone-shattering intensity. He shuddered above her while her body clenched around his and she stopped breathing altogether.

He collapsed on top of her, his big body continuing to jerk with aftereffects from their shared explosion. "That was amazing," he whispered against her ear.

She had to force air in her lungs to respond. "Yes," she wheezed.

"Damn . . . sugar, I knew you were going to be good, but I didn't realize you were going to near kill me."

She smiled, exhaustion rolling over her in an unstoppable wave. "Only fair . . . thought I might die there for a minute."

"Good thing you didn't."

"Mmmm . . ." she mumbled as she slid inexorably toward sleep.

She'd never been so tired in her entire life, but then, she'd never put her body through such an experience, either.

Hotwire nuzzled Claire's neck, kissing her softly. This felt so damn good. She was soft, tight, and blessed with a figure so beautiful it took his breath away. She was also sleeping.

Unable to believe the message his senses were getting, he lifted his head and looked down at her face. It was relaxed in the abandon of a replete woman exhausted by her lover.

He grinned.

He was going to tease her about going to sleep on him whenever he gave her a climax, but in a very non-PC way, he was filled with masculine pride at the thought of wearing her out from a single session of lovemaking. The little darling had climaxed so hard, her body had lifted his off the bed.

At the mere thought of how she arched and convulsed when she came, his semierect cock hardened in-

side her. It would take no provocation at all to change
that condition to full arousal. Despite having experienced the best sex he had ever known, the hunger he
felt for her had not abated.

On the contrary, now that his body knew the pleasure of touching and being inside her, it craved more.

His thoughts brought him up short. Had it been
even better sex than he'd had with Elena? Impossible.
He'd loved her. Time must have dulled his perception
of the pleasure he'd found in her arms. It was hard to
believe it had been more than six years. The memories
even felt like memories now, not a fresh reliving of too
much pain.

But there was nothing dull about the images in his
mind from the past hour. They and the piercing pleasure they elicited were sharp and edgy. They were also
bigger than simple sexual release and pure physical en-
joyment. He'd had plenty of both of those in the last six
years, but this feeling of intimacy afterward was different.

And it bothered him.

Had she felt the same? What was he going to do if
she started thinking she'd fallen in love with him? He
didn't want their friendship destroyed by expectations
he could not meet.

The problem was, he would get over these feelings,
just like he'd gotten over any tender feelings he'd felt
toward other women since Elena's death. Okay, so
maybe he'd never felt quite like this, but that didn't
mean it had any better chance at lasting than the other
feelings had. He wouldn't let it.

He'd made a promise to himself and to the woman
he had loved, though she had not been alive to hear it.
He'd never been tempted to break that promise, but he
was now. He didn't want to see Claire hurt.

You're a little late with that worry, a cynical voice inside his head taunted him. Women were different from men. They got sex and emotions all tangled up, and what woman wouldn't believe herself in love after sex that good?

His dick surged at the reminder, and satisfaction coursed through him despite the possible complications. Making love with Claire completely had been one for the record books. It had been so mind-blowing, he'd forgotten everything and he'd never done that—never been so oblivious to anything and everything but the feel of the woman in his arms.

He relived the sensation of her convulsing around him, of her inner flesh clamping his, and went iron hard inside of her. She moaned softly in her sleep and he groaned. A less scrupulous man would take advantage of the situation, especially with his memories of the way it had been only minutes before.

Exploding inside her scorching tightness had taken the top of his head off. His heat had added to hers and he had one of the longest orgasms of his life.

And then exactly what he *had* forgotten penetrated his consciousness and he went rigid above his sleeping lover.

Here he was, worrying like an adolescent with his first crush about *feelings* when he'd gone and done the unforgivable.

He'd forgotten the frigging condom.

How could he have been so stupid?

He'd remembered a glove every time he'd had sex since he was sixteen. Even when he and Elena had made love, he'd never once forgotten.

Cold chills washed over him as he berated himself for his stupidity. He had wanted to make it perfect for her and he couldn't have screwed up more badly than if he'd planned it. His sperm were swimming in her private pool right now and one of the little suckers could already have scored.

Claire could be pregnant with his baby.

The possible consequence was a lot less jarring than the realization of his error. Despite what she seemed to think, Claire would make an incredible mother. And the thought of her round with his child was an even bigger turn-on than memories of their intimacy. He was a hair's breadth from coming again and he hadn't even moved.

He willed his hard-on into submission as he considered Claire's reaction to his mistake. What if she *was* pregnant? She would not take possible single-motherhood in her stride.

Her life with her own mom had been too harsh.

And while she alone understood why, she doubted her abilities in that area. She'd questioned her suitability for motherhood as part of a parental unit; how much stronger would those insecurities be in the face of an accidental pregnancy? Understandably, she would want to give her baby the best of everything, including a whole family unit . . . a real home. Things he'd promised a dead woman he would never have.

Or had he? His promise to Elena had been that he would never love another woman like he had loved her.

In his mind that had meant he would never marry, never have kids. No woman would settle for his body without his heart.

But Claire had accepted him as her lover without protestations of love. Though he had to admit that in light of their circumstances, if she did equate incredible sex with that emotion, it might not be such a bad thing after all.

Her loving him could make it easier to do what he

knew she would consider acting on the best alternative. But even if she didn't love him, she would want to give the best to her baby. Her own heart's involvement wouldn't be as important to her as doing that. He was sure of it.

A band that had been tightening around his chest since Claire fell asleep in his arms loosened. He could keep his promise to Elena and still do the right thing by Claire. They could have a good life.

He was sure she'd see things the same way.

Chapter 14

Claire woke up to a slight throbbing between her legs and an unfamiliar inner sense of well-being that made her lips curl in pleasure before she opened her eyes. When she did, she discovered she was alone in a big bed. A deep sense of satiation and rightness permeated her as the late evening light of summer filtered through the lace curtains.

It was a beautiful room and the bed was deliciously comfortable. She stretched, luxuriating in the knowledge she had no more exams to study for, no job to go to. She could go back to sleep if she wanted to, or laze in the bed daydreaming until Brett came looking for her.

It was such a decadent feeling, lying naked in the oversized bed with no commitments pressing. She couldn't remember the last time she had felt so free of encumbrances. So happy. She wasn't sure she ever had.

She had spent years taking care of her mom both before and after the cancer struck. She'd gone straight to college after Noreen's death, too . . . not taking even a full month off before trading one all-consuming work-load for another one. She'd worked whatever hours were necessary to achieve her goals, both at school studying and at the jobs she took to support herself.

She had made love to Brett and, strangely enough, knowing there were no commitments for the future linked to it was peaceful rather than stressful. Before, when she'd had sex, the lack of reciprocal commitment had always hurt, but she didn't owe anyone but herself anything right now.

And she liked that. Brett only wanted the pleasure of sex and she wanted that, too.

For once in her life she was going to do nothing but enjoy . . . for however long that lasted. She was not going to worry about the future or holding on to Brett when he was ready to let go. He'd told her what to expect and instead of lamenting it now that they had made love, a big part of her was wallowing in the knowledge that she hadn't given more of herself away than she wanted to.

For the very simple reason that Brett had made it clear he didn't want it. No future. No commitments.

Freedom.

What an awesome concept.

Contrarily, the knowledge she didn't have to move made her want to. She wanted to see Brett, not to cling to him out of emotional neediness . . . but simply to be with him.

Only there was no sign of him in the room and no light coming from the bathroom. Nor did she hear anything from the outer room. Which did not mean he wasn't in the suite. The man could be as silent as smoke when he wanted to be.

She scooted into a sitting position and winced at the

slight ache in muscles used differently than they had
been in a very long time. A shower was no doubt in
order, but for a few brief seconds, she allowed herself to
wallow with happy abandon in the fact that Brett had
made love to her.

Thoroughly.

Passionately.

And beautifully.

He was a thrilling lover, completely wild with his car-
nality and capable of sparking the same reaction in her.
No woman could ask for more in the man she chose to
share her body with. She could still hear his shout of release echoing in her head.

Wow. If she'd ever known that sex could be so wonderful, she wouldn't have dismissed it as unimportant
in her life . . . that was for sure. But then, could it have
been this life-altering with any other man?

Somehow, she didn't think so.

Which was a slightly sobering thought. Was it complete freedom if she only experienced it with one man?

Dismissing the question as irrelevant in the face of
more happy feelings than she'd ever experienced in
one sitting, she climbed from the bed and spied a thick
white hotel robe laying neatly across the bottom corner.
She pulled it on and went looking for Brett, but he was
nowhere in the suite.

A note on the dining table told her that he'd gone to
pick up some necessary items for spending the night.
She hoped one of the things he was getting was a canis-
ter of tea. She could really use some right now.

There was a silver teakettle on the stove and she wondered if maybe the suite came equipped for it. She
searched the cupboards and found a fully equipped
kitchen but no food. However, in the last cupboard she

discovered a small basket filled with tea bags and enough coffee for two pots. Perfect. She put the water on to boil and took a shower while it was heating.

She washed her hair with the fragrant shampoo provided and then lathered her body, amazed at the way her skin tingled where she touched it. She'd never had these lingering effects from sex before. Not that she'd had sex all that many times, but her meager experience had been equally dismal in the pleasure department.

Her present feelings were really amazing. They'd made love almost three hours ago and she'd been asleep since . . . the fact that her body was still sensitized boggled her mind.

She went to wash herself. She was awfully sticky. She didn't remember being this wet either, but the first time he'd made her climax, she'd woken up a lot stickier than when she'd had sex before too. There was even more moisture between her legs now and it was stickier.

Had he forgotten the condom? The whole experience had been so hot, so out of her frame of reference, she had never once thought of it. She didn't remember him taking the time to put on protection, but she didn't really remember how she'd gotten totally naked either. It had just happened.

Of course it hadn't, but making love with him had been mind blowing . . . apparently literally. She could not imagine him being so irresponsible. It just wasn't in character, but then maybe he'd been so turned on he'd lost track of reality too. Embarrassment washed over her at how much she liked that thought. But it would mean she was special to him, because she was positive he didn't go around having unprotected sex.

She couldn't even be sure he had this time.

The teakettle started whistling when she was drying

off and she dashed toward the kitchen to shut off the burner as the door to the suite opened.

She stopped in her tracks and stared as Brett entered the suite carrying several bags.

His blue eyes were unreadable in a face too stoic for the aftermath of the kind of lovemaking they had enjoyed.

"Are you going to turn that off?"

Belatedly, she realized the teakettle was whistling shrilly now. "Oh . . . yes."

She rushed over to turn off the burner and move the kettle to an already cool one. The whistle stopped immediately, leaving an odd silence between them. What was he thinking? Why did he look so serious? He had forgotten the condom. It was the only thing that could make him look like that, wasn't it?

She certainly hoped so.

He dropped a couple of the bags he had in his hands on the kitchen counter and carried the others into the bedroom. She was still standing there, staring after him, trying to determine what to do or say next, when he came back.

"Were you trying to make tea?"

"Yes."

"I bought some for you. The kind you like."

"Thank you." The words were stilted, the moment awkward.

She was practically naked, and he was acting as if they were polite strangers. As if they had not checked into this hotel for the express purpose of making love. As if they had not made love with near soul-destroying intensity. Why?

Was it the condom thing? Or was he now trying to act like it hadn't happened because he wished it hadn't?

"I'll make the tea while you finish drying off from your shower."

It was not the most loverlike of responses, but it was considerate, she reminded herself. "All right."

He didn't say anything else as she headed back to the bathroom.

She stopped at the door. "Brett?"

"Yeah, sugar?"

The endearment was encouraging.

"Do you regret doing what we did?"

"Making love?" he asked as if there could seriously be some doubt about what she was referring to.

She spun to face him. "Of course making love. What else did we do?"

"Well, we had lunch at a Chinese restaurant, flew kites on the beach, got them all tangled, and checked into a hotel to stay overnight." If he didn't sound so serious, she'd think he was teasing her.

"Why would you regret any of those things?" she asked, irritated he was making it so hard.

"I wouldn't."

"Then why bring them up?"

"Why bring up regret at all?"

Which did not answer her question and she was smart enough to see that. "Because I want to know."

"If I regret making love to you?"

"Yes."

His blue eyes bored into her. "It's a waste of time to regret actions that cannot be changed."

Her stomach cramped. "Are you saying you wish they could be?"

He was certainly *acting like* he regretted making love. Which meant he probably didn't want to repeat the experience. A knot of pain formed inside her, a huge mockery of her newfound sense of freedom. She'd believed she could handle him moving on, but it had never crossed her mind he would want to do it so quickly.

Her heart cried out in denial.

"Go get dressed, Claire. And then we'll talk."

"Fine."

Hotwire sighed. She was angry and it was only going to get worse.

He had a plan to mitigate the consequence of his stupidity, but fixing a problem that should never have become a problem wasn't something he liked doing. Nor was he used to being in this position.

At least not with him as the instigator of the debacle.

She came out less than a minute later, wearing the hotel bathrobe and looking ornery. She'd finger combed her red curls, but even wet, they showed signs of having a will all their own.

He wished she'd put on one of the outfits he'd gotten her. She was too damn alluring wearing a garment he'd always associated with the bedroom. And he was not going back in there until they had some things settled between them.

He hadn't started making her tea yet and found himself moving out of her way so she could do it. He wasn't going to mess with the aura of mulish irritation surrounding her, no sir.

For a woman who was pretty much a disaster in the kitchen, she sure was particular how she made her tea. She even timed how long she left it to steep before adding one perfectly level teaspoon of sugar to her cup and two heaping ones to a second mug he assumed was his.

She finished about the same time he finished putting

away the few groceries he'd bought while he'd been out shopping.

She handed him the heavily sweetened tea. "Here. We can talk in the other room."

He took the mug from her, noticing how careful she was not to touch him.

He frowned. "I don't bite."

She glared right back. "Maybe I do."

He had to clamp down on an urge to laugh. That would not be a smart move right now, but she was the cutest testy person he'd ever seen. He sat at one end of the couch, but regretted his choice the second Claire followed suit. So close, she was way too tempting for his peace of mind or his self-control in the face of their need to talk.

Sitting in the spot right next to him, she faced him with her legs tucked up next to her. "So, does any of this grim fatalism you've been subjecting me to since coming in have something to do with the fact you didn't use the condoms you bought?"

He'd been about to take a sip of his tea, but put it down right quick. He had no desire to scald himself as shock coursed through him. "You realized I didn't use one?"

And was taking it this calmly?

"Not at the time, no." She took a sip of her tea, her gaze steady over the rim of her mug. "But it did when I was in the shower. It probably should have occurred to me earlier, like when I woke up, but I was too busy wallowing in how good it had been. I never got as wet as I did the night you gave me pleasure to help me sleep, so I wasn't entirely sure, but I suspected. I guess I'm slow about some things."

"Your brain is really fast."

"Not fast enough to remind you to use protection, apparently."

"It wasn't your job. I was the experienced one. It's entirely my fault."

She frowned at him. "You don't honestly believe that, do you? Because if you do, it's a terrible insult to my intelligence. I'm an adult and I'm responsible for my own actions, or lack thereof. And while I may not have a list of lovers as long as my arm, I'm no naïve virgin. I know the importance of using protection when having sex."

"You didn't know what you were getting into, how overwhelming it was going to be." Hell, neither had he, but he should have had an inkling, considering how hot he'd been for her. And that was what he had to focus on here. *He should have known better*; therefore, he had been the one to make the mistake. "You said yourself, you'd never before had sex worth writing home about. I should have protected you, but I screwed up. Big time."

They weren't easy words to say. He worked hard never to have to say them, so when they were necessary, they were like sandpaper on his voice box.

"I don't understand how this is your personal faux pas. You were as lost to what was happening between us as I was."

"But I shouldn't have been."

She eyed him speculatively. "Are you saying you aren't normally?"

"No," he gritted, feeling like a fool.

"Do you forget the condom very often?" She didn't sound worried.

In fact, if he didn't know better, he'd think that was relief darkening her brown eyes . . . and a certain amount of smug satisfaction. But no woman would react that way to learning she had just had unprotected sex, especially a woman as practical as Claire.

"Of course not. I never rely on my partner for birth control."

"So, I don't have to be concerned about contracting any nasty diseases?"

"No," he said, even more affronted by this question than the last.

Did she seriously think he would make love to her without warning her about such a thing? Not to mention the fact that he was a lot choosier about his sex partners than she seemed to give him credit for. "I am not carrying an STD."

"Good. Neither am I."

"Glad to hear it, but that's not the main issue here."

"So, what you are saying here is that you think because I was less experienced in the art of sex and mind-blowing orgasms that I was allowed to be brain-dead when it came to protecting myself from pregnancy?"

"No." For a woman with intelligence as fine as hers, she made some strange assumptions. "I did not say you were brain-dead."

"Then you agree that forgetting the condom was both our faults . . . both our responsibilities?"

"No."

"You're being ridiculous." She was getting all squinty-eyed, and calm patience was not the emotion emanating from her right now.

"I'm being honest. It's not easy to admit I made such a huge mistake, but I'm not going to shirk from it, either."

"What does that mean?"

"I'll make it right."

"In what way?"

"I think we should get married."

Chapter 15

Hotwire wanted to curse.

That had come out wrong. He hadn't meant to blurt it out without any buildup. Even if theirs wasn't the romance of the century, a woman deserved to be asked to be married with some finesse. Like over dinner with candlelight and a warm kiss, or two.

But he'd already blurted it out. Now he needed to go with the momentum . . . such that it was.

Her eyes were wide with shock. *"What?"*

"I *want* you to marry me. Please." At least that sounded better. Saying *please* was a good touch.

Only she didn't look even remotely more reconciled to the idea. Shock was still the only expression he could read on her face.

"Because we forgot to use a condom?" she asked in a voice that echoed astonishment.

"Because you might be pregnant."

She gasped, as if he'd said something offensive. "How likely do you really think that is?"

"You tell me."

"What do you mean?" she demanded belligerently.

"It's *your* female cycle."

"Oh." She went still, as if counting the days, and then her brow wrinkled and she bit her bottom lip. "I'm right in the middle of my cycle."

"So the timing couldn't be worse." Damn it. He'd done it again. "I mean, the chances we made a baby are pretty high."

"No. The possibility of conception exists, yes, but statistics show that men and women make love all the time during the optimum days in a woman's cycle without her getting pregnant. Why do you think fertility specialists are in such high demand here in the United States?"

"It's a high risk," he insisted. "Not everything is about statistics, Claire."

"And because of what you consider a high risk, not even a definite reality, you're willing to sacrifice your future and marry me?"

"It wouldn't be a sacrifice."

"Right. You don't love me—you told me so—and you never once thought of marriage before forgetting the condom."

He wasn't going there. She was right, but admitting it would only add fuel to her arguments. He'd already messed up enough in this discussion. "Claire, you can't tell me that after your childhood, you would take single motherhood lightly."

"After my childhood, the prospect of being a mother at all is not something I want to contemplate."

"Are you saying that you would terminate the pregnancy?" He'd never considered that possibility.

Maybe he should have.

Her expression filled with horrified revulsion. "I don't eat meat because the thought of killing animals is so abhorrent to me! Do you really believe I could kill my own child?"

"Some people—"

"Are not me. I do not see abortion as a viable form of birth control."

"I don't, either."

"Then why bring it up?"

"You said you didn't want to be a mother."

"I said it wasn't something I wanted to think about, not that I wouldn't do my best to be a good one if I had a child."

"I knew you'd feel that way."

"What way?" she asked warily.

"That giving our baby a chance at the best possible life would be worth whatever you had to do to ensure that."

"And you think that good life includes me marrying you?"

"After growing up with your mom the way she was, you'd want to give your child two parents it could count on."

"Are you trying to say that after your *normal* upbringing, *you* don't feel that way?" The way she asked it made him feel like he'd insulted her.

"I didn't mean to imply—"

"Let's get something straight here—my mom wasn't a rotten parent because she was single. She was a rotten parent because she drank. I don't. I won't. And I don't have to get married to give any child of mine a life worth living."

"But marrying me would make it easier. Admit it. You're just finished with school . . . you haven't established a career yet. *You need me.*" Couldn't she see that?

She scooted away from him as if he were diseased. "I'm not your charity case. You don't have to marry me out of some mistaken sense of chivalry or fear I'll follow in my mother's footsteps and rely on the largesse of the state to provide for my child."

"That is one fear I will never have," he said forcefully. "This is not about me thinking you'd be anything but a terrific mom. You're too strong and too smart to ever make your mom's choices, but why should you have to make any hard choices at all? The mistake was mine and there is nothing chivalrous in making it right."

"It was both our mistakes!" She glared at him. "And I don't need you *making it right.*"

What the heck was the matter with her? "You're acting like I've grossly offended you."

"You have."

"Asking you to marry me is an offense?" he demanded, none too happy at the moment himself.

"You didn't ask. You informed me it was the best solution to making up for a *mistake* you *regret* making."

"I didn't say I regretted it."

"And you didn't say you *didn't* regret making love, either. I understand your attitude now, but I don't appreciate it any more than I did before. What we did, we did together, and you can't deny it was something you wanted as much as I did."

"I don't regret making love with you," he practically shouted, unable to understand how their conversation had become a full-blown argument. "And I sure as heck wanted it."

She should be happy he wanted to marry her. Intimacy meant more to her than she was willing to admit, and he'd known that from the beginning. It was why he had tried to keep from acting on his desire, but he hadn't been able to keep his libido in lockdown mode living with her twenty-four-seven.

"Tell me about the other men you've had sex with."

"What?" She stared at him as if he'd grown two horns. "Why?"

"I want to know."

She frowned and shifted on the couch so her legs were in front of her, her feet on the floor. "There were only two."

"Who were they?"

"They were both boys I dated in high school when I was young and stupid enough to believe in love and happily-ever-after despite what I'd seen."

"Did you love them?"

"I thought I did."

"Who broke it off?"

"Me."

"Why?"

She sighed. "What does it matter?"

"It just does," he said, pretty sure he knew what she was going to say.

He'd known Claire for a couple of years now and had learned a lot more about her in that time than he was sure she realized. She was loyal to the point of fanaticism.

And she was ultra-committed in her friendships. Just look at the way she watched over Queenie, how hard Lester's death had hit her, and her willingness to sacrifice her own comfort to make Josie happy by being in her wedding. Even though it had meant going to work on no sleep.

"I broke up with each boy when I realized he wasn't as committed to the relationship as I was."

"Not because the sex was bad?"

"Of course not."

"I didn't think so. You were expecting a long-term commitment and they refused to give it to you."

"Yes, but that was a long time ago. I've grown up since then."

He locked his jaw in frustration. Yeah, right. Growing up did not mean changing a person's basic personality makeup. Her puritan soul should be rejoicing that he wanted to wrap their intimacy in the bonds of marriage, but she was fighting him with her typical intransigence. It made no sense to him.

Even if she didn't love him, and he could see now that had been an arrogant assumption on his part, she *did* care and she *did* want him. Marriage meant she got him for a lifetime.

And he got her.

How was that a bad thing?

"So you're saying that you like the idea of uncommitted sex with me?"

She smiled for the first time in several minutes. "Yes, that's exactly what I'm saying. I realized when I woke up that for the first time in my life, I'm free. Really free. No major commitments, no one to take care of, no goals to live up to with backbreaking work. If I want to backpack across Europe or take a job working in another state, there's nothing to stop me. I can go anywhere, be anything I want to be."

"Not while someone is intent on either harming or nabbing you, you can't."

"That situation won't last forever, and when it's over, I—"

"Can go anywhere, do anything. Yeah, I heard it the first time," he interrupted, his mood going sour with the speed of light. "And what about me?"

"Well, it's pretty obvious you regretted intimacy, so maybe it's best we don't go there again." At least she looked like the prospect of not making love again bothered her.

He had that much. "I don't regret it."

She snorted.

"I don't." His gut tightened with the desire to prove to her how much he didn't regret it. "The only thing I'm sorry for is ruining our first time together by forgetting something so important." He sighed, hoping she'd get it this time. "I screwed up and I won't let you stand alone paying the price for my mistake."

She jumped off the couch, her eyes snapping dark, furious fire. "I don't know how you can begin to imagine I would want to marry a man who sees it as the only way to make up for the biggest mistake of his life."

"I didn't say that."

"You didn't have to."

"Damn it, Claire. We don't have a choice. It's the only way to fix it."

"Marriage is not a wrench to tighten a leaky pipe. It lasts a lifetime, Brett."

"And you don't think I'd make a good long-term risk?"

"I didn't say that."

"It sure sounded like it, but maybe that's not the problem. Maybe you don't think I'd be a good father."

For just a second, her eyes softened. "Of course you would be."

"That's all I'm asking for . . . the chance to be a father to our child in the fullest sense of the word. I can't stand the thought of being a temporary or part-time fixture in my baby's life."

Her lower lip trembled, but she bit it. "You don't even know if I'm pregnant."

"My gut says you are." And in this case, he did not mind listening.

"I don't think you can trust your gut on this one."

"Why not?"

She sighed. "You're too far gone in guilt mode. In your mind a pregnancy is a foregone conclusion because you see yourself as having really messed up."

"At least you admit it."

"I admit nothing." She looked ready to cry and he didn't understand why. "I'm only pointing out that is how you feel."

"Damn it, Claire—"

"Stop swearing at me. I don't like it."

"I apologize."

"Fine."

"Now, will you please start being reasonable?"

"It's not reasonable for you to tell me we're getting married because of the remote possibility I could be pregnant. It's highly unlikely and if we don't make love again, I don't think we have anything to worry about."

"We are definitely making love again."

"Now who is being unreasonable?"

"You think it's unreasonable to face the truth? How do you imagine I ended up forgetting the condom? I want you so much and touching you is such a huge turn-on for me that I can't even guarantee the *next* time we make love that I'll remember. The only thing I can guarantee is that there will be a next time. In my mind, that is more than a decent basis for getting married."

"If you married all the women you had sex with, you'd have had to move to a Muslim state where polygamy was legal a long time ago."

"I only want to marry you."

"But you *don't* want to marry me. It's just your guilt talking. Besides, what about your promise to Elena? If you break it, you'll feel even guiltier."

"I never promised not to get married."

"Then what did you promise?"

"Never to love another woman like I loved her."

"In other words, you want to marry me, but not only do you not love me now, you have no intention of ever loving me?" She made it sound like he was offering her a skunk's entrails.

"We have passion, friendship, mutual respect. Those are good foundations for a marriage. And you just got through telling me how you don't believe in love ever after anymore. That aspect shouldn't bother you."

"You're right, it shouldn't." But it sure looked like it did. "Regardless, I'm not marrying you." She said it quietly, with a conviction he refused to bow down to.

Like hell she wasn't marrying him. It was the best solution, even if she wasn't pregnant. She needed him and one day soon, she'd see that. "We'll see."

"No, we won't see."

He just shook his head. "I bought stuff to make dinner, but if you would rather eat in the restaurant here, I bought you clothes to wear, too."

"You bought me clothes?" She sounded totally disoriented by the change in topic.

Good. Keeping her stunning mind off-kilter just might help his cause.

"Uh-huh."

"But you don't know my size."

"Sure I do." He could read the tags inside her clothes as easily as she could.

She frowned. "You didn't need to do that. I could have worn my stuff from earlier."

"If you want to eat in, you don't have to wear any clothes at all." And he let her see with a look just how much the idea appealed to him.

"We can eat in the restaurant," she slotted in so fast, the words all came out in a jumbled rush.

"If you're sure that's what you want."

"I'm sure, but I don't see why I can't wear my own clothes."

"I bought you a dress." And he'd had a lot of fun doing it.

"Dresses aren't really my thing."

"I wouldn't say that. You looked amazing at Josie and Nitro's wedding." The woman had killer legs.

"She paid people to do my hair and makeup."

"It isn't images of your hair that have me waking up hot and sweaty with a boner hard enough to drill through iron ore."

"You wake thinking about me? Excited . . . *that* way?"

"How can you be surprised after the way we spent the afternoon?"

"Wanting me when I'm around you makes sense, but you're implying you think of me when you're at home and stuff."

"*And stuff* is right. When I'm traveling. When I'm on assignments. I think about you a lot, sweetheart."

"You think about me . . . *that way* . . . at work?"

Hotwire rolled his eyes. Was she serious? "Are you saying you didn't think about me?"

"No."

He loved her honesty. He'd never known anyone who had that little artifice. She said what she meant. She never played emotional or mind games. Her integrity was part and parcel of who she was and who she saw herself to be.

He got up and grabbed her arm and started tugging her toward the bedroom, where he'd dropped the bags with the clothes he'd bought. "Come on. Let's get you dressed."

"I'm perfectly capable of dressing myself."

"No doubt." He grinned and winked. "But I'll enjoy helping."

"I don't think that's a good idea."

"You're that set on eating dinner in the restaurant?"

She pulled away and looked at him with an expression he didn't like. "It's not just that. If you try to help me dress, it could lead to other things and I don't think that's a good idea right now."

He stalked her toward the bed and she backed up, her eyes widening. He cupped her cheeks and stopped her retreat. Did she really not understand how impossible it would be to go back to a platonic friendship?

"We've got a saying back home, sugar. There ain't no use shutting the barn door after the cow done got out already."

"We aren't on a dairy farm here."

"I didn't mean to say we were, but we've made the sexiest kind of love. Going back to a platonic friendship would be like trying to play pro football without touching your opponent. It's a contact sport, sugar, and so is our relationship."

"I've got an even better saying for you . . . only a complete fool compounds a mistake by making it again."

"Making love wasn't the mistake and you can bet your bottom dollar it's going to happen *over and over again.*"

She opened her mouth to deny him and he didn't want to hear it. So, he kissed her.

For some reason, she'd gotten it into her head that him wanting to marry her made sex between them a bad thing. It didn't make any kind of sense to him, but one thing he'd learned growing up around the females in his family . . . the way a woman's mind worked was not something a mere man could ever hope to understand.

She didn't respond immediately to his lips, but he hadn't gotten to where he was by giving up on a battle before the first real skirmish. He gently increased the pressure, encouraging her to kiss him back. She held out longer than he would have, but after a lot of tender coaxing on his part, a small sigh escaped her.

Relaxing against him, she finally responded with the sweet passion that he had become addicted to. He kissed her until he was in danger of laying her back on the bed for another bout of lovemaking. While he would have liked nothing better, he had promised to take her to the restaurant for dinner.

He broke their lips apart and stepped back. "Maybe you're right about one thing, anyway . . . if I help you dress, we'll never make it out of here."

She nodded, her breathing every bit as ragged as his. "Where's the dress you bought me?"

"It's not actually a dress, but a skirt and sweater, and you don't have to wear it if you don't want to. I just thought you might like fresh clothes for dinner is all."

"If you want me to wear it, I don't mind," she said, surprising him. "It can't be worse than what I wore for Josette's wedding, but I'm not sure my shoes are going to look all that great with a skirt."

"I got sandals to go with it." He showed her a second bag that held a single shoebox.

"They're not high heels, are they?" she asked, suspiciously eyeing the bag dangling from his left hand.

"No."

"Okay, then. Um . . . thank you." Her expression chagrined, she took both bags from his outstretched hand and disappeared into the bathroom.

The sleeveless white, clingy sweater top and pleated skirt in a black, pink, and white swirl pattern had looked cute on the mannequin, and he'd known it would look killer on Claire. He hadn't been able to resist buying it, even though he wasn't sure she would willingly wear a skirt.

He smiled at the thought of her doing so to please him. That had to mean something.

When she came out fifteen minutes later, he was very glad he'd given in to the urge. He couldn't peel his eyes away from her. "You look beautiful."

She shook her head, a frown wrinkling her brow. "I look like a girlie wannabe."

"You are a sexy, beautiful woman. You are not a wannabe anything. Feminine is definitely your style."

She looked down at herself as if she couldn't quite believe what she saw. "I would never have bought this outfit for myself, but I like the sandals."

"The salesclerk assured me you could play basketball in them." He'd been told they were every bit as comfortable as they were pretty.

"I'll have to give it a try sometime," she said tongue in cheek, and he grinned in response.

"I'm glad you approve of the shoes, but as far as the outfit goes—from the sparsity of your closet at Josie's house, I'd say you don't make a habit of buying *anything* clothes-wise for yourself."

She shrugged. "I have enough to keep me from going naked and that's all that matters. I'd rather put money toward my computer equipment. You should understand that."

"Sure I do." But when they got married, he'd make certain she had enough money for both. He liked seeing her in girlie stuff, as she put it. "But my sister would take a second job if it meant the difference between having enough money to shop for clothes or not."

Claire gave him a blank look and then shrugged. "To each her own, I guess."

"You'd best be prepared. She and Mama are going to have a heyday taking you shopping when we are in

Georgia. Daddy bought stock in a recent mall development, saying it was because he wanted to get some of
that money back."

"I don't remember saying I was going to Georgia
with you."

"You will. Your causes are too important to you for
you to dismiss a chance of doing them some good with
my money."

She crossed her arms under her breasts, stretching
the white fabric of her top over her generous curves.
"You're playing dirty."

"I'm not playing at all. I want you in Georgia with
me."

"And you think bribing me is the way to get me
there?"

"The way that'll leave you least angry at me, yes."

"You wouldn't really kidnap me."

She didn't know him very well if she believed that.
He'd left his southern gentleman manners behind over
a decade before. "I'll do whatever it takes to keep you
safe."

She sighed, as if giving up. "All right."

The relief he felt was all out of proportion. "You
agree? You're coming to Georgia? No more arguments?"

"Not about that, but I'm not sure about shopping
with your mother and your sister. I imagine paying you
back for these clothes is going to make a big enough
dent in my bank balance."

He frowned at that. "They're a gift."

"No."

"Yes." He put his hand over her mouth. "No more arguing. Please."

He loved sparring with her, but he knew where an altercation between them would lead right now, even if she didn't. And it wasn't the restaurant.

"I called for dinner reservations while you were in the bathroom. We've got to get going if we want to be on time."

Claire tried to breathe normally as Brett guided her behind the hostess with a hand on her waist. First, he had kissed her stupid back in the suite, and then he'd been giving her looks hot enough to scorch her since she came out of the bathroom wearing the girlie clothes he'd bought.

Their argument had done nothing to diminish the sexual tension between them. And he'd kept some part of him in contact with some part of her since leaving the suite.

They'd only had to travel one floor in the elevator, but he'd made the short time a long lesson in seduction. He'd held her nape and caressed her with his thumb in a way that sent tingles all over her body.

Between his touching and sex-laden looks, she felt like a cat dancing on hot bricks. He was probably right that making love again was inevitable. She wasn't ready to concede that point just yet, though. And his idea that they should get married was totally out of the question.

He might be offering her a future she'd just started dreaming about, but he was doing it for all the wrong reasons. A man should ask a woman to marry him out of desire, not guilt.

He was too hard on himself. It was as if the concept that he was as fallible as the next man was anathema to him. He expected perfection from himself. And the one woman he'd been engaged to had been as close to perfect as they came, from what Claire could tell. Besides which, Brett had loved Elena.

That shouldn't bother Claire, but it did . . . especially in the face of his assertion he would never love her.

She couldn't live up to the other woman's standard, or even come close. *She* would not have given up the possibility of a lifetime of Brett's love for a long shot cause that had already been compromised.

Claire wasn't that self-sacrificing, but Elena had been and Brett was. She wouldn't let him sacrifice his future for her. Eventually, he would end up resenting her, especially if she became a bone of contention between him and his family.

And no doubt his overachieving, old-southern family would pee kittens if he tried to make the daughter of a suicide victim and a verified drunk one of them.

She was not going to let that happen . . . not any of it.

Chapter 16

The hostess stopped at a table that overlooked the ocean. "Will this do?"

"It's perfect," Claire breathed, loving the view and approving the fact that the table was not off in a secluded corner somewhere.

She needed all the help she could get in fighting her cravings for Brett. Being in the full view of the rest of the restaurant should help.

A half an hour later, she was questioning her easy confidence. Brett managed to make even the simplest gesture sexy. Not only had he made buttering bread look like it should be an indoor sport for adults only, but by the time he ate three bites of the appetizer, her gaze was glued to his lips.

Memories coursed through her of how those lips felt against her skin.

His legs kept straying to her side of the table, too. He would apologize, but then moved them with a subtle caress that left her breathing erratic and her heart rate elevated. As if it wasn't elevated enough just by his presence.

They were eating their main course when she gave up and just sat back to watch him. She might not have a lifetime with him, but that didn't mean she couldn't enjoy the here and now.

"What?" he asked, all innocence, one blond brow raised in inquiry.

"You're really good at the seduction thing."

"Seduction thing? I'm merely enjoying my dinner, darlin'." He smiled and her toes curled in her sandals. "The seducing comes later."

She shook her head, not buying it for a minute. "You are *so* trying to prove that I cannot resist you."

Both brows went up at that. "Can you?"

"Probably not, but I don't think you are being fair."

"What's not fair about eating dinner?"

"It's the *way* you eat."

His leg slid along her naked calf. "You think?"

She stifled a gasp and tucked her legs under her chair. "That smug attitude is going to get you into trouble."

"In what way?"

"It would serve you right if I insisted on sleeping alone tonight."

"Are you going to?"

That had been her plan. Things had gotten out of control, and she didn't see rampant sex helping get them back to manageable levels. However, she wasn't sure it would hurt, either. Nothing, not even rigid celibacy, was going to undo the fact that they had made love without protection the first time.

She took a deliberate sip of water and then carefully put her glass down. "The jury is still out on that one."

"Is there anything I can do to sway the vote?"

"Don't pretend you aren't already doing it."

"But I can turn it up a notch, if you think it'll make a difference."

The fiend.

"Do that, and I'll need an asbestos suit to keep sitting here." She was already hot enough to melt metal. "I'd rather you cooled off."

"We can go for a swim after dinner. That ought to cool both of us off."

"In the ocean?" She shuddered. Even in the height of summer, the water was cold enough to numb a person's extremities.

"In the hotel pool. It's outdoor and it's heated. It overlooks the ocean, but there's a glass wind barrier."

"Wow." It sounded really neat. And swimming in a public pool had to be safer than eating an intimate dinner for two with a man who could seduce a woman with the way he buttered rolls. "I wish we could."

"Why can't we?"

"I don't have a swimsuit."

"Sure you do."

She groaned. "You bought me one of those, too?" There went her nest egg to tide her over while she looked for a job. "But we never said anything about going swimming."

"A man can hope."

"I suppose it's a bikini."

"There's another kind of swimsuit?"

"Yes," she said in exasperation. "The modest one-piece or tankini . . . the kind I usually wear, not that I go swimming all that often."

Which had to have been glaringly apparent when she gingerly climbed into the shallow end of the pool while he dove in at the deep end and swam the length with sure strokes.

She wasn't even very good at dog paddling, so she played in the shallow water while he swam several laps without stopping. Some teenagers were playing a dunking game, and yet, Brett never bumped into any of them.

The kids climbed out and headed for the hot tub just as he went under water about halfway down the pool. In the gathering darkness, she couldn't see where he was.

Suddenly, he erupted out of the water in front of her, spraying her with cool droplets. "Why don't you swim with me?"

"I don't know how."

"But you said you wanted to come swimming."

She smiled. "Not everyone swims in a swimming pool. I like playing in the water."

The second she said it, she knew it was the wrong thing to utter.

His expression took on predatory intent. "Do you, now? What a coincidence—so do I."

"I don't think we're talking about the same kind of playing." And it certainly wasn't the kind that would cool her off.

He crowded her up against the pool wall, his big body blocking out her awareness of anyone and anything else. Even the cool water around her only registered on a periphery level.

His hands cupped her face. "Do you want me to teach you how to swim, or would you rather *play*?"

Oh, man. He really was lethal. "What sort of play did you have in mind?" she asked in a husky voice she barely recognized.

His hand slid down her back and cupped her bottom through the bikini pants. "I'm sure we'll think of something."

"In a public swimming pool?"

"We could always go back to the room."

It was tempting. Incredibly so. She wanted to just melt against him, but the lure of learning how to swim shimmered in her mind. It was something she had always wanted to do, but had never gotten the chance.

She put her hands against his wet chest, the warmth there making her fingertips tingle. "Would you really teach me to swim?"

His expression took on that same cast it had when he helped her study. "Sure. How come you never learned?"

"No opportunity."

"It's about time you did, then."

She licked her lips. "Yes."

He swung her up against his chest and she gasped in shock. "Brett! What are you doing?"

But it was obvious what he was doing. He was carrying her to the deep end. Right in the middle.

"This might be a good time to tell you that the sink-or-swim approach to anything, including swimming, itself has never appealed to me."

He smiled down at her and shook his head. "Don't you trust me, darlin'?"

"When you talk in that honeyed drawl, I'd trust you to do anything." No doubt to her detriment.

"Is that right?"

She sighed and rested her head against his wet chest. "Yes."

"Hold your breath, Claire."

"Why?"

"Just do it."

"Okay." She took a deep breath and held it.

He let go.

She dropped in the water and expelled her breath in shock. She started sinking before she could even yelp.

Strong hands immediately pulled her to the surface.

"The first thing to remember when you're learning to swim is that oxygen is buoyant . . ."

An amazing hour followed during which he rarely took advantage of the scanty nature of her swimsuit and made a genuine effort to teach her to swim. By the time they called a halt, she was executing a rudimentary forward stroke and could float on her back very nicely.

She held onto the edge of the pool and grinned at him. "That was great! Thank you."

"Thank *you*, sugar. Watching your body move in that scandalous bikini was better than a wet dream."

"I can't believe you said that." She sent a wave of water cascading over him with the sweep of her hand.

He didn't so much as grunt, but moved in with the silent speed of a shark. He landed hard against her and she lost her hold on the side of the pool. She grabbed on to his shoulders so she wouldn't sink, the scandalous bikini and his swim trunks no real barrier between them.

He took hold of the pool edge on either side of her. "You're going to pay for that, sugar."

"I am?" Acting on instinct, she brought her legs up and locked her ankles behind his back. The apex of her thighs settled just above the waistband to his shorts. His muscles there immediately clenched and he made a sound that was part growl, part moan.

She smiled. "And just how are you going to make me pay?"

His head lowered until his lips were a breath from hers. "I'll think of something."

"I'm sure you will," she said softly with as much seductive promise as she could conjure in her voice.

Then quickly, using her hold on his torso to leverage herself above him, she shoved down on his shoulders, leap-frogging over his body to land in the water behind him.

She popped to the surface just like he'd so recently taught her and burst out laughing at the sight of him doing the same thing. Her dunking maneuver had been a complete success. The look in his eyes promised retribution, and she turned to make a mad scramble for the stairs at the shallow end.

She didn't make it.

Strong arms lifted her from the water. "That was sneaky, Claire."

She was too busy laughing and gasping for air to answer.

He flipped her until she landed cradled against him, her arms and legs locked firmly against his strength. His triumphant smile sucked more air out of her than the swimming had.

"You're gorgeous," she sighed, not having meant to say any such thing.

"Compliments are not going to win you mercy," he informed her, but the warmth in his blue gaze said otherwise.

She was completely helpless in his arms, and yet she wasn't worried at all. "Maybe I don't want mercy."

"I'm not falling for that ploy again."

She batted her eyelashes in a way she'd never done before. "What ploy would that be?"

He lifted her and leaned down so once again their faces were so close she could feel his breath. "The *wouldn't you rather kiss me than dunk me* gambit."

"Wouldn't you?" she asked, her voice husky with genuine desire.

"Any sane male of the species would, but a man can't have his woman thinking she can get around him so easily. It's bad for his self-image."

"Like that would ever be a problem with you," she scoffed. "What if I told you that nothing you could do

would tarnish your image as a bad-ass former mercenary tough enough to get the job done, no matter what
it is?"

He took a deep breath as if inhaling the fragrance of
her skin, not chlorine fumes from the pool. "Then I
might have to kiss you anyway."

"Consider yourself told."

The words were barely out of her mouth when his
lips slanted over hers with enough heat to make the
moisture on her skin turn to steam. He was so darn
good at this stuff. He devoured her mouth until she was
moaning against his lips and trying to free her arms so
she could touch him.

She heard a wolf whistle and his hold on her loosened. Relief that her arms would be free surged through
her. Only, instead of getting a chance to touch the muscular body so temptingly close, she found herself tossed
in the air and landing with a splash in the pool.

She came up spluttering and laughing, her feet easily touching bottom. She heard more laughter and saw
that the teens had exited the hot tub and were whistling,
laughing, and calling out encouragement to her or Brett,
depending on if they were girls or boys.

She looked from them over to Brett.

He looked ready for a frontal attack, but she was too
smart to go for a payback gambit she was sure to lose.
She had something far more effective in mind.

She waved at the teens and smiled sweetly at Brett.

His eyes narrowed in instant alertness.

His toss had left her closer to the steps, and she
started backing toward them now. "Amazing how effective a dunking can be to cool a person's urges. I'm so
chilled, in fact, that I think I'll go warm up in the hot
tub now that it's empty."

Brett moved toward her, his expression revealing

that he'd latched on to her weapon of choice immediately.

"I'd be happy to warm you up."

"Oh, that won't be necessary. Why waste a perfectly good hot tub moment for *something else?*"

The teenagers were laughing as they spilled into the rec room off the pool area. A couple of the boys called advice to Brett over their shoulders while the girls called, "You go, girl," to Claire.

She climbed out of the pool, adjusting her swimsuit with downright provocation before tripping over to the room with the still-bubbling whirlpool.

Brett came in just as she was lowering herself into the steaming water.

Their skirmish momentarily forgotten, she moaned in pure bliss at the feel of it surging around her. "This feels so good."

"I know something that feels better."

She had to stifle a smug smile. "Do you? I can't imagine what."

"You're not one of the seniors you take care of at Belmont Manor, sugar. I don't buy that you've forgotten this afternoon so quickly."

"Oh, that." She waved her hand airily. "This is much less exhausting."

"You sure about that?"

She wasn't, but that didn't stop her from nodding. The hot water felt like it could drain every last bit of energy from her.

He grabbed the handrail and moved onto the top step. "Maybe I'll have to prove you wrong."

"Excuse me, but the pool area will be closing in ten minutes."

Brett stopped and turned to face the maintenance man who had spoken from the doorway.

"You mean we have to leave?"

"I'm afraid so."

Claire couldn't hide her disappointment. "Oh."

The hot tub felt so good after the exertion of her swim lesson that she hated being told she'd have to climb out again in only a few minutes.

"I'm sorry, ma'am," the maintenance man said before turning to go.

Brett followed him out to the pool area, and when he came back a few minutes later, he looked very pleased with himself.

"I guess I have to get out now," she said reluctantly.

The lights around the pool went out and all but some floor lighting around the hot tub went out as well.

"I suppose that's a hint." She stood up to go.

Brett's smile shone in the darkness. "Relax. I worked something out with the maintenance guy. We can stay as late as we want as long as we don't go out to the pool area where the security cameras are."

She didn't ask how he'd arranged that and didn't really care. As long as she got to soak in this blessed heat longer than ten measly minutes, she was happy. "Great."

Brett climbed into the hot tub and headed straight for her. He lowered himself next to her and right into her personal space. "Now, what was it you said about hot tubs not being as tiring as bedrooms?"

She leaned back against the wall with nowhere to go. "Um . . . I believe I was discussing what we were doing in the bedroom."

His arms came around her, one hand at her neck and the other on her back. "So am I, sugar. So am I."

She swallowed nervously. "We can't do that here."

"Are you sure about that?" he asked again, and suddenly her top was loose and the bubbles in the water jetted it away from her body.

She screeched and tried to lunge for it, but he was in the way. "Brett . . . my top."

He kissed her, stifling her complaints. He tasted so good and knew exactly what to do with those lips that she let her top float away while her hands were busy exploring the hard contours of his chest.

But when his hand began to caress her now naked flesh, she gasped and wrenched her head away from his. "Brett! We can't . . . not here."

"Sure we can."

"But the teenagers."

"Are now in the game room, which has been locked off from the pool area. In fact, no other guests can come in through the other entrance, either. Ernie locked them."

"Ernie?"

"The maintenance guy."

"But how are we going to get out?"

"The doors lock from the other side. We can leave, but we can't get back in."

"Oh."

He kissed the corner of her mouth. "Yes, oh . . ."

The warm bubbles were caressing her breasts as effectively as Brett's hands, and Claire's arguments were fading in the face of a renewed desire that swamped her senses. "You're sure no one can come in?"

"Positive."

"What about Ernie?"

"No chance."

"Oh . . ." the word morphed into a moan as both of his hands cupped her slippery, wet curves bobbing in the water.

"You're so perfect, Claire."

She shook her head, but she reveled in the knowledge that he enjoyed her body as much as he did. Brett's appreciation for her body was open and honest. It was also enhanced by genuine affection and a desire to give as much or more than he received. It was amazing.

Her eyes, which had closed in pleasure, opened to watch him. His expression was one of devastating desire. And the sight of her naked breasts in his hands was so beguiling she felt a gush of wet warmth between her legs that had nothing to do with the water bubbling around them.

"Oh, Brett."

He smiled, his satisfaction at her response gleaming in his eyes. "Feel good, sugar?"

"Better than good."

"Put your head back and concentrate on nothing but my touch and the caress of the water against your skin."

"But I want to touch you, too."

"Not this time, sugar."

She would have argued, but what he wanted her to do was too tantalizing. So, she put her head back on the concrete.

"Hold on a second." He shifted and leaned over her. "Lift your head."

She did and he slid something under it. She realized it was a folded towel and it felt ten times better than the hard concrete.

"Better?"

"Much."

"Good. Now, I want you to relax. No matter how good it feels, keep your muscles from tensing up. Can you do that for me, sweetheart?"

"I can try," she said in a passion-drugged voice she barely recognized as her own.

He went back to touching her and he didn't only concentrate on her boobs. He touched her everywhere, his fingers sliding against her wet skin with devastating effect. He found the erogenous zones he'd explored that first night in the hotel with his massage and then some. She did her best not to tense up and whenever she did, he would change his caresses to a kneading massage until she relaxed again.

It was like the time he'd touched her in the hotel, only now she knew the pleasure that awaited her, and she wasn't suffering from a head injury that dulled the sensations.

It was a lot harder to remain relaxed, but she soon realized that in some strange way, forcing her muscles to stay loose magnified the pleasure.

Her bikini bottoms went the way of her top and she didn't even murmur a protest. She trusted him to have ensured their privacy completely before starting this.

Brett would never expose her to the humiliation of being caught en flagrante delicto.

But even though her bottoms were gone, he made no attempt to touch her mound or vulva. It was as if he was intent on stimulating every other part of her body. Just as when his hands roved over her breasts, they somehow always missed her nipples. The bubbling water touched everything, though. She found herself spreading her legs to increase the gentle caress of the bubbles and moaned in desperate pleasure as one of the jets hit her sweet spot from behind.

"Oh . . . oh . . . goshhhhhh . . . that's so gooooood."

He laughed softly in her ear as his mouth wreaked havoc along sensitive nerve endings. "Let's turn you around, sweetheart."

She didn't understand what he wanted, but steady hands guided her around so that she knelt on the bench and rested her head on her forearms against the towel. He pulled her thighs farther apart, adjusting her stance until the jet hit her clitoris in a steady stream and she cried out in pleasure.

His hands went back to work on her, brushing her inner thighs, then her calves, then even the soles of her feet before moving to knead her stomach and then her freed breasts, while his lips and teeth explored her nape and the vulnerable area behind her ears.

She could feel his erection pressing against her through his shorts. She ground herself against him with frustration, wanting to feel his naked flesh against her. *Why did he still have his swimsuit on?*

She couldn't make her mouth form words to ask. She was rapidly losing touch with coherent thought as the excitement and need built inside her to nearly unbearable levels. She hung, suspended on the verge of climax, the bubbling jet caressing her sweet spot but not giving enough stimulation to send her over. His caresses had turned every one of her nerve endings into a raw conduit for pleasure, but he didn't trespass on the flesh that needed it most.

She began to writhe, first pressing her bottom against him and then leaning forward, trying to increase the pressure of the water jet on her clitoris. Neither helped, and she found herself crying out her need, begging Brett to take her.

Chapter 17

But he didn't.
He reminded her to relax.

"I can't!"

"Shh . . . baby, yes, you can. It will be worth it. Trust me. *Please.*"

She shook her head violently. She couldn't do it, and the kneading massage wasn't helping anymore.

"Shh . . ." he soothed her over and over again as his hands stilled on her completely. "Come on, sugar, you can do it."

Then he whispered a litany of sexy words in her ears, telling her how good it would be if she would just hold on a little longer, if she would only relax this one last time.

Taking several deep breaths that made her chest ache, she forced her rigid muscles to loosen.

"That's right, darlin'. You're doing so good." He started touching her again, but kept reminding her not to tense up until she was whimpering and her vocabulary had diminished to one word. *Please.*

He was playing with her nipples now, but it wasn't enough. The delicate pinching and rolling of her engorged peaks only added to the maelstrom of need coursing through her. Her breath got choppy, she couldn't get enough air into her lungs, and her pleas were coming out guttural and low as primal desires wracked her body.

She bit the back of her hand to stop from screaming in tortured pleasure. But then the jets stopped and she did scream. She needed the water's caress on her clitoris.

Rocking her hips back and forth in the now still water, she hissed with frustration. "Brett, turn them back on. Please. I can't stand this!"

She felt herself being lifted and then laid on her back, her legs dangling in the water as her bottom balanced on the edge of the hot tub.

He put the towel back under her head, but she could have told him it didn't matter. No amount of discomfort could compare to the agonizing need in her lower body.

He shifted to kneel between her legs, pressing them wide open with a hand on each of her inner thighs. The now cool air made her clitoris tighten and she tried to close her legs, but his hold prevented her.

Then Brett's mouth closed over her swollen, aching flesh, his tongue lapping up a wet warmth that did not come from the hot tub. It felt so good, she almost fainted.

"Oh, yes . . . please . . . please . . . Brett . . . please . . . oh, gosh . . . please!"

He licked her like an ice cream bar, his talented tongue further stimulating her swollen labia but not quite giving her the relief she sought.

She arched up toward his face and cried gutturally, "Now, damn it, Brett . . . do it!"

And he did, two fingers sliding inside her and pressing against a nerve center that made her scream again with pleasure. His lips closed over her clitoris, his teeth holding it in place for his tongue to thrash. And she exploded with an orgasm so intense everything went black around the edges while her body shook with the climax.

But she didn't faint, and the sensations did not abate like they had that afternoon. Her orgasm went on and on, and on, and on, and on, and he didn't stop what he was doing with his mouth, not for a second. She thrashed violently against him, but still the convulsions kept tightening her insides and making her hips buck under his mouth.

She lost all sense of time and place while she went through one crashing wave of sensation after another. Finally, she could stand no more and she collapsed against the hard concrete, her limbs totally boneless, small whimpers coming from her throat in involuntary bursts.

He immediately changed the way he was touching her, sliding his fingers out of her. He gentled her with his lips against her labia, and then with sure hands as he pulled her back into the soothing water. She sat in his lap, with trembling legs straddling his thighs, and received a massage that brought her sawing breaths back under control and her speeding heartbeat out of the danger zone.

"That was incredible," she said against his neck, her voice choked with emotional tears she couldn't begin to stem.

"Yes." His voice sounded raw and strained.

"Are you okay?"

"Better than okay."

"I . . . you didn't . . . do you want . . . I could . . ." A yawn choked off her words.

He laughed. "Yes . . . definitely you, you incredible woman. And I did. It's been years since that happened in my shorts, but baby, you are one sexy lover."

She nuzzled him. "Thank you."

"It's the truth."

"For what you did."

"We both did it, or didn't you notice?"

All she'd noticed was that she'd just experienced the impossible at his hands.

"If you hadn't touched me like that, I could never have . . ." Her voice trailed off. She had no idea how to describe what had just happened.

"Had an extended massive orgasm?"

That worked. "Yes."

"We'll have to do it again sometime soon."

"Don't know if I'd survive," she mumbled against his skin.

"I have it on good authority you would."

Tension filled her despite how wrung-out her body was. "Other women have proven it?"

"Not by me." He soothed her renewed tautness with smooth, skillful caresses on her back. "But I read a book."

"You *read a book* on doing *that*?" He had to be kidding.

"Yep. I was on assignment. It was that or a book on the history of goatherding. The sex manual won hands down."

"Glad you read it," she mumbled as her brain shut down.

* * *

Hotwire felt Claire go lax against him. She'd been limp before, but this had the quality of sleep. For the second time, she'd fallen asleep after making love. Well, now he knew what to do if she ever got insomnia . . . and he was still going to tease her.

He couldn't help feeling smug about the way he'd worn her out. A man liked to know he made an impression on his lover. Considering her response in and beside the hot tub, he'd made a heck of an impression on Claire.

He smiled in the semidarkness before lifting her back out of the water. He carried her to a bench beside the hot tub and laid her on it. Her naked, sprawling abandon was enough to make his dick twitch with renewed interest despite his recent powerful orgasm.

He went out to the pool area and grabbed the two hotel bathrobes Ernie had left earlier on his instruction. He pulled his on and then fished Claire's swimsuit out of where it was floating on the edge of the hot tub and put it in his pocket.

Then he fed her loose body into her robe. She was plenty relaxed now. Feeling like the general of a particularly successful conquering army, he wrapped the robe around her and tied it. He was careful to cover her completely before carrying her out of the pool area and down the hall to the elevators.

Thankfully, the elevator was empty when it arrived, and no one else got on as it took them to the floor of their suite.

She woke up . . . sort of . . . when he took her into the shower to wash off the chlorine. She mumbled and grumbled as he rinsed both of their bodies and washed her hair. Her eyes closed while he was rinsing the suds away, and he was sure she'd gone to sleep standing up.

He turned off the shower and dried her off before

tucking her into the king-size bed. She mumbled his name and curled onto her side. He finished drying himself off and joined her. She didn't wake when he pulled her into his arms, but snuggled into him with a soft sigh.

It felt good. Better than good, it felt right and she would have to recognize that eventually.

Claire woke at dawn to Brett's touch.

She smiled sleepily. "Hi."

He was propped on his side, facing her. His fully alert blue gaze was filled with sensual promise and the kind of warm welcome she couldn't let herself start thinking meant something more than it did. But her heart did a strange little twist anyway.

Without warning, he rolled on top of her, his naked body warm and vibrant. "Hi, yourself."

She slid her legs apart, making a spot for him in the cradle of her thighs. "I could get used to waking up this way. It's nice."

"Keep thinking that way and we're going to get along just fine, darlin'," he said in his slow southern drawl that was like sweet honey to her ears.

She rocked her pelvis upward, groaning with pleasure at the same time he did. "I'd say we get along pretty well already."

"You may be right, but I'm a competitive man. I'm always looking to improve."

Images of the night before came into her head and heat suffused through her. "Impossible."

He shook his head and then kissed her. He was lazy and slow, but didn't hold back from making love and bringing them both to the ultimate pleasure as soon as she was ready. Afterward, unlike the day before when making love had exhausted her, she felt energized and ready to face anything.

When she said so, bouncing out of bed and heading to the shower, he laughed and followed her. They played in the shower like two children, exploring each other and teasing until they made love again, this time fast and furiously, with him holding her up against the tiled wall. She wondered in a brief moment of sanity whether every time would be different and so wonderful.

Incredibly, he'd remembered a condom in the shower. She couldn't have imagined making love the way they had, so the thought of preparing for it totally threw her.

When she asked him about it, he winked and told her, "I guess I've got a more active imagination than you, but I can't conceive of being *anywhere* naked with you that I wouldn't want to make love."

She just shook her head and dried off, feeling more lighthearted than she could ever remember being. Spending time with Brett felt *good*.

They checked out of the hotel after a scrumptious breakfast from room service and headed back to Portland in Brett's car.

She watched over her shoulder as the small town disappeared from view. "I wish we could stay longer."

Though she didn't mind leaving before running into the maintenance guy, Ernie. She felt shy about him knowing what she and Brett had been doing in the hot tub the night before, but not embarrassed enough to regret doing it. And she sincerely doubted Ernie had even an inkling of what had really gone on.

Even she couldn't quite believe it. She'd known Brett was an experienced lover, but nothing could have prepared her for the way he'd made her feel in and out of the hot tub.

Her mind filled with memories and she lost herself in them.

"Claire . . ." he said with slight exasperation.

Her head snapped round and she looked at him. "What?"

"*I said,* I would bring you back sometime. What were you daydreaming about?"

"I'm not telling." But if her blush didn't give her away, he wasn't as observant as she thought.

"I bet I can guess," he said with that slow smile that always made her heart go crazy.

"I bet you can, too. I don't care what you say . . . nobody can learn how to do something like that out of a book." Though she hated the thought he'd put in real-time "flight hours" with another woman—or women—to get so adept at it.

"I told you last night, I've never done that with another woman." His tone was so serious, she had to believe him. "Though I tried a less intense version of the technique that night you refused to take your pain medication."

"You were good at it then, too."

"But last night was better," he said, his voice laced with satisfaction.

"Yes." It had been incredible. "Why only me? Did you just read the book?"

"I read it eighteen months ago and the simple answer is, I wanted to. *With you.* I've spent a lot of time fantasizing that scene with you, but I've got to be honest . . . it was way better than my daydreams. And I didn't think that was possible."

She hadn't thought the whole thing was possible. "You're an unbelievable lover, Brett."

"Don't give me all the credit, sugar. All I did was follow the suggestions I'd read and a few ideas I'd thought up on my own during some unbridled fantasizing. You're the one with enough feminine passion to power a small city."

Unbridled fantasizing? He thought her passion could power a small city? She sucked in a worried breath. "Do you think I'm a nympho?"

He burst out laughing and didn't stop for several miles.

She frowned at him, not finding her worries remotely as funny as he did.

"You're joking, right?" he finally asked, unchecked amusement glinting in his blue gaze.

"No. And why can't I be a nympho?" she asked, offended for a different reason altogether.

"Do you want to be one?"

"No."

"Then don't worry, you are in no risk of going that direction."

"How can you say that after last night?"

"You are twenty-eight years old and until yesterday, the only two lovers you had were high-school boyfriends. That is not nymphomaniaclike behavior."

"Maybe I'm like the alcoholic who doesn't realize she is one until she takes her first drink and then ends up dying from alcohol poisoning within a few short years."

So, it hadn't exactly been her proverbial first drink, but she could imagine becoming addicted to Brett's lovemaking way too easily. She didn't like the prospect one bit. Being addicted to a man who was still pining after his lost love was not the way she wanted to spend the rest of her life.

He shook his head, laughing like a demented hyena again. "You're not going to die from enjoying sex with me."

"I thought I was going to have a heart attack last night."

"You didn't."

No. She'd fallen asleep instead. She had to admit that didn't seem all that dangerous. "Well," she grumbled with a pout, "you make it sound like other women aren't like me."

"They aren't."

"Doesn't that make me a deviant?"

"No. It makes you unique and special. You do not have abnormal desires, but are so sweetly responsive you make me shake when I touch you. Frankly, sugar, you're the lover of this good ole' boy's fantasies."

He couldn't mean it. "*I'm not Elena.*"

He was silent for several seconds, his expression losing any sign of amusement, and then he sighed. "Believe it or not, I'm not looking for another Elena."

Oh, she believed him. Once you'd had perfection, you didn't go looking for the same bolt of lightning to strike twice. "It doesn't matter."

"Yes, it does. Or you wouldn't have brought it up. I need you to listen to this, okay?"

"All right." What choice did she have? She was the goober who had brought it up, but if he went into a long dialogue about how different she and Elena were, Claire was afraid she just might cry.

"I don't spend my time with you comparing you to her. You are yourself, Claire. I don't want you to be anyone else and you can believe me when I say that I have never made love to a more responsive woman or one who fit me better sexually."

She was more sensual than his lost love? "*Never?*"

"Never. You knock me flat on my butt with your passion."

It was her turn to laugh. "Yeah. Right."

He wasn't flat on his butt when he was turning her inside out with his touching in the hot tub.

"You don't believe me? I've never once forgotten the

condom, not even when I was a randy teen. Being with you blows my rational mind with the power of detonated C-4."

He'd never forgotten the condom, not once? "Was Elena on the pill?"

"No."

"Oh." If what he was saying was true, and she didn't believe he would ever lie to her . . . the passion they shared *was* unique for him.

Special . . . as he'd said.

How long did lust last, though? Not long enough to cement a lifetime, she was sure. But then she couldn't imagine ever feeling less entranced by his touch.

Was that lust . . . or love?

They were certainly a pair. She didn't believe in romantic love, but denying its existence had no power to diminish the fear that it was that exact emotion responsible for her current turmoil. He did believe in love. He'd made no bones about how much he'd loved Elena, but he'd told Claire he would never love her.

So, she didn't believe in the emotion, but she was afraid she loved him anyway, and he did believe in it, but he was not similarly afflicted. What a mess!

And where did it leave them? Where did it leave her?

She had a choice, she supposed . . . break off her relationship with Brett now because of probable future pain or live in the present and worry about the future when it arrived. It was no choice, really. The here and now was too good to give up for a future without him, especially when such a future looked bleaker than her past had ever been.

Not wanting to dwell on that reality, she said, "I heard you on the phone to Ethan this morning."

Brett gave her a measured look before fixing his attention back on the road ahead. "He thinks he might have a lead on the men in black at the funeral. He and my contacts in the FBI are tracking it down."

"That's great news."

"Yes, it is. Hopefully, my operative who took Queenie to Nevada has had similar success."

"What is he looking for?"

"Collins has instructions to make a list of everyone who had seen Lester the month before he died. We could go back farther, but my gut tells me that a civ wouldn't have waited that long to neutralize the risk of Arwan revealing him once he realized Lester was talking so freely about his past."

"I'm sure you're right, but do you really think Queenie will be able to remember everyone Lester saw, or even knew about them all?"

"According to you both, he wasn't a man who socialized much. It shouldn't be that hard, and my operative is trained to coax information from the deepest memory banks."

"Wow."

"But he's not limiting himself to Queenie . . . he's also talking to other people at Belmont Manor, both residents and employees. In addition, he'll be going over the logs of Lester's visitors, both outsiders and medical professionals."

"What about me?"

"What about you?"

"I spent a lot of time with Lester."

"You were only with him at night. You said yourself he rarely saw anyone else on your shift, even when you weren't there."

"That's true, but there were exceptions."

"Make a list of them and we'll cross-reference it with the list that Collins comes up with."

"Okay." She leaned over the seat and grabbed her

backpack from the floor behind her. "I wish I'd brought my laptop. I like typing more than writing."

"Poor baby. You should have a PDA."

"Yeah, but they cost money, and keeping my computer equipment up to date is hard enough on my budget! The laptop you gave me was a whole generation newer than my old one. I'm still wondering how you got Josette's homeowner's insurance to pay for it."

"Just be glad they did."

"I am." She was also fairly certain Brett had not required full payment, but the one time she'd brought up paying the difference, he'd gotten majorly cranky and refused to discuss it.

She pulled one of the composition books from her backpack and flipped it open. It was the black one she used for her programming class. Brett would probably laugh if she told him she bought different-colored comp books to take notes in and coded them by class types.

Even Josette had found Claire's obsessive organization amusing, but Claire hadn't minded. Josette was never mean about anything—she just knew how to laugh and that was a trait Claire liked in a friend.

She flipped through the written-on pages, looking for a blank one, and it took a few seconds for her brain to register what she was seeing. The pages were not filled with her notes on computer programming, but with names, dates, and locations in a neat print that was definitely not her handwriting.

She stopped turning pages and read one in its entirety.

Her skin grew clammy with shock as cold permeated her body. "Brett?"

"Yeah, sugar?"

"You said you thought having Lester's kill book would help with the case?"

"Yes."

"Well, I think we have it."

"What?" He looked sharply at her and then back at the road.

"You remember how you thought Lester might have hidden his own book and then forgotten he'd done it?"

"Yes."

"Well, he did. In my backpack."

"That's not possible. You would have noticed by now."

"No, I wouldn't. My black composition book was for my programming class. I finished my final project before the first attack in Josette's house. Remember, you turned it in for me?"

"But you've been in and out of your backpack tons of times since then."

She explained about the color-coding for her classes. "My eyes just skipped over it because I didn't need it."

"I can't believe this."

"I can't, either."

"You've had it all the time."

She nodded and swallowed against a sour taste in her mouth. "The guy in the bathroom at the college was right, but how could he know?"

"You said you thought that was your notes for your programming class. Does that mean they're missing?"

She rifled through the bag. There was no second black composition book. "Yes, the notes are gone."

"Maybe Lester switched the composition books."

"Mine could be back at the hotel."

Brett shrugged. "It could be, or whoever went looking for Arwan's kill book found your composition book instead and that's why he came after you."

"Lester wouldn't have deliberately put me at risk like that."

"Sugar, his mind was going . . . for all we know, he started making the switch and forgot what he was doing halfway through."

"We'll never know, will we?"

"No."

Her heart hurt because no matter what way she looked at it, the man she'd loved like family had deliberately used her as a blind to hide his secrets.

Brett grabbed his cell phone and made a call. She listened with half of her attention as she realized he was talking to Collins and finding out how close the operative was on a completed list of people Lester had seen in the last month.

She started reading through the kill book. Lester had notes beside some of the jobs, and it didn't take her long to decipher his notation code and determine which jobs had been for the government and which had been for private citizens. He hadn't only worked domestically, but had traveled the world with his profession.

Her stomach churned with acid as she flipped from one page to the next, no longer reading but merely taking in the reality of what each page represented.

Brett turned off his phone and set it down. "Collins says he should have the report for me when we get to Portland."

"He's a fast worker."

"He's been busy while we've been studying for your finals."

"I kept you from the investigation, didn't I?"

"I trust him to do a thorough job and . . ." His voice trailed off suggestively and he winked. "It was fun helping you study."

She tried for a smile and failed. "I'm glad," she said anyway.

"What's the matter, Claire?"

"Nothing."

"Wrong answer."

"It's just . . ." She paused, trying to gather her thoughts while keeping her roiling stomach under control. "It didn't seem real before this, that Lester was an assassin. But the names of the people he killed are in here."

Chapter 18

She held up the kill book, its harmless appearance so incongruous with what it held that she shook her head.

"He listed the people who hired him for the jobs and why they hired him. He was very meticulous. You can't tell though, what he felt about any of it. It's all so cold and emotionless. He was my friend, and he killed every person in here."

Anguish ripped through her. How had Queenie stood reading through this book?

"You look a little shaky," Brett said, his voice laced with concern. "Do you want me to stop the car?"

Her stomach twisted. "Maybe you'd better."

He pulled into a rest area and stopped the car away from the bathrooms, near some trees. She shoved her door open and stumbled out of the car, doing her best to control the urge to be sick.

She made it to a picnic table and sat down on the bench. It was summer and there were other people in the rest area, but none of them paid her any attention.

For that, she was grateful. It was bad enough that Brett was witnessing her mental distress.

She rubbed her arms, feeling chilled despite the warm sun beating down on her. Her mind raced with images of the old man she had cared so deeply about killing each person he'd listed, and she couldn't stand it. She hugged herself, trying to hold the feelings inside, trying not to fall apart from the truth.

He'd once told her that he saw his job as the same as being a soldier, but he'd been paid better. He'd seen his kills as another way of waging war for his country. It wasn't the same, though. Not everyone in that book was a threat to national security or the greater good of mankind. They couldn't be . . .

And who had Lester been to think he could make that distinction, or that the men who had hired him could?

She couldn't come to terms with the reality the composition book represented, because she still loved that old man and grieved his passing.

She didn't realize she was crying until Brett sat down beside her and pulled her against his chest. "It's okay, sugar. You can cry it out. Mama always says that tears are God's way of washing away pain a little bit at a time."

His tender understanding released the floodgates, and she sobbed in the circle of his strong arms. He held her, petting her and saying soothing things until she eventually got herself under control.

He wiped her face with fresh tissues. "All right now?"

She sniffed and nodded, though she wasn't sure she was all right. "I can't believe he killed all those people. I really cared about him, Brett. He was my family."

"Oh, baby . . ." He rocked her back and forth like she really was a small child, and she found comfort in it even though she knew she should be handling this on her own.

This was her grief, not Brett's, but somehow he'd made it past her every barrier, and her emotions were frighteningly open to him.

"How could he do that?"

"The war changed him. Queenie said it best . . . battle left him scarred and changed his conscience. You can't judge another person's life by your own."

"I don't want to judge him." She really didn't. She just wanted to understand, but she didn't know if she ever could. "It hurts to know what he did. It had to have hurt him, too. You know it did."

"You're probably right."

"Then why did he keep doing it? He was an assassin for decades!"

"I don't know, sweetheart, but he was living the life he thought he should live." He sighed and rubbed her back, no doubt understanding way better than she could. "He gave up the hope of a wife, of children, and gave up his family so he could do what he did. He had to believe in it."

"Yes."

"His choices weren't yours, sugar, but they didn't make him a monster. He wasn't a cold-blooded killer or without honor or conscience, he just had a different set of standards he lived by."

"He was a good man—*he was*," she said fiercely, her feelings of loyalty toward the old man not diminishing because she'd been forced to come face-to-face with the reality of her friend's life choices.

"Yes, he was, and he loved you. Queenie said so."

"Yes."

Brett eventually got her back in the car, but when she

went to pick up the kill book, he took it away with a shake of his head. "Concentrate on making a list of people that you know Lester saw in the last month."

She was only too happy to do so and take her mind off the names written so neatly in the composition book.

Hotwire drove while his mind churned with the ramifications of Claire's reaction to seeing the kill book.

The reality of Lester's past as Arwan had devastated her. She didn't understand why he had become an assassin or how he could have lived his life doing one job after another.

Would she be any more capable of dealing with Hotwire's past? It was far from pristine. He'd gone solo like Lester had done, and although Hotwire had never once killed for money, he had been forced to kill in self-defense and the defense of others in his years as a mercenary.

Would Claire be able to understand and accept that?

He'd never been ashamed of his life as a soldier, both for his government and as a private operator. He'd believed in his job in the Rangers and he'd taken that core set of beliefs with him into his life as a mercenary. He had used his skills to protect, to save, and to defeat the enemy.

Some would look at his past and see shades of brutality when in reality, he'd only done what had to be done at the time.

It wasn't a carbon copy of Lester's path, but it was close enough. He remembered the discussions he and Claire had had about violence as a solution to a crisis. She said she wasn't a pacifist, but if she wasn't, she was damn close.

For the first time, he wondered if her refusal to marry him had something to do with her inability to accept his past. It made sense, but it also worried the hell out of him.

He'd been pretty confident of overcoming her emotional misgivings, but how could he convince her that his past did not make him a monster?

The prospect that he would have to bothered him. A lot. He'd spent his whole adult life excusing and explaining his career choices to his family and he'd always felt a barrier between himself and the rest of them because of it.

He didn't want to feel the same separation from Claire.

Brett was strangely subdued as they made their way to his hotel suite. He hadn't said much since her emotional outburst at the rest area.

She'd never made friends easily . . . at least, not since her dad's death. She had a hard time trusting people, and letting them get close required a level of risk that she'd always shied away from. She knew better than most people how easy it was to lose the people in your life who were supposed to be constant.

She'd let Queenie and Lester into her heart, and then Josette, whom she'd shared more with than anyone else . . . besides Brett. She hadn't realized how lonely she'd been until she'd become friends with Josette, though. Her time with Queenie and Lester had always been limited to her work hours, but Josette's friendship had permeated every aspect of Claire's solitary existence. She didn't want to be alone anymore.

She wanted more than Brett's body; she wanted his friendship on a level that scared her spitless because it made her vulnerable to losing him. If he walked away, it would hurt. So much. No matter what label she wanted to put on the feelings she had for him. She wished she could turn her emotions off as she'd done during the final years of taking care of her mom, but she didn't know how.

Brett let them into the suite with his key card, and a few seconds later, while she was still busy stretching the kinks from the nearly two-hour car ride, he swore.

She spun to face him. "What's the matter?"

"The suite was searched while we were gone." He was glaring down at something beside his computer.

"Did they take anything?"

"It doesn't look like it, and unless they were better at computer security than I am, they weren't able to log onto either of our systems."

"Good." She hated this feeling of violation, and for whatever reason, the thought of a faceless person poking around in her computer files was even worse.

Brett powered up his system. "Unless the civ took a crash course in subtle searching methods, I think we're looking at the men in black as culprits."

"When you find out who they are, I want to tell them a thing or two."

"Me, too, sugar. Me, too." The dark menace in his voice made her shiver.

"Are you still convinced they weren't responsible for my attack?"

"I have a hard time seeing one of our government agents trying to smother you with a pillow."

"You can say that after seeing Arwan's kill book?"

Brett's face closed up. "Yes."

She turned away, not wanting to deal with what felt like a rejection. "My list is on the last page of the purple composition book if you want to compare it with Collins's report."

"Where are you going?"

"I thought I'd watch television in the bedroom." She waited to see if he'd ask her to stay and help him.

"Fine."

She nodded and went into the other room.

She was lying on her stomach, her head at the end of the bed, and watching a home decorator show when he came in to find her, his expression grim.

She rolled and scooted into a sitting position. "Did you need something?"

"You hungry for lunch?"

"I didn't realize it was that late." She looked down at her watch and realized she'd been in the bedroom for more than an hour. "I guess I could eat something."

"Do you want to order or do you trust me to order for you?"

She shrugged. "I trust you."

"Do you?"

Her brow wrinkled in confusion. "Yes."

"I've been going over Arwan's notes."

She noticed that he used the assassin name to refer to Lester in that role as well. It seemed right, because from what she could tell, Lester had been two different people . . . at least, he'd lived two very separate lives. "Find anything?"

"I'm not sure about the case yet. I'm going over it as I type it into a database that I will cross-reference with Collins's report. But I did find something I thought might interest you."

"What?"

"Arwan didn't take every job. In fact, he was very particular about the jobs he did take. He refused to kill unless the danger to national security or the security of others could be proven to his satisfaction."

"What about the private jobs?" she couldn't help asking.

"There weren't that many, but the reasons for the contracts being taken out were ones that Arwan believed justified his involvement."

"Like what?" She desperately wanted to understand.

"Like a man who beat his wife to death and was doing a damn fine job on his children until their grandfather hired Arwan to take him out. There weren't as many laws in place to protect domestic abuse victims back in the fifties as there are now. That grandfather saw no other way to protect his family, and Arwan agreed."

She shouldn't feel relief, but she did. The idea of vigilante justice wasn't acceptable, and yet, how could she condemn a grandfather for wanting to protect his grandchildren from their violent father? A man who had already killed his wife . . . the man's daughter.

Her eyes filled with tears and she averted her face so Brett wouldn't see them. "You're right. Knowing that helps a lot. Thank you."

"If it helps so much, why won't you look at me?"

She shrugged and surreptitiously wiped at her eyes. "No reason. I'm just watching the show."

"And that's more important than what I told you about Lester?" he asked.

"Arwan, you mean."

"They were the same man."

So much for her theory. "Well, yes, but . . ."

Brett sat down beside her and tugged on her chin until she was looking at him. "Why are you crying?"

"I'm relieved—I shouldn't be, but I am."

He shook his head. "I'm never going to understand you, am I?"

She shrugged. "Probably not. I don't think our brains are wired the same way."

"Does that bother you?" he asked with a probing intensity she didn't understand.

"Not really. Josette informs me that it's a man-woman thing."

"And you think that's all it is?"

"Yes." She didn't get the underlying significance of his question, but she could sense that he wanted something from her. Some kind of assurance, but she didn't know about what. And since she didn't know what it was, she didn't know how to give it, either. "What is it, Brett? What do you need?"

His eyes went smoky, just that fast. "I always need you."

As his mouth took possession of hers, she was sure that needy passion wasn't what his odd looks had been about, but she didn't hesitate to respond to him. He made her burn and she was only too happy to go up in flames.

Afterward, they ordered lunch and took a shower while they were waiting for it. He kept dropping the soap and then going searching for it, his mouth and his hands managing to caress every square inch of her in the process. She was leaning against the wall, panting after a shattering orgasm, when room service knocked on the suite's door.

Brett did a quick dry-off and then wrapped the towel around his waist to saunter into the main living area. The man had no shame, but he sure was fun.

She finished her shower, threw on a tank top she usually wore under other things and a pair of shorts she never wore in public.

His wolf whistle of appreciation when she went into the living room made her grin and get all shivery at the same time. He was still wearing the towel while he set the food out and she did a little whistling of her own. That elicited retaliation in the nicest possible way, and she thought later it was a good thing her food had been cold already, because they sure didn't get to it immediately.

After lunch, she called the professor who wore the same cologne as the guy who had attacked her. Once she knew its name, Brett insisted on running downtown and getting a bottle so he could smell it, too. He wanted to be on the alert.

After sniffing it and pronouncing it way too girlie for a real man, he recapped the fragrance bottle and tossed it in the bag.

When they got back to the hotel, she did the comparison of her list with Collins's report while Brett finished entering the names from Arwan's kill book in the database.

The phone rang a little later and Brett answered it while she saved Collins's report with her additions in it. There had only been two, and she figured they were both useless, one being a doctor who had worked with Lester since he first became a resident of Belmont Manor and the other a small group of politicians who had visited the Manor a few weeks before. They hadn't been there during her shift, but Queenie had told her about the visit. It had upset her. While they had not been Lester's visitors per se, they had seen him.

She smiled as Brett hung up the phone. "Who was that?"

"Ethan. He identified the men in black at the funeral. They work for a director with a lot of clout in Washington."

"Who is he?"

"Raymond Arthur. Ethan ran a background check on

him. He's a former military hard-ass with some questionable mission directives in his past."

"What do you mean?"

"He isn't known for showing scruples when it comes to getting the job done. I wouldn't be surprised if a good portion of Arwan's later hits were ordered by him."

"Do you think he would have had Lester killed to keep the government's secrets?"

Brett's expression was grim. "It's possible. This guy sounds like the type that would have thrived during the secrecy surrounding our efforts in the Cold War."

"What are we going to do about it?"

"We're going to call on him while we are on the east coast, and we are going to force a meeting with his two agents. One of them has gray eyes and a medium build."

"Like the man who tried to smother me with a pillow?"

"Yes. If they are responsible, there will be hell to pay from here to the next election." The soldier who went into battle and knew how to do whatever it took to win gazed out from Brett's glacier-cold blue gaze.

She could almost feel sorry for the government agents in question.

Claire's tension grew with every mile the SUV traveled away from the small municipal airport where Brett had landed his plane.

His parents lived about an hour and a half southwest of Savannah, on the outskirts of a small town named for one of Brett's ancestors. She couldn't even imagine. What must it have been like growing up as a member of the town's founding family? Brett wasn't a conformer, and she wondered if it had been hard for him.

He didn't talk a lot about his family . . . all she really knew was that they were definitely a bunch of over-achievers and he loved them.

But the prospect of meeting the rest of his family had her stomach in knots. It shouldn't and she knew it shouldn't. She and Brett weren't a couple. Not really. He hadn't even said anything about his marriage proposal since leaving Lincoln City.

This was probably the one and only time she would ever meet these people. So, his family's opinion of her should not matter, *but it did.* She smoothed down her white t-shirt and the khaki cargo pants she'd worn to travel, wishing her wardrobe stretched to a pair of real slacks.

Brett was silent, too, his usually charming exterior going grim the closer they got to his family home. Was he embarrassed to be bringing her?

"I can stay at a hotel, you know. I don't have to horn in on your mother's birthday weekend."

His head jerked as if he'd been deep in thought. "What?"

"The bad guys aren't going to know where I am. I can stay in a hotel."

"You're staying at the house." That's all he said and then he went back to brooding.

She watched the green scenery go by for another mile. "How close are we?"

Right then, he turned the car into a long drive lined with trees. "Very close."

As he pulled the car to a stop behind a huge white mansion, she felt her heart speed up until it was going faster than the Road Runner fleeing Wile E. Coyote.

"Your parents live here?" she demanded in a voice that sounded as awed as she felt.

"Yes."

"You grew up *here?*"

"Yes." He got out of the car and came around to open her door, but frowned when she made no move to step out. "It's just a house, Claire."

"It looks like a scene from *Gone With the Wind.*" She and her parents had lived in a pretty nice house in West Portland prior to her dad losing his job, but it had been nothing like this.

"No chance. My mother and sisters think Scarlett O'Hara gave southern women a bad name."

"Because she was so selfish?"

His brows rose, as if he hadn't expected her response. "Yes."

"Okay . . . so it's not a movie set, but it is beautiful—and *huge.*" She sighed and stared at the house and its incredible surroundings, unable to imagine growing up in such a place . . . and then leaving it.

He smiled, his eyes narrowing with a speculative gleam. "If I promised to bring you here every holiday and two weeks in the summer for our kids to run riot, would you marry me?"

She gasped. "I thought . . ."

"What did you think?"

"That you'd forgotten about that ridiculous idea," she blurted out. But the image he painted of their *children*—not just child, singular—playing in the green, green grass, or climbing one of the huge trees around the mansion, was totally tempting.

"I'm reserving my resources."

"What do you mean?"

But he didn't get a chance to answer, because two boys with dark hair and identical grins had come hurtling from the direction of the house and threw themselves against him with gleeful cries of, "Uncle Brett, Uncle Brett."

A small, blond girl followed the boys, her shorter legs not letting her reach Brett as quickly as the other two. When she did, she stood back, sucking her thumb and watching the boys and Brett engage in an impromptu wrestling match.

Claire climbed from the car and closed the door, snagging the little girl's attention. She smiled shyly around her thumb.

Claire dropped to her haunches so she and the child were at eye level. "Hi, my name is Claire. What's yours?"

She popped her thumb out of her mouth. "Jenny."

"That's a pretty name. Is it short for Jennifer?"

Jenny nodded. "Those are my brothers, Derek and Kyle. They're bigger than me," she said confidingly.

"I see. They like to wrestle with their uncle, don't they?"

"Uh-huh." She looked at Claire for several seconds before asking, "Are you Uncle Brett's girlfriend?"

"No . . . um . . ." Claire hoped her consternation did not show on her face. "I'm, uh . . . his friend. That's all."

Jenny didn't say anything to that, but popped her thumb back into her mouth, her expression solemn.

"Hey, sugarplum." Brett had come to stand with one boy hung under each arm like a bag of oats. "Where's your mama?"

"She's inside," Jenny said around her thumb.

"I'm right here, actually."

Claire surged to her feet and Brett released his hold on his nephews as they all turned at the sound of the melodic voice. His sister was a beautiful woman, dressed elegantly in a pale pink suit and heels, with a superficial resemblance to Brett that was unmistakable.

The woman put her hand out to Claire. "I'm Eleanor

Adams-Stanton, this disreputable person's older sister and these three adorable cherubs' mother."

Claire shook hands with her. "Claire Sharp. It's a pleasure to meet you."

"She said she's not Uncle Brett's girlfriend," Jenny piped up. "Nana was wrong."

Chapter 19

Looking supremely unconcerned by his niece's comment, Brett ruffled the girl's golden curls. "Claire was being shy, sugarplum. She's my girlfriend, all right."

Eleanor's brows rose. "Maybe she's not shy so much as ashamed to claim you?"

The twinkle in her blue eyes so like Brett's indicated the words had been meant to tease, but a tiny clenching of his jaw said that he'd taken them to heart.

Claire moved a step closer to Brett. "Of course I'm not ashamed to claim him."

"But you said you wasn't his girlfriend," Jenny repeated.

"Weren't," her mother corrected with a gentle pat on her daughter's shoulder.

"It's all pretty new and it's not exactly official," Claire said by way of an explanation.

"What does that mean?" one of the boys asked. "How do you get an official girlfriend, Uncle Brett?"

"It means, you hooligan, that I'm still working on

convincing her to marry me. Once I do, it will be as official as it gets."

His sister's eyes widened in shock, and then a grin at odds with her elegant demeanor spread across her face. "Mama is going to be thrilled."

"Do you have to wanna marry a girl for her to be your girlfriend?" the other boy—she thought it was Kyle—demanded.

"No, but I'm going to marry Claire and she *is* my girlfriend. She's just not used to it yet."

"Oh." The young boy looked at Claire. "I have a girlfriend, but I don't wanna marry her."

Claire was going to kill Brett, but thought she'd wait until there were no children around to witness the deed.

She smiled at Kyle. "That's probably best. You've got years before you should start thinking about marriage."

"My daddy says the same thing, but he likes being married to my mama a lot, so I don't know."

Eleanor laughed, looking pleased by her son's remark, and then took Claire's arm. "Come along. Mama is dying to meet the first woman Brett has ever brought home to the family."

First woman? He hadn't told her he'd *never* brought another woman home to the family. No wonder his sister was looking so much like the cat that ate the canary.

Claire shot him a hot glare over her shoulder.

He just shrugged, a smile creasing his face in sexy lines. Then he mouthed, *I warned you.*

And he had, but he hadn't warned her he intended to tell his family he wanted to marry her. Being the first woman he brought home would have been bad enough, but that just cinched it. Brett had put her in an untenable position. She supposed that's what he'd meant by saving his resources.

He planned to turn the women in his family loose on her and from her brief glimpse of Eleanor, that was a scary proposition. The next time Claire got Brett alone, she was going to make his ears ring.

Jenny's tiny hand slipped into hers and squeezed. "I like you. You'd make a nice auntie."

Claire felt a funny little flip in her heart. She smiled down at Jenny. "I like you, too."

But she went speechless when they walked into the mansion. Even coming in through the back hall was impressive. The moldings were solid wood and carved from a time when workmanship really meant something. As they filed into the spacious entry hall, her breath caught. Its huge dimensions were eclipsed by the grandeur of the staircase and artwork gracing the walls.

"Oh, my."

"It's lovely, isn't it?" Eleanor asked without so much pride as a practical appreciation for the beauty.

"Yes."

"It's hard to believe Brett left all this to live in an army barracks, and who knows what other forsaken places, when he was eighteen."

"Sometimes a person's dreams require sacrificing things that matter."

He was suddenly beside her, his arm going around her waist, the "hooligans," as he called them, tearing off ahead to enter a room off the opposite side of the cavernous entryway.

"You two stop running right this instant," their mother called in a stern voice, but was overridden by a southern drawl so like Brett's that Claire sucked in a shocked breath.

"Leave them be, Ellie. They're too full of energy to move in slow motion all of the time." A man who looked as she imagined Brett would in twenty years, with some silver in his blond hair and a few laugh wrinkles around his eyes, stepped out of the room.

"I don't recall you ever allowing me to run in the house," Eleanor replied wryly.

"Certain privileges are reserved for grandparenthood," the man who had to be Brett's father said, and then turned to her. "You must be Claire."

"Yes."

They shook hands, his grip firm but not crushing. "Loren. I would like to say that my son has told us a great deal about you," he said as he led her into the living room, "but he's been typically closemouthed, and now you will have to endure a family's curiosity as we satisfy ourselves about you."

Were they going to give her the third degree? That scenario was the last one she wanted to contemplate. "I—"

"You make it sound like we're going to cross-examine her, and I realize being a lawyer and then judge for so many years is hard to overcome, but do try to be civilized. You're scaring the poor dear to death. Can't you see how tense she's gotten?" This came from a woman sitting on a low sofa, Kyle and Derek on either side of her.

She was every bit as elegant and beautiful as Brett's sister, but her eyes and hair were dark and she was probably a good three inches shorter than her daughter. Though she looked much too young to have given birth to either Eleanor or Brett.

She shook her head at her husband. "Sometimes I wonder where you hide that charm that convinced me to marry you."

"Brett's must have gone missing, too. He hasn't been able to convince Claire to marry him at all and he's looking for us to help."

"What?" His mother stared at Claire as if she were an apparition.

"I never said that," Brett denied.

"You yourself told me you hadn't convinced her. What else could you have meant but a plea for help?" Eleanor sat down on one end of a matching sofa opposite the one her mother and children were sitting on.

"My son asked you to marry him?"

Claire could only nod. Reminding them all, including the man she was now clinging to like a lifeline, that she had said no did not seem politic.

"Well, glory be, my son got some of his father's wits after all. Those are the wits that he had before so many years in a courtroom drained most of them away," she said with a haughty look at her husband.

Incredibly, he didn't appear offended at all, but grinned and slapped his son on the back. "This is wonderful news, son." He turned his grin to Claire. "What do your parents think of Brett?"

"Her parents are both dead," Brett quietly stated.

"Oh, I'm sorry." His mother's dark eyes swam with sympathy. "I will not be offended that I am only meeting you for the first time, then. When he told me that he'd known you for over a year, I naturally thought that Brett had met your family already and kept you a secret from us. I couldn't understand why, except that he has this silly little idea that we're too prying. It shouldn't have bothered me, I know . . . but I'm only human and I've been waiting so long for this son of mine to settle down."

"We've only been friends, Mrs. Adams. Really."

"Until recently," Brett added. "Though I think we both knew for quite a while that we wanted more."

"Do call me Felicia and you may call Brett's father Loren. Why, you're practically family."

"Please . . . I . . . Brett . . . I mean . . . Please don't get your heart set on marriage. I don't think it would work," she said all in a rush.

"Why?" his sister baldly asked.

Claire swallowed, trying to find the right words. "Our backgrounds are too different, for one thing."

"There aren't that many women who are ex-mercenaries like his friend Josie. Surely you wouldn't limit him to waiting for one to come along."

Brett's hold on her tightened and tension emanated off of him. Despite the fact he said he wanted the marriage, he wasn't any more comfortable with this conversation than she was. Maybe he would remember that, and the next time he was tempted to call in reinforcements, would keep his big mouth zipped.

"I didn't mean that."

"Then what did you mean?" Felicia asked gently, her dark gaze probing.

Claire swept her arm out to indicate their surroundings. "I mean this. Your lifestyle, the way you raised Brett . . . it's like a fantasy. He owns his own jet, for heaven's sake, and I can't even afford a used car at the moment."

"This is about money?" Loren asked, his expression puzzled.

"No. Yes. Not entirely."

Brett's father laughed, a warm, rich sound. "You're as confused as Brett's mother was while I was courting her. That's a good sign, son."

"I hope so." Brett pulled Claire onto the sofa his sister had sat down on.

His father lifted Derek and put him in his lap, taking the seat beside Felicia. "We're not royalty, Claire . . . or the Kennedy clan." He chuckled at his own joke. "My ancestors helped found this town and built this house for themselves and the generations that came after them, but we're no different from your own parents."

Claire just shook her head. He had no idea how wrong he was, but no way was she going to tell him.

Instead, she said the one thing that she could say with total honesty. "I used to think I was a nonviolent person, but there are times I could happily boil your son in oil. I really think whether or not we marry is something that has to be settled between the two of us."

Thankfully, the conversation moved on to other subjects after that, and Claire found herself really liking his family.

When Felicia declared that Claire needed time to unpack and refresh herself before dinner, Eleanor insisted on showing Claire to her room. For some reason that made Brett nervous, or so the somewhat strained smile he gave her as she left with the other woman implied.

Eleanor led Claire up the large, winding staircase. "Brett said that you were Josie's roommate."

"Yes."

"So, that's how you met?"

"Uh-huh."

"When did you start dating?"

"Um . . ." Their first date had been their trip to the beach . . . if you could call it a date.

She wasn't sure admitting that at this point would be the most impressive piece of information she could impart. Brett's sister would think he'd lost his mind, proposing so soon. Claire wasn't sure she didn't hold that opinion herself.

"We admitted we were attracted to each other at Josette and Nitro's wedding," she said after some furious thought.

"Weddings have that effect on people."

"I suppose."

"So, why haven't you said yes yet?"

Claire tripped on the top step and grabbed for the balustrade. "I'd rather not talk about that."

"Well, that's one thing you and Brett have in common."

"What?"

"Neither of you likes to answer questions about your feelings. We've still never gotten a complete answer out of him about why he chose to be a soldier instead of going to medical school like Mama and Daddy expected."

They'd thought Brett ought to be a doctor? For astute people, they had been singularly blind about their second son's calling in life. "I'd think that was obvious."

Eleanor stopped in front of a closed door and looked keenly at Claire. "In what way?"

"He's a warrior at heart. You only have to know him a few hours to see it." And she couldn't imagine he'd changed all that much since he was a young man, filled with idealistic dreams of serving his country. "He even flies a kite like a commanding officer with a new recruit."

"You went kite-flying?" Eleanor asked, sounding shocked.

"Yes."

"But Brett doesn't do stuff like that. Sure, he plays with the children when he's here, but before they came along he didn't play at all. People mistake all that Adams charm for a laid-back attitude, but my brother does not have a laid-back bone in his body. He spends very little time relaxing. Even when he was younger, he was always practicing his martial arts, or horseback riding, or skeet shooting, and he did everything with an eye to being the best there was. None of that was play to him."

Claire thought of their walk in the park, their time on the beach, the fun they had in the pool and then the hot tub the night before. "He relaxes with me."

"You must be a very special woman."

Claire shook her head. "Oh, no. I'm pretty average. I just finished getting my first college degree, and I work in an assisted-living care facility. Maybe Brett relaxes more than you think he does with his other friends, too."

"You're more than friends if he wants to marry you."

Claire could feel the heat crawling up her cheeks because she knew exactly what the other woman was alluding to. "Yes."

Eleanor smiled kindly and then opened the door to their left. "Here you are. Brett's in the room next to you and you share a connecting bathroom. Jenny's on the other side, but don't worry about sounds carrying. The house is old with very solid walls."

"Um . . . I . . ."

"Brett watches you like a hungry mountain cat. He'll be sneaking along the balcony or through the connecting bathroom, come nightfall, or I'm not the astute observer of human nature the constituents that voted me in as a judge think I am."

Claire just shook her head. Southerners were a lot more forthright than she'd ever believed, and she said so.

Eleanor laughed. "Only within the family."

"But I'm not . . ."

"You will be. He may not have convinced you he's a

solid bet yet, but he will. Brett's nothing if not tenacious, and he's had to fight too hard his whole life to be a person different from the one the rest of us expected him to be. That kind of stubbornness has become second nature to him now."

"I'm no slouch in the stubborn department myself."

"Of course not. Brett wouldn't be happy married to a wilting violet."

"I don't think he would be happy married to me, either."

"He disagrees, and I have a feeling you don't give yourself enough credit."

Claire shook her head. "You make quick judgments."

"It comes with the job. I drive my family crazy sometimes, but they put up with me."

"Where is your husband?"

"In Raleigh on business. He'll be down in time for the festivities tomorrow, though."

"Oh. I look forward to meeting him."

"He's dying to meet you, too. He's always said that if Brett ever married it would be to a woman very different from his family, and he was right. I don't mind telling you, there are a few Georgia peaches who are going to be crying in their champagne at the party tomorrow."

"I—"

Eleanor waved her hand, as if dismissing any regrets Claire might want to express. "Brett wouldn't be happy married to a local girl. He wanted to travel the world and he has. He likes living in Montana now, though goodness knows why. It's not the most populated state in the union and the winters are so cold."

"It's beautiful and I think he likes isolation—besides, he said you all liked to ski."

"Yes, but a few weeks every winter in the snow is a far

cry from spending months on end driving through foot-high drifts."

"I don't think he spends that much time at home."

"No, I don't suppose he does." Eleanor indicated Claire's cases, which had been delivered to the room. "What are you wearing to the party tomorrow?"

"How formal is it?" If it was very formal, she could wear the dress she'd worn in Josette's wedding. It didn't look in the least bridal. If it was more casual, she'd wear the outfit Brett bought her at the coast.

"Mama likes to dress up."

Claire crossed to the suitcase and pulled her single formal dress out. "Will this do?"

Eleanor nodded, definite approval in her eyes. "Yes, that will be perfect. Please don't think I'm being nosy, but I know how important things like this are to a woman."

Claire let out a small breath of relief while she tried to contain her astonishment at the last bit of Eleanor's speech. Brett's sister thought nothing of asking her why she wouldn't marry him, but apologized for asking about her clothes.

Amazing, if totally incomprehensible.

"I'll leave you to freshen up before dinner."

"Thank you."

Claire was finishing hanging her clothes in the old-fashioned wardrobe when Brett came into the room . . . via the balcony door.

He walked right over and pulled her into his arms for a scorching kiss. His lips devoured hers with a desperation she didn't understand, but gladly gave in to.

Long moments later, he broke off the kiss. "Man, I needed that."

"Missed me?" she asked, tongue in cheek.

"Yes," he said with real feeling.

She laughed. "Right. We've only been apart about forty-five minutes."

"It was the longest three-quarters of an hour of my life."

"Pull the other one." He had been in some tense situations where time would have crawled by.

"I'm serious." He looked down at her with an intent expression. "I kept picturing what my sister was saying to you and I got nervous as hell."

"You didn't need to." Claire wrapped her arms around his neck and felt a smile curving at her lips. "She just asked why I refused to marry you, informed me you wouldn't be able to hold back from coming to my room after dark, but that I wasn't to worry because even though Jenny is on the other side of me, the walls are thick and she wanted to know what I planned to wear to your mother's birthday party tomorrow."

He groaned, looking truly pained. "That's what I was afraid of. On the bright side, she and Mama must have decided you would make a good addition to the family or she never would have been so open with you."

"More like they both see you as unbending as a piece of granite and figure you'll wear down my resistance to marriage, so they might as well accept what cannot be changed."

"And are *you* going to accept what cannot be changed?"

"What do you think?"

"That you're not resigned." He sighed. "But don't kid yourself about Mama and Eleanor. If they didn't like you, they wouldn't resign themselves to anything."

"They spent one afternoon talking to me. How can they have made up their minds so quickly?"

"Sometimes that's all it takes. And for all Mama likes to pretend I never mentioned you, I did. I told them plenty when I called to inform them you would be with me at the party, too."

"You talked about me *before*?"

"You were my friend, Claire. Yes, I talked about you."

"I can't imagine what you found to say."

"You rival me for computer acumen—what do you think I talked about?"

"Oh." For some stupid reason, she was disappointed he hadn't mentioned her more as a woman . . . but what would he have said? *Mama, I've got this friend with bad hair and no dress sense and she likes to spend her off days visiting the elderly.* Not likely.

"I also told them you were damn sexy and it always surprised me you didn't date."

"I was too busy."

"You were never interested in another guy," he said smugly.

"So what if I wasn't? That doesn't mean I can't live my life without you."

"Are you sure about that?"

An honest answer would get her in deeper, so she kept her mouth stubbornly shut.

He wasn't bothered. He just grinned, looking much too smug for her comfort. "That's what I thought."

"Don't get cocky. It's not becoming. And your family would die of apoplexy if they found out you wanted to marry the daughter of a man who committed suicide rather than face his own failures and a woman who drank herself to death for pretty much the same reason."

"They already know it and they're just fine."

Chapter 20

Claire's heart stopped beating. *"You told them about my parents?"*

"No. And I never will if you don't want me to, but they know I want to marry *you* and you are that woman. They've met you and they like you and that's all that matters. Not who your parents were."

It wasn't that simple. She knew that, even if Brett didn't.

"Your sister is a public official. The press digs up all sorts of unsavory stuff when election time rolls around. What if they make my background public and embarrass her?"

"She's not a U.S. Senator, for crying out loud. We don't get those kinds of mudslinging campaigns and media exposés around here. Even if we did, she'd just go on record as saying she thinks it's amazing what you've made of your life, considering what you had to overcome to do it. Because it's true, Claire. You're an incredible woman. You beat the odds and I admire you a lot."

Her eyes burned with inexplicable moisture. "Thank you."

He kissed her. Swiftly and hard. "Now, tell me what you think of my family."

"I like them, but I understand why you live in Montana."

He nodded. "They're nosy and I like my privacy."

"Exactly." She broke away from him, needing some space.

His comments had really touched her, but she wasn't sure if he was right. She had no problem believing her background was not a problem for him, but she wasn't sure—despite what he'd said—that his sister would be so sanguine.

She stopped in front of a painting of a small child playing in the dirt, her frilly white dress smudged and her face suffused with innocent joy as she made a mud pie in what appeared to be a real pie tin.

There was something familiar about the little girl.

"That looks like Jenny."

"It is."

"The artist is very talented."

"Thank you."

She looked at the signature. *H.B. Adams.* "Is he a relative?"

"You could say that. H.B. Adams is me."

She spun to face him. "What?"

"I took up painting years ago as a way to escape when my brain was filled with too many ugly images associated with war."

"What does the *H* stand for?"

"Hamilton."

"Your first name is Hamilton?"

"Hey, it's not as bad as my brother. He got stuck with Loren Quincy Adams, the Fourth."

"Does he go by Loren or Quincy?"

"They tried to stick him with Quincy and then Junior, but he fought for Loren. They compromised on L.Q., but if any man could go by Quincy and make it work, it would be my brother. He's the perfect judge's son."

"And you don't think you are?"

"They wanted me to be a doctor. Did my sister tell you that?"

"Yes."

Despite the fact he'd asked the question, his eyes widened. "Wow, she really wasn't pulling any stops. Anyway, I disappointed them all when I chose to join the army right out of high school. I wouldn't even finish college first and enter as an officer. My father and I fought for weeks before I simply walked out of the house one day and came home enlisted."

"But you did what you needed to do. You succeeded at it, too."

"You consider dropping out of the Rangers and becoming a mercenary a success?"

"The way you did it, yes. You kept your ideals, your integrity, and your honor. You're the kind of man I'm glad is defending my country, Brett."

"So, my past doesn't bother you?"

She felt her own eyes flair. "Of course not. Why should it?"

"You're as close to a pacifist as it gets, sugar. I thought maybe the violence in my past might disgust you."

"You aren't a former gang member. You only ever did what you had to do to protect your country, or the people you were trying to save."

"But you were so upset once the reality of Lester's life hit you."

"He was an assassin, not a soldier, and right, wrong, or indifferent . . . I don't see those things the same way.

Besides, you helped me come to terms with the other life he lived."

"Then why won't you marry me, damn it?"

"Because you don't love me." As she said the words, she knew they were true.

It shouldn't matter, but it did. More than anything else, and she couldn't deny that truth any longer. She wanted to marry him, could not imagine anything more wonderful than spending the rest of her life with this man. Only she could not live that life weighted under the burden of loving a man who loved a dead woman.

"And you still love Elena."

"Elena is gone."

"From life maybe, but not your heart."

"We're good together, Claire."

"It's not enough."

"You could be carrying my baby."

"And I might not be."

"I'm not sure I care anymore. I'm tired of being alone, Claire. Can you understand that?"

"Yes." Too well.

"You complement me in a way no one else does, and I need your body like hell on fire."

"Lust burns out."

"Who says?"

"You can't build a lifelong commitment on physical need," she asserted doggedly.

"Bull. We have a better chance of making our marriage survive than a couple who loves each other, but has no spark in the bedroom. Just ask Lise. Her first marriage was like that and when her husband found passion, he left her."

"That's terrible."

"But it's life. We're friends. We have a lot in common."

She laughed at that.

"Okay . . . so we aren't carbon copies of each other, but that would be boring."

"Heaven forbid you should ever get bored."

"There's no chance of that with you in my life."

"You know . . . I met this man at Josette's wedding."

Brett's expression turned fierce. "Who? I don't remember you meeting someone else."

"Yes. He was the classic 'no commitment' kind of guy. First he kissed me senseless and then told me he wasn't in the market for a relationship."

Brett looked ready to spit nails by the time she was done talking, but slowly understanding dawned in his eyes. "You know why *I* said that."

"Yes. You loved Elena and will never love another woman like that, but for some reason you've decided that no longer matters where I'm concerned."

"Don't make it sound like I'm shortchanging you. I'll be a good husband."

"And a good father."

"So my family tells me." There was such longing in his expression that her own heart contracted with the pain of it.

She about suffocated on the swell of love for him that poured through her. Far from being a fairy tale, love was a force to be reckoned with, one that could hurt as much as it helped. She wanted so much to make his desires come true. He would be a terrific dad and an awesome husband . . . except for the fact that he didn't love her.

Claire needed Brett. She couldn't deny it, but what would happen if one day he woke up and hated the choice he'd made? What if she was the mother of his children and he decided he wanted to walk away? The thought ripped a hole in her heart and it hurt so much she had to turn away.

Her dad had walked . . . in the most permanent way possible, but Brett would never do that. He wasn't weak. And she wasn't her mother, but her love made her so much more vulnerable to him than she wanted to be. He could hurt her. Marrying him could hurt her. Badly.

He wasn't offering her a two-sided marriage of convenience. Heck, he wasn't offering her a marriage of convenience at all. He said he needed *her*. This wasn't just about the forgotten condom, or the lovemaking, except in that he wanted it to continue. He also liked her and cared about her . . . as a friend. He wanted to be with her.

But her need for him was all wrapped up in her emotions and that made the prospect of marriage unequal, even if it wasn't as dispassionate a proposal as she had first thought. She would be the lover, but never the beloved, and wouldn't that make it easier for him to walk away?

He was there immediately, his hands gentle but firm on her shoulders. "What's the matter, sugar?"

"Nothing new."

"So tell me what's old."

"I can't."

"Why not?"

"It would hurt too much," she said honestly.

"Are you sure about that?"

"Yes."

"You're sure it isn't because I'm a soldier?"

"No." She bit her lip. "I admire you, Brett . . . more than I can say. I l-like pretty much everything about you."

"Then marry me."

She shook her head from side to side, her emotions running riot inside of her. "I can't!"

"Why can't you?" He turned her to face him, his expression so tender it made her ache. "Explain it to me, sweetheart, please."

Tears spilled hotly down her cheeks. "I love you, Brett."

Something flared in the depths of his eyes. "That should make it easier for you to marry me, not harder."

"It would . . . if you loved me, too."

"Why?"

"Because if we got married and I let my love grow and then you got tired of me, or found someone else to love and decided to walk away, it would hurt too much."

"So, you don't want to take a chance at happiness because you're afraid I'm going to leave you high and dry someday?"

"What would be holding you?"

"You," he said fiercely. "And me. I'm a man who keeps a promise once he makes it, Claire. I won't break the ones I make to you on our wedding day. I'm not like your father," he said, showing he knew what scared her the most.

Her heart wanted to hope, but the cynical part of her mind that had learned too indelible a lesson early on said that her dad had probably made the same promises to her mom.

The feelings warred inside of her until she felt like she was being torn apart. "I don't want to talk about this anymore."

"Fine. We won't talk," he growled and then his lips locked over hers.

He kissed her until she was like a pliant doll in his arms.

When he broke his mouth away to kiss along her jaw-line, it took her a few seconds to gain enough breath to talk. "Brett, this isn't a good idea."

He cupped her face with hands that spoke of more than passion, but without the words, her mind refused to allow the message a path to her heart. "We're done talking for right now, sugar. Now, use your mouth in a more productive way."

The need in his blue gaze obliterated her reticence and she kissed him with all the passion his touch invoked, allowing the pleasure to numb her mind and give her temporary peace. Her last coherent thought was that being in Georgia had not put a halt to their intimacy at all.

They were on time for dinner . . . just. Brett wore a suit and she wore the skirt outfit he'd bought her in Lincoln City. She was glad she had when she saw the chic dresses his mother and sister wore to the table. She felt that for a woman who had spent most of her life oblivious to fashion, she had become inordinately interested in clothes.

Strangely, it didn't bother her.

It was a surprisingly enjoyable evening. And despite her assertion to the contrary, Claire found herself promising Brett's mother and sister she would join them on a shopping trip to Savannah the day after the party.

Brett spent the evening treating her like she really was someone special to him, not just a woman he had the hots for and had convinced himself he had to marry. She tried not to get caught up in the fantasy, but by the time he came to her room late that night, she was lost to the feeling of being someone unique and important in another person's life.

Her mom had needed her, but no one had ever made her feel central to their happiness like Brett did when they made love.

He held her afterward, their heated bodies close together, and brushed at tears she was getting used to dealing with. "What is it, sugar?"

"It's just so beautiful when we make love."

"Yes, it is."

"But it's not real. It's an illusion," she said to remind herself as much as him.

He rolled on top of her and slid into her body with an erection that should not have been possible yet. Then he leaned up on his arms. "What the hell isn't real about this?"

"It's just sex. It's not love."

"You love me."

"But you don't love me."

"And you think that makes the passion between us something less than what it is?"

"Doesn't it?"

"Don't kid yourself. This is real. What we feel *together* is real. This . . ." He thrust into her. "*This* is no illusion."

"But . . ."

"Damn it!" He thrust powerfully, sending shards of pleasure piercing through her. "Elena said she loved me, but she refused to leave her country even though she knew she was in grave danger. She died for a lost cause, but she refused to live for me. What we have is better than that kind of love. Can't you see that? It's honest and it's reciprocal."

As he increased the pace of his lovemaking, driving her to a passion-filled place that had little room for rational thinking, her mind latched on to one last thought. If he believed this was *better* than love, maybe that was because he did love her but didn't want to use the word to describe what he felt.

Maybe he couldn't stand the thought of breaking the promise he had made to his dead fiancée. Or maybe saying the words made him feel too vulnerable because the one woman he had admitted to loving had chosen duty over him, not the other way around.

Claire's thoughts splintered as her pleasure spiraled, but this time when she climaxed, words spilled from her mouth, unplanned but not unwelcome. "I love you, Brett. I love you so much!"

"You are so beautiful. So perfect for me," he husked, awe in his voice, and then he came, too. Afterward, he said nothing more, but he held her close until she slept.

When she woke, he was gone, but she couldn't forget what he had said. Was it possible that Hamilton Brett Adams could love Claire Sharpe?

The prospect made her jittery with joy, but fear that she was setting herself up for an emotional calamity stopped her from dwelling too closely on the possibility.

She arrived downstairs for breakfast only to discover an unexpected group of visitors. Wolf, Lise, Nitro, and Josette were eating with the rest of Brett's family when Claire entered the dining room.

Josette jumped up from the table to hug her. "Claire! It's so good to see you. I heard you've had a very eventful couple of weeks."

"That's one way of putting it, but what are you two doing back? And here? I thought you were going to be gone for at least a few more days."

"We couldn't miss Ms. Adams's birthday party," Nitro said, and incredibly, Felicia nodded as if she had expected nothing less.

Over breakfast, Claire saw that she and Loren treated both Wolf and Nitro like members of the family and, by extension, their wives. No one seemed to find it odd to embrace two ex-mercenaries in the family bosom, but then Brett was ex-merc, too.

Still, Claire liked his family all the more for accepting his friends and by doing so, tacitly that aspect of his lifestyle as well. She couldn't help wondering if Brett realized the significance of it, though.

After breakfast, he gathered his guests together in a room in the back of the house to discuss the case.

"Have you come up with any connections between the list in the kill book and the people who saw Lester that last month?" Nitro asked.

"Yes, but only superficial connections. Some visitors share last names with people in Arwan's notes, both the kills and the ones who hired the jobs done, but it will take longer to find out if any of those superficial connections go deep enough for suspicion to be attached to them. We're also looking to see if there are connections that are not so obvious, and, of course, that's going to take longer, but we've got help."

"Who?" Josette asked.

"Lester's nephew. He came to the funeral and we met him," Claire said.

"Can he be trusted?" Wolf asked.

"I ran a background check on him and he's clean." Brett handed a manila file folder to Wolf. "Whatever job he holds for the government is deep, but there are no red flags anywhere."

"What does your gut say?"

Brett didn't hesitate. "Never trust someone until they've proven themselves."

"Exactly," Nitro said with a firm nod which Josette emulated.

Claire gasped. "Then none of you can trust me because I've never proven myself."

"On the contrary," Brett said, "you could have sold Josie out to the media after the mercenary school was bombed, but you protected her instead. You were in enough trouble without watching out for Queenie, too, but as soon as you realized she was in danger, you insisted on helping her. You don't have a lot of friends, but the ones you do have can count on you. You're as loyal as they come, Claire."

He seemed very satisfied by that knowledge.

Lise smiled, rubbing her pregnant tummy. "I usually reserve my research skills for my books, but if you point me the direction to look in, I can help search for connections between the two lists."

Claire knew Lise was due in just a few weeks. She couldn't believe the pregnant woman had come with Wolf to help in the investigation. "You people are amazing."

And they proved just *how* amazing over the next few hours while they each did what they could to help with the investigation. They worked through lunch, although Wolf made Lise take a nap in the early afternoon.

She grumbled, but she looked tired and left with a smile after he gently rubbed her tummy and told her he thought Junior was sleepy.

When it came time to get ready for the party, they had established three possible connections that looked like real leads.

Josette offered to come to Claire's room so they could get ready together. They had each showered and put on their dresses when there was a knock on the door. It was Eleanor, already perfectly put together, but with a large basket full of beauty paraphernalia dangling from one arm.

She smiled, her eyes dancing with anticipation. "I had an idea for Claire's hair and thought I'd see if y'all were ready to go yet."

The hair in question was still damp and Claire grimaced. "As you can see, not even close."

"I love your natural curl, but it needs a little taming. I think if you put a little product in it and then let it dry naturally, you'd really like the results."

"Product?"

"Curl enhancer, lightweight hair gel, and when it's dry something that will make it shine without making it stiff."

"You think my curl needs to be enhanced." She didn't mean to use a tone of voice that implied Brett's sister was unhinged, but she couldn't help herself.

Claire's hair was curlier than Shirley Temple's would have been after sticking her finger in a light socket.

"You want to enhance the actual curl, as opposed to the kinks and twists."

"Oh."

Eleanor lifted the basket. "Are you game?"

"Definitely." Claire sat down on the edge of the bed and let the other woman apply whatever goop she wanted to her hair.

"Now we'll let it dry while we're doing makeup."

Josette's eyes lit up at that pronouncement and what followed was forty-five minutes of hysterical fun. Eleanor happily showed Josette three different ways to apply eye shadow. They settled on one that gave Josette's eyes a slightly tilted, exotic look that both Eleanor and Claire pronounced perfect.

The former mercenary asked scads of questions

about all the girlie-type products in Eleanor's basket and insisted on trying a few of them out. After she was done, her usually straight, unstyled hair was swept up with a few curling wisps framing her face and she had finished her makeup with a dark lip gloss that complemented her strikingly made-up eyes.

When it came to doing Claire's makeup, Eleanor said she wanted to go with the natural look. Claire wasn't sure exactly what that meant, but it sounded good to her. She was willing to believe she'd like it more than the extensive grooming she'd received for the wedding. And she was right.

When she went to look in the mirror, she was shocked at how feminine the halo of ringlet curls around her head looked. It was totally natural and yet *not*. Her curls were tamed, or at least looked like an actual hairstyle, and her brown eyes looked dark and intriguing, highlighted by the subtle shadows and liner on her lids.

"Wow," she whispered.

Eleanor stepped behind her and grinned at her in the mirror. "My brother is going to drool so much, you'll need to carry an extra handkerchief for him."

Josette laughed. "I think you're right."

Eleanor turned to face her, still grinning. "Your husband will probably just pick you up and carry you back to your bedroom. I've seen how that man operates."

Josette twirled in front of the mirror, her skirt floating around her highly toned legs. "He'll have to catch me first and that's not as easy as he likes to think it is."

Chapter 21

Hotwire's breath seized in his chest as Claire walked into the ballroom. Josette was on one side of her and Eleanor the other, but both women faded to the outer edges of his vision as his entire being centered on the only woman he craved like an addiction. Man alive, she was beautiful.

He liked her hair . . . it looked more natural than at the wedding, and if she was wearing makeup, he couldn't tell. He liked that. Claire didn't need enhancement.

She was stunning all on her own.

Her body encased in the sexy number she'd worn to be in Josette's wedding, her feet shod in the dangerously high stilettos, she walked slowly forward. Her hips rolled seductively because of the shoes, and while other men noticed, her attention was fixed solely on him.

And the look in her eyes made him want to sweep her into his arms and carry her back up that huge staircase. There was such tenderness there and approval for what *she* saw.

She had said she loved him and he was starting to believe that might be true.

His first reaction when she'd said the words was that she was confusing physical ecstasy with love. After all, if she loved him, wouldn't she want to marry him?

But maybe she did. Maybe she really *was* just scared he was going to lose interest one day and walk away. Her parents had done a number on her for sure, but that was never going to happen. Every time they made love, he wanted her more, not less. And he didn't just crave having his body buried in hers so deep neither of them could tell where the other one started and they left off.

He craved her affection, her attention and her presence. As he'd told her . . . it was better than love.

He felt a jab in his ribs and turned to glare at Wolf. "What the hell was *that* for?"

"Lise has asked you three times if you and Claire have plans to see each other after the investigation. I'm guessing the answer is yes."

The smirk on Nitro's face said he'd been speculating, too.

Hotwire shrugged. "You could say that. I asked her to marry me."

It was the first time he'd seen his friends dumbfounded. Both men's mouths dropped open and then snapped shut without a word being uttered.

"You did what?" Wolf demanded after a short silence, his arm wrapped possessively around his wife's pregnant waistline.

Hotwire rolled his eyes. Like he'd stuttered the first time? He didn't think so. "I asked her to marry me."

"Boy, you are one fast worker," Nitro said. "I distinctly remember you telling me that you and Claire were nothing more than friends."

"I was wrong."

Nitro did a double take. "You sure you aren't sickening?"

"There's nothing sick about my attraction to Claire."

"Hell no, there isn't . . ." He paused and grimaced. "Pardon the language, Lise. But, Hotwire, you admitting you were wrong is one for the record books."

"Only for petty-minded people who keep track of that sort of thing."

Wolf laughed, but Nitro just shook his head. By then the women had reached them and Hotwire forgot about his friends' reaction to his news. Claire was standing right in front of him, her soft, silky skin in touching distance, the gentle fragrance that he recognized as only her, luring his senses.

"Hi," she said, looking nervous.

"Hi, yourself." He reached out and pulled her into him for a quick kiss. He couldn't help himself, though he guessed he'd catch hell for it later from Mama. He spoke low, close to Claire's ear, "You are so beautiful, you look good enough to eat for breakfast, lunch, and dinner."

She gasped and turned pink. "Brett!"

"It's all right, sugar. Our friends understand."

Her gaze skidded to Nitro and Josie, and his followed. Neither was paying Hotwire and Claire the least attention.

Josie's hand was on her husband's arm and his attention was focused one hundred percent on her. "You look beautiful, sweetheart."

Hotwire recognized that tone as one he used often with Claire. It was the *I want to get you away from here and strip you naked* voice.

Josie preened, former hardened mercenary nowhere

in evidence. "Thank you, Daniel. I don't suppose you want to dance?" She turned to the others. "He taught me on our honeymoon."

She sounded very proud of herself.

Nitro didn't need any further urging, but took his wife onto the ballroom floor and pulled her into his arms without so much as an attempt to use a formal dance hold. It didn't take a rocket scientist to figure out what kind of dancing that couple did best.

"What about you, Lise?" Wolf asked. "You feel like dancing?"

"Maybe once," she said with a smile, but turned to look at Hotwire. "I really enjoyed talking to your parents. Your father has so many interesting stories."

Wolf laughed. "You better watch out, or he's going to end up in a book."

Hotwire winked at Lise. "Don't you worry, Lise darlin'. Daddy wouldn't mind that at all."

Wolf scowled at the *darlin'* and Lise said, "He looks so much like you. I felt like I knew him right away."

"There isn't much resemblance when we open our mouths," Hotwire scoffed.

"You don't think so? I'm not so sure. I caught myself feeling like I was talking to you several times."

"I know what you mean," Claire said, turning within the circle of his arms to face the other woman. "If there wasn't the age difference, they could be mistaken for twins."

Hotwire just shook his head.

Wolf tugged Lise out onto the dance floor before she could say anything else.

Hotwire pulled Claire back around to face him. Looking at her close up made him feel sucker punched again.

She wasn't looking at him, though; her focus was on

something across the room. His parents? "Do you want
to go wish Mama a happy birthday?"

"No. Well, I mean . . . yes, but not right this second. I
need to talk to you about something." But her gaze was
still on his parents across the room.

"You look exquisite tonight, Claire."

That got her attention and she smiled at him, albeit
distractedly. "I think we established that you liked me in
this dress at Josette's wedding."

"Is that why you wore it? For me?"

"What do you think?" she asked in a breathy, warm
voice that went straight to his groin.

"I think it's going to kill me to stay at the party long
enough not to offend Mama."

Claire patted his chest in what he was sure she thought
was a comforting manner, but all it did was turn him on
further. "You're strong enough to survive an assignment in a jungle infested with predators, both men and
animals. You can handle a few hours of unrequited lust."

"You sure about that?"

"Positive. And if you get exhausted from the effort, I
believe I know just how to revive you."

"You're teasin' me at your peril, woman."

She laughed, the seductive sound an aphrodisiac of
unequaled potency. Then she grew serious. "Listening
to Lise made me remember something I believe could
be important."

"About Lester's case?"

"Yes."

"What is it?"

"A couple of days before Lester died, Queenie and I
were talking about him. She was worried his mind was
slipping further into dementia, but I wasn't sure I saw it.
I mean, he definitely had his bouts of senility-driven dialogue, but that had been going on for a long time.

Only something he had done very recently had really worried her."

"What was it?"

"There was a group of politicians who came to Belmont Manor. They were on a committee charged with assessing the living and care options in Oregon for the elderly."

"So?"

"Well, Lester pulled one of the men aside and started talking to him. He called him by the wrong name and really made a pill of himself, according to Queenie. One of the orderlies had to coax him back to his room. It was odd, because as a general rule, Lester refused to speak to people he didn't know and a lot of people he did."

"But he acted like he thought he knew this guy?"

"Yes. Which is what worried Queenie so much. She said the politician didn't know Lester from Adam. Not only that, but even though the politician is only in his forties, Lester talked like the guy was one of his clients from his days as Arwan. Queenie was sure it meant that Lester was moving into total senility."

"And you don't?" It sounded like dementia to him.

"No. Think about it, Brett. If someone who had known your father as a younger man, but hadn't seen him since, ran into you, they might mistake you for him at first. Our brain plays tricks on us like that and even though you are so much younger, their first reaction wouldn't be to take that into account. Neither was Lester's and because he *was* going senile, he was convinced he was speaking to a man he had met many years before."

"So far, none of those politicians has any known links to any of Arwan's hits."

"No, but one of them shares the last name of a client

Arwan turned down. It was in the late eighties and Lester had all but retired. I don't know how the man contacted him, but Arwan refused the job."

Hotwire said a word that his mother would have washed his mouth out for, remembering exactly what Claire was talking about. "You're right. We dismissed the possible link as unlikely to generate a real suspect."

"Because Arwan turned down the job."

"But he kept a record of it being offered, and even if the politician didn't know about the kill book, he saw Lester as a threat because Lester had remembered meeting the man's father and was just senile enough to say something."

Claire's big brown eyes were filled with regret. "He signed his own death warrant when he unwittingly greeted a man from the past."

"Most civs wouldn't want the fact that their father had tried to hire a hit man to come out, but a politician would be doubly vulnerable. Heck, you were even worried about my sister being adversely impacted by your past."

"Exactly. And what if his dad followed through with hiring the hit? Just because Arwan turned him down doesn't mean that he gave up on the idea of getting rid of someone who was in his way. For all we know, he took care of the job himself."

"There was a farmer standing in the way of land development in a small town in Eastern Oregon and the client wanted him disposed of," Hotwire said, remembering what he'd read in the kill book.

"That town isn't so small anymore and I bet that land development had a lot to do with it. The state representative probably built his political base on his father's success revitalizing that area."

"We're doing a lot of speculating here."

"It wouldn't be hard to check any of this out."

"No, it wouldn't. But it will have to wait until after the party." His family would never forgive him otherwise, and the politician wasn't going anywhere. "Now, sugar, I want to dance."

"I don't know how."

"Just hold on to me and sway to the music."

"I can do that."

And she did . . . beautifully. The feel of her in his arms paid hell on his good intentions, and it took all of his self-discipline to break away from her when the music moved into a slightly faster rhythm.

That didn't stop him from dancing with her again and again throughout the festivities. He was either a glutton for punishment, or hopelessly addicted.

An hour's worth of research after the party verified all of Claire's suspicions.

The farmer in question had died of a heart attack even though he'd had no history of heart problems. The land developer had become something of a town father and when his son entered local politics, no one had been surprised.

The son was medium build with gray eyes . . . he also had aspirations to the governorship, which was motive for a man with little conscience to silence Lester and anyone else who might be able to blow apart the house of cards his father had built. The question was . . . did the politician have no conscience?

There was still the agency director in D.C. to take into consideration. According to Ethan, whether he had a conscience or not was also questionable.

Hotwire shut down his laptop and closed it. "That's it, then."

"This guy is the most solid lead we have," Wolf said, supporting his dozing wife as she sat sprawled across his lap.

"I want to talk to the feds before we go after him."

"I'm still not convinced that director had nothing to do with the attacks on Claire," Nitro said, echoing Hotwire's thoughts.

"I got a voice mail from Ethan. He said he has Raymond Arthur ready for a meet in D.C.," Hotwire said.

"When?" Claire asked.

"Tomorrow."

Her face fell. "I promised your mother and sister I'd go shopping with them. I'll have to cancel."

"There's no reason for you to go. In fact, I'd rather you didn't."

"Why not?"

"You'll be safer here. I don't want to take you into the lion's den until I know they aren't hungry."

"Smart man," Nitro approved.

"Why don't I go shopping with Claire and the others?" Josie asked. "I can keep an eye out for trouble while you all fly up to D.C."

"Why do Wolf, Lise, and Nitro get to go and I don't?" Claire asked.

"I told you, I want you safe," he said at the same time as Wolf growled, "Lise will not be going."

Lise's eyes widened and then narrowed in a way that promised retribution for the high-handedness of Wolf's pronouncement, but she didn't argue.

Claire frowned. "I'll miss you." Then she brightened a little. "But I've got to say that though I've never actually looked forward to shopping, after this afternoon with Eleanor and Josette getting ready for the party, I really am."

He pulled her from her chair into his lap. "I'm glad

you're getting along with my sister, sugar." He liked the thought of her missing him, too.

"Are things going to get mushy around here? Because if they are, I think I'll take my pregnant wife to bed."

"*Bed* being the operative word," Nitro said in a deadpan voice, but everyone laughed anyway.

"Are you saying that's not where you want to take me?" Josie asked with a coquettish smile that threw Hotwire.

He'd crawled beside this woman through the rain forest, mud caked on their clothes, both of them armed to the hilt and feeling mean enough to chew nails. She didn't look mean now. She looked like a woman who enjoyed taunting the man she'd married.

Hotwire had to stifle a grin he was pretty sure Nitro wouldn't appreciate. Marriage had changed some things about his friend, but not everything. He could still be a mean son of a bitch when he wanted.

Nitro swung his wife in the air and carted her from the room slung over his shoulder, the only sound coming from the couple her shrieking laughs and promises of reprisal.

Lise tried to argue she was too heavy when Wolf cradled her against his chest and carried her out of the room, too, but he paid her no mind.

Claire looked at Hotwire, her expression warm and intimate. "Are you going to carry me out of here, too?"

"That depends."

"On what?"

"Where I get to carry you."

She batted her eyelashes and his dick jumped in his pants. "Bed?"

"You said the magic word." He stood up in one fluid movement with her tightly held in his arms.

He took her to his bedroom where he proceeded to do what he'd wanted to the first time she'd worn this dress . . . peel it off her and then spend a long time making love to every inch of her beautiful body.

They left for D.C. with Lise holed up in her and Wolf's room writing, while Josie kept her promise to accompany the other women shopping.

Hotwire wasn't surprised that Wolf got his way, not after how neatly he'd convinced his wife to rest the day before. Wolf was not a stupid man, nor did he make the mistake of thinking he'd married a dumb woman. Hotwire had taken note for the future, the thought of having to use similar techniques with Claire a sweet one.

Maybe he should get a pregnancy test kit and ask her to use it. Some were highly accurate within hours of conception. The image of Claire large with his child flashed in his mind, sending arousal rushing through him while a funny feeling twinged in his chest.

Man, that would be sweet.

They flew into an airport outside D.C. and rented a car to drive straight to the park where they were to meet Ethan.

He was waiting for them by the fountain he'd told Hotwire to look for. Three other men were also there. The one in the middle had steel-gray hair and an expression colder than the arctic in his gray eyes.

Raymond Arthur.

The other two men were the agents who had attended Lester's funeral. Ethan's ability to get all three there brought him up another notch in Hotwire's estimation. He had to have some pull in Washington.

"Hotwire." He put his hand out. "Good to see you again."

Hotwire shook his hand. "Claire sends her regards."

Ethan smiled slightly. "I bet you hated passing them on, though."

"I'm not that bad."

A scoffing sound came from his right.

Hotwire frowned at Wolf, who looked too innocent to be believed, and then made the initial introductions. Ethan introduced the other agents as well.

Raymond Arthur frowned at Hotwire, his expression filled with impatience. "You have something that belongs to us."

Hotwire crossed his arms over his chest, and raised his brows in question. "Do I?"

The sense of impatience emanating off the other man grew. "Let's not play games. You've got the kill book and we want it."

"That's unfortunate, because you can't have it."

Raymond turned to Ethan. "What the hell is this? You said they were prepared to cooperate."

Ethan shrugged. "Maybe Hotwire's definition of *cooperate* is different than yours . . . or maybe he changed his mind when he came face-to-face with your charming personality."

"Bullshit."

Ethan just looked bored.

Raymond turned back to Hotwire. "Tell me what you want in exchange for the kill book."

"Stop trying to piss me off. I'm not going to give you the kill book under any circumstances. Ethan is a different matter, however, but that has nothing to do with you."

"Then what in the hell am I doing here?"

"I want some information from you."

The expression in the director's eyes was not promising, but Hotwire wasn't worried. "Claire Sharp has been attacked twice. I want to know if your men are responsible."

"They're not. I read their reports and although they searched her house and your hotel room, they never physically accosted her," Ethan said.

"Not even four days ago at her college after she took a final?" Hotwire pressed.

Ethan ignored the singeing glare he was receiving from the director. "Not unless they left it out of their report."

Hotwire turned to the two men in question and asked, "Were either of you watching her at the time?"

The younger agent nodded once.

"Did you see who went into the bathroom with her?"

He looked uncomfortable. "No."

"Why?"

The look he gave his director was met with stony fury. The agent tugged at his collar and swallowed. "I thought she was taking her test. It was supposed to last over an hour. I decided to grab some food. When I got back, she was already gone and neither of you returned to the hotel that night."

"She finished her test early," Hotwire said with some pride. She was so damn smart.

"Yes, well. I didn't know she'd been accosted in the bathroom."

Hotwire nodded and then looked at the director. "Dismiss your men."

Raymond did so with a flick of his hand. The two agents left.

Hotwire had been able to determine that neither was currently wearing the exclusive cologne Claire had identified with her first attacker. One thing about expensive cologne . . . being oil-based, it lingered on a man's clothes, even when he wasn't wearing it. There was not even a trace of the unique scent on either of Raymond's men.

Besides, neither gave the impression of a man who would sweat with fear at the prospect of accosting a woman to gain information from her.

He focused his attention on Raymond. "I want you to leave Claire and Queenie alone."

The response he got was pithy and foul, but he smiled anyway. "There's a reason the FBI hires me for certain jobs. You don't want to mess with me or my own."

Nitro and Wolf gave Raymond identical looks of icy disdain as they nodded in agreement with Hotwire's words.

"It's a crime to threaten a federal officer."

"So is hiring an assassin to kill someone your agency can't touch."

"You work freelance for the government."

"Not as an assassin and you'd do well to remember that distinction. I have nothing in my past that wouldn't bear scrutiny. We both know you can't say the same."

"Are you going to make the kill book public?" Raymond asked with a damn good poker face.

"Not at this time."

"What does that mean?"

"It means I want the bastard who attacked Claire nailed. If the kill book is necessary evidence, I'll use it."

"There is no point in me staying here any longer, then."

"Not once I have your word you'll leave Claire alone."

"You would trust my word?"

This time Wolf's snort was loud and derisive.

"No."

"Then why ask for my promise?"

"Because then there can be no mistake in our understanding. If you screw with me, I'll come after you with everything I've got."

"You have my word." Raymond then spun on his heel and walked away.

Hotwire pulled a memory fob out of his pocket and handed it to Ethan.

"What's this?" the other man asked.

"The database from the kill book along with the results of the cross-reference search we did on it with the people your uncle saw during the last month of his life."

"Does it tell me the name of the man who attacked Claire?"

"Yes." Hotwire related the politician's history and the name of the cologne Claire had smelled on her first attacker. "I want him locked up."

"I'll take care of it, but it might be a good idea to keep Claire out of sight for a while longer."

"I will."

"With what you've got and knowing who the civ involved is, it shouldn't be too hard to gather enough evidence to neutralize him."

"That's what I figured."

"I'll call you when the arrest is made."

Hotwire handed him a card. "This has my contact information in Montana."

"Is that where you'll be?"

"Yes." He was going to take Claire to his home and convince her to marry him come hell or high water.

They were in the car on the way back to the airport when Nitro said, "So, what's the holdup with you and Claire getting hitched?"

"She hasn't said yes."

"Why not?"

"She says it's because I want to marry her for the wrong reasons."

"And what would they be?" Wolf asked.

Hotwire would never admit this to anyone else, but he trusted Wolf and Nitro with his life. "I forgot the condom the first time we made love."

"She's not on the pill?"

"No. Her last lover was in high school."

"You're kidding." Wolf whistled. "She's twenty-eight, right?"

"Yeah."

"That makes it what . . . *ten years?*"

"She didn't think much of sex and she was too busy taking care of her mom to have a social life, then too busy trying to fit four years' worth of school into three."

"I guess."

"So, the fact that you forgot the condom and are her first lover in a really long time made you feel like you had to propose marriage?" Nitro asked, having made no comment at all on Claire's dearth of sexual escapades.

"I want to marry her."

"Does she know that?"

"Of course she does. I asked her."

"But she thinks you want to marry her because you forgot the condom and she might be pregnant, right?"

He thought over the last few days. "I think she knows I want her regardless."

"Have you told her you love her?" Wolf asked.

Chapter 22

"What we've got is better than love."

"What the hell are you talking about, better than love?" Nitro demanded incredulously.

"I can't love her."

"Why not?" Nitro asked.

"If you don't, you have no business marrying her," Wolf said.

He didn't want to deal with Wolf's assertion, so he focused on Nitro's question. "I promised Elena that I would never love another woman as I loved her."

Nitro shook his head. "Whatever pseudo promises you made to each other in the first flush of love don't carry weight now. I'm sure you meant it when you said it, but neither of you realized she would die and you would have the rest of your life to lead alone."

"I didn't make the promise to her when she was alive."

"What did you do, make an oath on her grave?" Wolf asked.

"You could put it like that."

"But that's stupid. You didn't owe it to her to spend the rest of your life without love just because she died before you did."

"I owed it to her because it's my fault she died."

"Bullshit," Nitro snapped. "Elena chose to stay in a volatile situation for the sake of her belief in her cause."

"I was supposed to go back for her, but I got sent out on another mission before I could and she was killed because of it."

"You had no choice, but she did," Wolf said with certainty. "She had connections. She could have gotten herself out of the country a lot sooner than she tried to, but she didn't. She put her cause above you, not the other way around."

Claire had said the same thing, or at least part of it.

Hotwire sighed, coming to terms with a truth he'd hidden from because it had hurt too much to deal with at the time. Elena's duty had come before him, and he hadn't wanted to face that because it meant she hadn't loved him as much as he loved her. After all, he'd begged her to leave her country against the express orders of his superiors.

"That doesn't change the fact that I don't feel the same way about Claire as I did about Elena."

"How is it different?" Wolf asked.

"For one thing, I've got about zero self-control when it comes to making love with her. I want her all the time and I can't shut it off even when we're working on the case."

"That's not a bad thing. I feel the same way about Josette."

"I didn't say it was bad. In fact, I told Claire it was better."

"That's what you mean by better than love?" Wolf asked.

"Yes, and you know, when I'm with her, I feel at peace with myself, not like I'm always trying to prove that I'm worthy of her affection. It feels good."

Nitro and Wolf both gave him strange looks, and then Nitro asked, "What else?"

"The idea of her being pregnant with my baby is the biggest mental turn-on I've ever known. With Elena, I wanted all of her to myself. Neither of us wanted to have kids right away."

"You think you don't love Claire because you want her to have your baby?"

"Not like I loved Elena. There's nothing selfish in what I feel for Claire. I want her to be mine, but most of all, I want her to be happy."

"And let me guess . . ." Wolf said. "Claire isn't perfect, but you don't want her to be because you like her just the way she is?"

"Yes. How did you know?"

"I feel that way about Lise."

"Do you miss her right now, even though you only saw her a few hours ago and you're going to see her again pretty soon?" Nitro asked.

"Damn right," Hotwire said.

Both men looked at him as if expecting him to say something. "What?" he finally demanded.

"Just what do you call these feelings you have for Claire?" Wolf demanded.

"Do they have to have a name?"

"They don't have to, but they do," Nitro said.

"What? It's not merely lust because as much as I want her, I like her, too."

"Are you really that stupid?" Nitro asked with a frown.

"There are none so blind as those who will not see," Wolf added with a smirk Hotwire wouldn't mind wiping off his face with a fist if he wasn't driving a car.

"You two are both starting to get on my nerves. I need your help figuring out how to convince Claire to marry me, and you're busy mocking me."

"Why don't you try telling her you love her?" Wolf asked.

"I told you—"

"More than you've ever loved any other woman," Nitro added, rolling right over Hotwire's denial.

And suddenly he could see his blind stupidity in glaring Technicolor. Oh, hell. He did love Claire and he should have seen it ages ago, but he'd hidden from that truth as effectively as he'd hidden from the reality of his relationship with Elena. But instead of pain at the realization, he felt an overwhelming sense of rightness.

"I'm head over heels in love with Claire Sharp."

Wolf laughed. "Smart man."

"Finally, that computer brain of yours came up with the right equation," Nitro said, a genuine smile warming his usually taciturn features.

"Well, hell . . . now I'm going to have to convince Claire."

"It shouldn't be too hard. She loves you, too."

"That's what she said, but I told her I didn't love her. I don't think she's going to be a pushover to convince."

"But you can do it."

Of that Hotwire had no doubt and he was pretty sure he knew just the way to go about it.

Exhausted from shopping, Claire flopped down on the sofa in the living room. "I didn't know buying a few clothes could be such a marathon sport."

Eleanor laughed from her seat at the other end of the couch. "Mama and I have closed down more malls than you can shake a stick at."

"Well, there's no sense making the long drive into Savannah unless you plan to utilize your time wisely while there," Felicia said.

Josette laughed. "That's one way of looking at it. I suppose Claire and I are lucky you two didn't decide to close the malls down today."

"Well, you'll pardon me for saying so, but it was obvious neither of you were used to the rigors of marathon shopping."

Claire laughed at that. She was in pretty good shape, but Josette was more physically fit than any other woman Claire had ever known. Only Felicia was right—neither of them had been up to the other women's weight shopping.

"I've got to say that I've been on easier twenty-mile marches through the jungle than shopping with the two of you," Josette said.

"Now, this sounds intriguing," Lise said from the doorway.

The other women greeted her with a warm welcome.

"Are you done writing for the day?" Claire asked.

Lise nodded, yawning behind her hand. "Yes. One more minute in front of my keyboard and my mind is going to melt."

"Well, you're just in time for some tea."

As Brett's mother spoke, a young woman who worked for the family carried a tray with glasses and a large pitcher of sweet tea into the room. When each of the women had a glass of the refreshing beverage in hand, she left.

Lise sipped hers with a look of bliss on her face. "I love southern sweetened iced tea. They just don't make it the same anywhere else."

"Of course not," Felicia said complacently.

"It's yummy, all right, but I keep expecting to be offered a mint julep," Josette said with a smile.

"We'll have them after dinner, if you like," Felicia said.

Josette smiled, but Eleanor fixed Claire with her steady regard. "The more time I spend with you, the more convinced I become that you and my brother are meant for each other."

"I concur," Felicia said.

"I've thought so for a long time," Josette said smugly.

Claire frowned at her. "You of all people should know why we aren't."

Josette had to know about Elena. Besides, Claire hadn't told the whole story of her childhood to Josette, but she'd told her ex-roommate enough that the other woman should realize Claire could never fit into Brett's family.

"Why is that?" Lise asked, and then blushed. "I'm always doing that, asking whatever pops into my mind without thinking if it's something I should do first."

"It's all right," Claire said. "I don't mind, but you know Brett is still in love with his dead fiancée, and then there's the fact that my background just doesn't fit with his."

"What do you mean by that?" Felicia asked.

"My dad committed suicide when he lost his job and we were faced with bankruptcy."

"Your poor mother," Felicia sighed.

"Yes, well, she didn't exactly rise to the occasion. She became an alcoholic and died of liver cancer almost four years ago. We had a lot of trouble with the cops when I was growing up ... mom was not a happy drunk."

Felicia shook her head. "You had a difficult childhood, but you can't think Brett cares about where you come from."

"I was more concerned about how you would react to it . . . or Eleanor, being an elected official and all."

"Oh, pooh. You're the epitome of the American dream, Claire. You lifted yourself out of an ugly situation and have created a different life for yourself. I'm impressed, and anyone who isn't can vote for the competition."

Josette laughed. "I like that. You know, I didn't know all of that, but it explains some things that used to confuse me. One thing I want to know, though . . . how did you take care of your mom for so many years without learning a thing about how to cook?"

Claire burst out laughing. "Believe it or not, Mom was mostly a raw-vegetable-and-fruit vegan. We never ate meat and nothing got cooked except rice and potatoes. I don't know how she ever justified the distilled grains in alcohol to herself, but she was fanatical about food. I learned to bake potatoes in the microwave and we had a rice cooker there at the last. But my real problem in the kitchen is the fact that I'm too easily distracted by what's going on in my head."

"Well, that explains it," Josette said.

"I can understand that," Lise added with a rueful smile.

Claire smiled at all of them, but focused on Eleanor. "Brett said you'd react this way to my past."

"He knows me well," his sister said, sounding pleased.

"He doesn't understand you all are proud of him, though. He feels like he's on the outside of your family sometimes, I think."

"You can help him to see differently, can't you, Claire?" Felicia asked. "He made his choices and he made a good life for himself, one to be proud of, but

sometimes it takes an outsider to break through barri-
ers built in the past."

"You think I have that much influence with him?"

"I'm certain of it."

"I'm sure you're wrong about Elena, too. He isn't in
love with a ghost, but a flesh-and-blood woman,"
Eleanor said with a significant look at Claire.

The men returned after dinner, and Claire was glad
to hear that Brett had turned the information about
the politician over to Ethan and the case would now be
handled through official channels. She wasn't so glad to
hear that Brett planned to keep her out of the way until
the perp was brought in.

"But I have to get back to work. They won't hold my
job open indefinitely."

"Now that you're done with school, it's time for you
to move on to a job more commensurate with your skills
anyway, sugar."

"That's just it. I've got to start looking for one." She
wasn't as enamored of the idea of going overseas, or dis-
appearing to another state now . . . the freedom she'd
thought she wanted didn't seem nearly as alluring as
trying to make her relationship with Brett work.

"You already have one if you'll take it."

She looked at him warily, wondering if they were
talking marriage again. She saw that as slightly more
than a mere job.

"With our company."

"But you've already got Josette working for you. You
don't need me, too."

"I need you, all right, but so does the company. Josie
is good with a computer, but you are incredible."

"He's right, Claire, you are," Josette said from her

chair on the long veranda along the back of the mansion. She didn't sound in the least offended that Brett had judged Claire's abilities superior to hers. "Besides, I'm not done with school yet and I don't want to work until I am. Even then, it's likely I'll help Daniel with his architectural design business rather than work for Hotwire and Wolf . . ."

"I thought we already had this settled," Wolf added.

"But I . . ."

"It sounds like a wonderful opportunity," Brett's father said. "Anything my son is involved in is going to be a success, and that means this would be the beginning of a really good career for you."

"Thanks for the vote of confidence, Daddy."

"Anytime, son. I guess it's no secret I'm very proud of the man you've become."

Brett stared, his mouth opening and shutting. "I think you really mean that."

"Of course I do."

"Thank you."

Claire felt happy tears prick her eyes and she blinked at them. Lise wasn't so reticent. She swiped at wetness on her cheeks. "That's so sweet."

Wolf laughed. "Pregnant women and their hormone-driven emotions."

Lise smacked his arm and got pulled into his lap with a brief kiss for her trouble.

Eleanor and her family had left right after dinner, so it was just the former mercenaries, their wives, her, Brett, and his parents.

They chatted late into the night, while fireflies danced just beyond the veranda, until everyone agreed it was time to go to bed.

*   *   *

The next morning, she woke up to find Brett leaning over her with a small white wand. "I have it on very good authority that if you pee on this here little stick, we can find out with ninety-nine-point-eight percent accuracy whether or not you are pregnant."

She stared at the stick and then at Brett. "And if I am?"

"I'll probably attack your body like a Saracen, so I hope you remembered to take your vitamins yesterday, sugar. But the thought of you carrying my baby makes my dick hard enough to bust the seam on my Levi's."

"You're not wearing any jeans."

"It's a good thing, then, isn't it?"

She did as he wanted and sat staring at the little white indicator for several long minutes after the patch in the window had changed color.

Brett pounded on the door and she came out, feelings she didn't understand roiling through her.

He looked expectant. "Well?"

"Um . . ."

"Pink is for pregnant and blue is for not. Which was it?"

"You really want me to be pregnant, don't you?"

"Yes, but if you aren't, I think I might enjoy rectifying the situation . . . with your approval, of course."

Oh, gosh . . . she believed he meant it, but did that mean he loved her or just really loved the idea of being a dad?

"It's pink."

He whooped loudly and lifted her to spin her around the room. "That's great news, baby!"

She buried her head in his neck and clung to him, scared and elated all at once. "Do you really think I'll be a good mom?"

He stopped spinning and cupped her face and made her look at him. "The best."

"I want to be. I really do," and that's what confused her so much.

She'd never thought to have her own children. She'd always told herself that she spent enough years taking care of her mom, she didn't need a family of her own. And she'd been afraid . . . knowing how transitory happiness and family stability could be. So, she'd never considered diapers and the merits of breast feeding, but all she could think about right now was giving birth to a small life that would join hers and Brett's irrevocably and forever, even if they never got married.

"I love you, Claire," he breathed against her lips and then kissed her.

When he lifted his mouth, she looked at him solemnly. "You don't have to say you love me just because I'm pregnant with your baby."

He stared back at her, not looking the least surprised by her denial—which said a lot, she thought.

"I'm telling you I love you because I do."

She wanted it too much to believe it. "Then why wait until now to say something?"

"Because I was an A-Class idiot earlier, but I don't expect you to make it easy on me to convince you. You're a woman, after all, and I screwed up. I will convince you, though, sugar. You can bank on it."

He didn't give her a chance to respond, but swept her into his arms and took her back to the bed to make love to her with a driving passion that left her breathless.

They flew out late that morning. Josette and Nitro went with Wolf and Lise, who planned to drop them at the nearest major airport so they could fly commercial home. When Claire asked why they weren't flying with her and Brett, he told her he was taking her to his home in Montana.

They didn't talk much after that, and she found herself dozing before they even reached altitude. Brett kept her awake a good portion of the night before making love and the short hours of rest were catching up with her body.

He touched her shoulder. "Claire, sugar . . ."

Her eyes fluttered open. Man, she was tired. "Uh-huh?"

"Why don't you go back and lie down on the bed? You'll get better rest than sitting up here with me."

"And my snoring won't interfere with the instruments," she joked around a yawn.

"You don't snore, but you are distracting."

She laughed. "All right, I'm going." She unbuckled her seat belt and headed toward the small bedroom in the back of the plane.

Pushing the door open, something teased at her senses, a faint trace of a smell she recognized but couldn't quite place. The bed looked so inviting. She stepped toward it.

"Your nap is going to have to wait, Miss Sharp."

She looked to her left where the voice had come from and gasped in shock. A man she'd never seen before stood on the far side of the bed, an ugly black gun in his hand and pointed at her. The wide cylinder at the end of the long barrel was a silencer. She'd seen one on the Internet.

If he shot her, Brett wouldn't even know. Then he could shoot Brett, too. The thought sent panic arcing through her. He could kill them both. She had to warn Brett.

She opened her mouth to scream and he lifted the gun and barked, "Don't!"

She stopped . . . not because he was threatening to shoot her, but because he hadn't already. He had to have some kind of plan and she wanted to know what it was.

"William Keely, I presume."

The man's gray eyes widened and then narrowed. "You know who I am."

"Yes—what I don't know is what you are doing on this plane."

"I have a couple of problems I need to take care of."

"Let me guess . . . me and Brett?"

His gray gaze was ice cold. "How did you find out about me?"

"We found the kill book."

"So he did record offers as well as jobs."

"Yes."

"I was worried he might."

"So you killed him?" she asked, feeling sick and furious at the man's lack of remorse.

"That would be telling."

"Assuming your plan is to kill me and Brett, too, what difference does it make?"

"Who said I wanted to kill you?"

"You've got a gun pointed at me."

"As a precaution."

"What I don't understand is why you haven't used it yet," she said, ignoring his last comment as total baloney.

"I don't want to use it, but that doesn't mean I won't. So, don't get any ideas about screaming. Not that your lover would probably hear you in the cockpit."

"But you're not taking any chances."

"No. You're being awfully cool about this."

She shrugged. "Conditioning. You and the men in black have put me through the wringer lately. I finished with panicked hysteria a long time ago."

"I don't remember you ever being struck with it."

"You mean the night you tried to smother me with a pillow."

The slight flaring of his eyes was the only indication she had that she'd made a direct hit.

"Your cologne gave you away. It's very distinctive."

He frowned. "How unfortunate, but it's not a private stock. A lot of other men use the same one."

"I guess. I'm not into stuff like that, but I've only ever smelled it two times. On you and one of my professors."

"I see."

Her gaze flicked around the room until it landed on what looked like a backpack in the corner behind him. A parachute pack. Her brain worked feverishly on why it would be there.

Chapter 23

Hotwire reached altitude and put the plane on auto-pilot. He started checking the instruments, a sense of unease niggling at the back of his mind. Something wasn't right. His security checks had been okay before takeoff. None of his alarm systems had indicated anything out of the ordinary, but something still didn't feel right.

He went back over their arrival at the airport, seeing the others off, boarding his plane with Claire . . . she'd been asking him about returning to Portland. He'd been expecting an argument when he told her he wanted to take her to Montana, but she'd surprised him by acquiescing. He'd figured out why it had been so easy a few minutes later when he caught her yawning. Logically, sending her back to take a nap was the right thing to do, but his gut was telling him otherwise.

Why?

He scanned the radar and saw an upcoming pressure system. It might get choppy, but he could fly around the system. No, that wasn't it . . .

He went back in his mind to the moment they'd walked onto the plane. He'd had a sense that someone had been in the main cabin, but his security system had verified there had been no entry since he and Claire left it three days ago. He'd looked around the cabin, but not so much as a seat belt had been out of place.

So, why had he thought someone had been on the plane?

Then it hit him. He'd smelled a very faint trace of something. It had been so faint, it hadn't registered with his conscious mind because he'd been too focused on explaining their trip to Montana to Claire.

He searched his memory bank for the scent . . . it had been girlie. He was up and running on silent feet to the back of the cabin as he realized what that pseudo-feminine fragrance had actually been.

The cologne of Claire's attacker.

He stopped outside the bedroom. The door was ajar and he could see Claire—not her face, but her body. No one was near her but he heard a man's voice.

"What made you suspect me?"

"You'd been to visit Lester the week before his death. He mistook you for your father, didn't he?"

"Yes. I didn't realize at first what had happened. It wasn't until he started spouting off about turning down the job that I knew who he was. My father had deplorable sense when it came to hiring the right employees for the right jobs."

"You aren't similarly afflicted, I suppose?" Claire asked, her voice showing no evidence of fear or nervousness.

He was so damn proud of her, but he was going to kill the son of bitch in there with her. The man had to be holding her somehow, and since it wasn't physically,

Brett guessed the guy had a gun. Otherwise Claire would have come running back to the cockpit.

"No."

"So, who did you hire to help you with this job?"

"Who said I hired anyone?"

"You got past Brett's security measures. That took some doing. I don't see you being a computer specialist."

"I'm not."

"Then . . ." She was fishing and he was impressed at how well she did it. If she could just keep him talking another couple of minutes, they should hit that pressure front and the plane was going to get jiggy damn fast.

Hotwire would make his move then.

"Tell me who else believes I'm responsible for the old man's death and I'll tell you who I hired."

"You go first."

"I decline."

Claire gave an exaggerated sigh. "You're not going to like hearing this, but maybe it will make you reconsider your plans for me and Brett. The suits in Washington know all about you and one of them is really annoyed with you."

Keely swore. "They don't have anything linking me to the old man's death."

"There's the kill book."

"Which is embarrassing, but not any kind of proof I killed a geriatric."

"Then there's your cologne . . . and the fact that you attacked me."

"You can't be sure it was me."

"You left footprints outside my house."

"My shoes aren't handmade, either."

Claire shrugged. "Tell me who sold Brett out."

"You're so sure it was someone who knows him?"

"My acquaintances are mostly going senile and dealing with the aftereffects of hip replacement surgeries and the like. None of them knew about Brett, either."

"I didn't, either, until he attended the funeral with you. From there, it was relatively easy to get the intelligence I needed to track you two down."

"Who gave it to you?" Claire repeated, with a stubbornness Hotwire recognized and applauded.

Another couple of seconds and he could move in.

Keely said a name that made Brett frown. It was another merc, a man who was as good with the computer as he was deadly. He had no scruples and even less conscience. He would kill his own family for the right price. Brett had been on a couple of missions where he'd been a member of the team, and he'd refused to work with the other merc after the second time.

He wasn't surprised at all that the other merc had helped a slimeball like Keely, but he was pissed as hell that he had been able to overcome Hotwire's security measures.

The plane jerked and dipped.

Claire cried out and fell, and Keely swore just before another bump sounded from the other side of the bedroom.

Claire crawled out of the bedroom at speed, surging to her feet as she gained the main cabin. Hotwire grabbed her and shoved her into the tiny galley. Keely came rushing from the bedroom, gun first. Hotwire knocked the gun out of his hand and then coldcocked him with a single punch.

"Secure him," he shouted at Claire as he ran for the cockpit. The plane was shaking wildly and he needed to make evasive maneuvers fast.

He got the plane settled and rushed back to Claire, to find that she had tied Keely and was trying to drag him toward the closet.

Hotwire gently pushed her out of the way and took care of dumping the man in the closet after making a thorough search for weapons, particularly anything sharp enough to cut his bonds.

"I already did that. I put what I found over there," Claire said, indicating the small table between two of the seats.

Hotwire didn't bother to look before jamming the closet door shut so it could not be opened. "That will hold him until we land."

"That's what I thought."

He took her into his arms and held her so tight she squeaked. He forced himself to loosen his grip . . . a little. "Sugar, that was one scary few minutes."

"Tell me about it. I was scared to death he was going to get bored talking and decide to shoot me and then you."

"I'm damn glad he didn't, but I don't understand why not."

"He wanted it to look like an accident. He had two syringes with him. I bet it's the same stuff he gave Lester to induce a heart attack. He brought a parachute pack . . . I think he planned to kill us with the poison and let the plane crash, making it all look like an accident."

"It sounds like you had it all worked out, sweetheart."

"Everything but how to get away from him and warn you."

"Turbulence worked nicely."

"Yes, it did, but I'm surprised you didn't fly under it or something. You're really good at avoiding that sort of thing, I noticed on the flight out."

He told her about his realization that something was

wrong and his plan to use the turbulence to make his move. Then he led her back to the cockpit, where he settled her into her seat before heading the plane for the airport near D.C. that he'd landed in the day before.

Once he reached the ground, he called Ethan on his cell phone and arranged for pickup of the prisoner. He and Claire had to make statements, and it was late the next day before he was allowed to take her to Montana as he'd originally planned.

Claire was relieved to discover that Brett's house was nothing like his parents' home. It was a simple, single-story ranch and she liked it. A lot. The living areas all had a sense of spaciousness that she really enjoyed and thought would be great for a family.

The décor surprised her, though. He preferred geometric lines and bright spots of color with warm overtones. The artwork on the walls was a mixture of his and other artists', but all of it was striking.

"Where do you paint?" she asked as he led her through the living room.

"My studio is in the back of the house. Would you like to see it?" There was an undertone in his voice she didn't get.

She looked at him questioningly, but said, "Yes."

He nodded, his own expression so serious and intent that it would have scared her if she hadn't had all the fear squeezed out of her the day before on a flight no one would call uneventful.

She followed him through a doorway into a huge room. It ran almost the entire length of the back of the house and was easily fifteen feet deep. This man took his need to relax through art seriously. Multiple sky-lights bathed the room in bright natural sunlight while the walls were covered with paintings in different stages of production.

Some oils were obviously not done. There were water-colors, too, and acrylics . . . but they all had one thing in common. Their subject: Her.

Every single painting she saw was of her. Some were of her sleeping. When had he seen her doing that? One was of her standing over a burning toaster, her expres-sion resigned. She remembered the morning not long after meeting him for the first time that she had burnt her breakfast toast. He'd teased her because she couldn't blame it on the toaster. She'd been reading a program-ming manual and pressed the button down twice in-stead of taking the toast out when it was done.

She moved around the room, her heart pounding as she looked at one painting after another of herself. Each expressed some different facial emotion. She stopped in front of one that showed her sitting on the end of the couch, her expression vulnerable.

"I was thinking about you."

"I didn't know that, but something in your expres-sion called to me."

She turned and her breath came out in a loud gasp as she saw a life-size oil, definitely finished. "You never saw me naked before. How could you have painted this?"

"I saw you a hundred times in my dreams. Amazing how accurate it is, isn't it?"

She couldn't answer. Her tongue wouldn't work, but he was right. For a man who had only his imagination to go on, he'd done an incredible job of portraying her nude body.

"A gallery in New York has been trying to get me to show for months, but this is my best work and I couldn't share it with the public, not without admitting that you meant way too much to me."

She reached out and touched the painting, running her finger along the line of the lifelike curve of her breast to a nipple beaded with desire. "I look like I'm waiting for you to come back to bed."

In the painting, she was in the middle of a big four-poster bed with sheets the color of the sunset, and while the top sheet covered one thigh, the rest of her body was completely open to his view.

"In my mind you were."

"I just cannot believe you painted all of these of me."

"It was the only thing that kept my sanity while I was so busy trying to hide from the feelings you brought out in me. I told myself you were simply an interesting subject."

She dropped her hand and turned to face him then. "What feelings?"

"I told you, but you didn't believe me. But I love you, Claire. I have for a long time. I blinded myself to it because . . ." His voice trailed off and his expression was pained.

"You didn't want to break your promise to Elena."

He sighed. "That was part of it, but it wasn't all."

"What else?"

"I loved Elena, but duty meant more to her than I did. I was afraid of the feelings I had for you . . . they were powerful, more powerful than anything I'd ever known."

"You were afraid I would hurt you?"

He frowned, looking way less than pleased to be discussing this aspect of his emotions, but he nodded. "I sensed from the very beginning that you could hurt me more than she had and that bothered the hell out of me. I was such an idiot, Claire. I told myself I didn't love you, that I couldn't, that what I felt for you was better than love."

"Maybe—"

"It *is* better than love, or at least the love I felt for Elena. What I feel for you is so much bigger, so much stronger, so much more than what I had with her. You're the whole package, sugar, the one woman who makes my life complete. Can you understand that? I need you."

She was going to cry, but she didn't care. She never would have thought her hardened ex-merc could speak so poetically. "I'm not perfect," she said with a choked voice.

"And I'm glad, because you are perfect the way you are for me. I love you so much, it scares me."

"It scares me, too. I love you, Brett. So much."

"I know, sugar, and I'll thank God every day for the rest of my life that you do. Do you know that?"

She couldn't answer and he didn't seem to need her to.

He kissed her and then picked her up with his lips still locked to hers. He carried her to a bedroom and laid her on a bed and she saw that it was the bed in the painting.

"Is this what you call living out your fantasies?" she asked as he stripped out of his clothes.

He started undressing her, his hands purposeful and insistent as he took off first her shoes and socks and then her pants and top. He left her in her bra and panties, feeling more exposed than if she were completely naked.

He stepped back and looked at her, his expression filled with desire and tenderness. "Every moment with you is living out a fantasy, Claire. The best kind. Now, put your hands above your head, sugar."

"Why?"

"Because I'm going to like looking at you that way."

She laughed, doing as he said, enjoying the way it made her nipples rub against the lace of her bra. "I like it, too."

"Now, keep them up there while I pull off your panties. Will you do that for me, sugar?"

"Yessssss."

He didn't remove her underwear right away, but first he traced all along the edges and then down over her mound, making her arch with need.

"That feels good," she panted.

"Yes, darlin', it does." He played with her through the small patch of silk for a long time, until she was writhing under him and wanting his fingers on her naked flesh.

"Brett, please . . ."

Hotwire inhaled the sweet fragrance of Claire's arousal and hooked his fingers in the waistband of her panties. He wanted to touch her silky, wet heat as much as she wanted his fingers there. Having her here, in his bed, was something he'd fantasized about repeatedly, but never let himself contemplate really happening.

But now that she was his, he would never let her go. He started pulling them down her legs, going slowly, letting the silk caress her thighs as he went. "You are going to marry me, aren't you, sugar?"

Her head was twisting side to side. "You . . . what?"

The panties came off and she spread her legs in open invitation to his touch.

He fluffed her curls and then dipped one finger into her honeyed heat. "Marriage. You and me becoming husband and wife. You're going to marry me."

"I love you," she groaned.

"And I love you." He thrust two fingers up inside of her.

She cried out.

"Say yes, Claire. I want to hear the words." He didn't know where the strength to talk was coming from, but he needed to know she was done balking at the last fence.

"Yes. Whatever you want, Brett. Anything. Just touch me."

He crawled up so he was over her, their bodies aligned. He kept loving her with his fingers, but didn't touch her clitoris or that special spot deep inside. "Now, that's an intriguing proposition, sugar, but what I need from you is a cognizant acceptance of my marriage proposal."

Her hands came down from above her head and she grabbed his penis and pulled it toward her opening. "Yes, I'm going to marry you, but I may kill you first if you don't make love to me right this minute."

He surged inside of her, kissing her at the same time. They came together almost immediately, their meshed mouths catching the other's cries.

Afterward, he rolled on his back so she was on top of him.

She nuzzled his chest. "I wonder if we are going to have a girl or a boy."

"It doesn't matter to me. I'm not building any dynasties. I just want healthy kids."

"Me, too." She lifted her head so she could look him straight in that incredible blue-eyed gaze. "I don't want a big wedding, like Josette's. I'd rather get married on the beach with just you and me and our friends. And your immediate family. Okay?"

His heart tightened in his chest. "That sounds great, sugar. Perfect, in fact."

"Can we go on a honeymoon?"

"Yes. Anywhere you want."

She sighed and closed her eyes, laying her head on his chest. "I don't care where. I just want to be with you and know that we're there because we love each other and want to be together for our whole lives."

"That sounds good, sugar, real good."

"Yes, it does." She hugged him tight and he wrapped his arms around her, accepting once and for all that there was nothing better than love, not the kind he shared with Claire, anyway.

They got married on the beach . . . in Mexico. His family came, and their friends. Queenie came, too, from her new home near Roswell where she, Josie's dad, and his wife printed a small monthly newsletter that specialized in conspiracy theories and exposing government cover-ups. After the wedding, Hotwire took Claire to an all-inclusive resort and taught her to snorkel and scuba dive while she helped him perfect his kite-flying techniques.

William Keely died mysteriously while in jail awaiting trial. There were rumors that he had connections that would not like being sold out for a deal he was negotiating with the D.A. The D.A. had been reticent to cut the deal because evidence had been mounting that Keely had killed more than one person in his rise to power . . . starting with the problematic farmer who had stood in the way of his father's land development.

Claire was just glad that some kind of justice had been served against Lester's murderer. When she said so to Brett, he commented that she was awfully bloodthirsty, for a pacifist.

She pointed out that she wasn't a pacifist.

She was just a woman who, when she loved, she loved deeply, and she was going to love Hamilton Brett Adams to the depths of her soul all the way into eternity.

If you liked this Lucy Monroe book,
you've got to try the others in her
READY, WILLING, AND ABLE series . . .

READY

Writer Lise Barton is used to coming up with wild
scenarios for her characters, but the one that's playing
out for her right now is no fiction. Someone is stalking
her, someone who knows where she lives and what she
does—who's even threatened her family. To protect
them, she packs up and leaves Texas for the anonymity
of Seattle—where it starts all over again . . .

Joshua Watt's mission is simple: Bring Lise home for
Thanksgiving or he'll never hear the end of it from his
sister. He's spent months trying to forget the taste of
her lips, but the minute he sees the fear in Lise's eyes,
the former Army Ranger takes control. His mission:
Protect Lise and try to keep his personal feelings out
of it. Because if there's one thing he's learned,
it's that sex and work don't mix. So far . . .

A crash came from inside the apartment. Then silence. He knocked again, louder this time.

Again there was no response.

He called out her name, but absolutely no sound came from the apartment.

Had she fallen and hurt herself? She wasn't always completely aware, and he'd seen her walk straight into a wall when her eyes were hazy with a certain look she got.

His fist against the door made it shake within its frame.

Still nothing.

He surveyed the locks on the door. They were too basic to be of any real use at keeping out the criminal element. He didn't even hesitate.

He had the door open faster than if he'd had a key.

A slight *whoosh* of air to his left sent him into immediate battle-ready mode. Reflexes honed by six years in the Army Rangers and a decade spent as a mercenary took over. He swung toward the faint sound, his hand coming up to block the blow.

He grabbed the poker before it connected with his head and had his assailant in a headlock before he realized it was Lise.

He tossed the cast-iron poker aside and spun her to face him, her dark blond hair flying around her face. "What the hell are you trying to do?"

Big hazel eyes stared back at him with a glazed look he'd come to know all too well in his profession.

Terror.

Her breath came in shallow pants and her sweatshirt-clad arms were trembling.

What the hell was going on?

"Why didn't you answer the door?"

Her mouth moved, but nothing came out.

He shook her gently. "Speak, Lise."

Her eyes blinked and then filled with tears.

"Damn it." He hauled her against him and wrapped his arms around her.

He'd really frightened her when he forced his way into her apartment. He hadn't considered that possibility when he picked her locks. He should have.

She was a small-town Texas girl living in the big city.

Obviously, she hadn't acclimated well.

Her body shook against him and he felt like a real heel.

"I didn't mean to scare you, little one."

Lise's fingers were digging into his shirt, holding the denim so tight, he'd lose the shirt before he lost her grip. She pressed her face into his chest as if she was literally burrowing into him.

"Joshua?" It was the first recognizable sound she'd made in over a minute.

"Yeah?"

"What are you doing here?"

"You told Bella you weren't going to Texas for Thanksgiving."

Lise shuddered. "No. I'm not going."

She didn't sound like she had a cold. Her usually soft voice was strained, but not in a way that could be caused by a scratchy throat.

He rubbed her back.

It just seemed like the right thing to do.

She responded by relaxing her hold on his shirt just the tiniest bit. He kept it up, talking to her in the same tone of voice he'd used to calm the little boy he'd liberated on his last mission. He used similar words, too, telling her it was all right, that he wouldn't let anything happen to her, that she was going to be okay.

It took almost as long as it had taken him with the boy before she relaxed enough to step away from him. When she did and he got his first good look at her face, he winced.

He'd seen snow with more color than her skin, except the purple bruises under her eyes. Her bow-shaped mouth trembled.

"Lise, you don't belong in Seattle."

"H-how . . ." She blinked, made a visible effort to gather herself in, and her quivering lips formed words. "How do you figure that?"

"It's pretty damn obvious to me you aren't settling into city living. You get an unexpected visitor and you're practically crawling out of your skin."

She shook her head and laughed hollowly. "Trust me, moving back to Texas won't help."

"Why not?"

"My problems travel with me."

"What is that supposed to mean?"

She didn't answer, but this time he didn't wait

around for a reply. He propelled her gently toward the bedroom. "You can tell me about it on the plane. Get your stuff together. We've got an eight o'clock flight."

"No." She twisted from his guiding hand and stopped, wrapping her arms around herself, covering the Dallas Cowboys logo on her sweatshirt.

"I can't go, Joshua." Her southern drawl was very pronounced, her voice on the ragged edge of hysterical.

"Why not?"

She swallowed and looked away from him, her body stiff with stress. "I'm afraid."

"Of what?"

"I don't want my family hurt because of me." Her eyes were both pleading and wild. "If I go to Texas right now it could put them all at risk, even little Genevieve."

He bit back an ugly word. "Explain."

"I'm being stalked."

WILLING

Josie McCall left her dad's mercenary school for a normal job in computers. But now that someone has torched the school and her dad is MIA, Josie's going to use every bit of her training to hunt down the culprits who took him. Josie knows a lot about explosives, hand-to-hand combat, and tracking. What she doesn't know about is sex. She has no idea what to do with the volcanic attraction she feels for her dad's new partner, Daniel Black Eagle. And that feels more dangerous than any bomb . . .

Daniel knows exactly what he'd like to do about that attraction. He can't get within five feet of Josie without wanting to touch, taste, and protect her. But right now he's got his hands full figuring out who set that bomb and took Josie's dad. Daniel's sure of one thing, though—he's not letting Josie McCall out of his sight for a single second . . .

"What do you think you are doing?" Her words came out funny, like hiccups, because her diaphragm was hitting his shoulder.

"You're too tired to hike back."

"I am not."

He didn't bother to argue, but she wasn't so sanguine.

"Listen here, Neanderthal man, I'm a trained soldier. A mile hike is nothing for me."

"You've been awake for twenty-four hours or more, inhaled smoke, saved your dad from a burning building and tracked perps at a running jog."

"So? I'm not a wimp."

"No, but you are a termagant."

"What's that?"

He smiled as he told her.

"I do not nag and I am not a shrew!"

"But you are overbearing on occasion."

"You can say that when you're the one carrying me

against my will?" she asked furiously. "If anyone's a termagant here, it's you."

"Men can't be termagants."

"You use pretty big words for a mercenary," she grumbled.

"I like to read."

"I do, too, but the word I want to call you is one I learned listening to soldiers."

He laughed, something he rarely did . . . except when he was with Josie. How could she think he didn't like her? She made him smile, and that wasn't easy.

"Put me down, Nitro, or I'm going to get mean, and I don't want to because you're helping me."

"Call me Daniel." He didn't like being reminded of his past when he was with her.

"What?"

"Daniel. It's my name."

"Hotwire and Wolf call you Nitro."

"I want *you* to call me Daniel."

"*Daniel*, put me down or things are going to get ugly." The tone of her voice said she meant what she was saying.

They were more than halfway back to the compound, so he stopped and let her slide to her feet, his hands loosely guiding her at the hips. When she was solidly on terra firma again, he should have let go, but he didn't.

And she didn't move away immediately, but stood staring up at him like an accident victim. It was a look he'd gotten very familiar with on their last mission, but he still didn't know what it meant. She licked dry lips, and his body told him what he wanted it to mean. She was too close not to notice the change, and she jumped away from him like a scalded cat.